MW01701531

The Vampire Gets His Mate

Book 1 in Misfit Island

J.L. Hendricks

This book is a work of fiction. All of the characters, organizations, and events portrayed in this novel are either products of the author's imagination or are used fictitiously.

Cover Design by Victoria Cooper

First Edition December 2022

Contents

Other Books by J.L. Hendricks

Worlds Away Series

Book 0: Worlds Revealed (join my Newsletter to get this exclusive freebie)

Book 1: Worlds Away

Book 2: Worlds Collide

Book 2.5: Worlds Explode

Book 3: Worlds Entwined

A Miss Claus Shifter Christmas Romance Series

Book 0: Santa Meets Mrs. Claus

Book 1: Miss Claus and the Secret Santa

Book 2: Miss Claus under the Mistletoe

Book 3: Miss Claus and the Christmas Wedding

Book 4: Miss Claus and Her Polar Opposite

The FBI Dragon Chronicles

Book 1: A Ritual of Fire

Book 2: A Ritual of Death

Book 3: A Ritual of Conquest

New Orleans Magic Series

Book 1: New Orleans Magic

Book 2: Hurricane of Magic

Book 3: Council of Magic

Island of Misfits

Book 0: Island of Misfits

Book 1: The Vampire Gets His Mate

Chronicles of the Fae Princess –

Trilogy Published by LMBPN Publishing

See these titles and get their links at https://www.jlhendricksauthor.com/

The Vampire Gets His Mate

Book 1 In Misfit Island

The real events of the October revolution and the subsequent outcome of Czar Nicholas II and his family are different from how I portray them here. This is a work of fiction and fantasy.

I hope you enjoy this story and keep in mind I have taken creative license to conjure up an alternative history.

Chapter 1

Russia, 1917

"Mmmm, I love a man in uniform." The sultry woman with smoky eyes, long hair as dark as a moonless night, and nails longer than anything Maxim had ever seen was running one down the front of his red uniform jacket. "And dark curls." Then she ran her fingers through his mussed-up brown hair and yanked on one lock of hair that had curled over the top of his crumpled uniform collar.

Instinct had his throat clogged. The woman in front of him was more than human, even though that wasn't possible. However, through his experiences, Maxim learned there was more out there.

Maxim Volkov was a soldier first and foremost. He protected the palace and the Czar. Well, that was until the October Revolutionists attacked. Now, he wasn't really sure who he was, or what he was supposed to do. "Please." The raspy words left his mouth, but he wasn't really sure what he was asking for. Did he want to die since he had failed at his one job? Or did he want a new life?

While the woman was beautiful, she was also scary. Her eyes were red-rimmed, and her teeth? Well, they were something out of a nightmare – stained red at the sharpest points. He tried to tell himself that it was from her lipstick, but a niggling in the back of his mind told him she wasn't a regular woman. One word entered his mind, but he couldn't believe it – *Вампир*. Vampires were what the soldiers spoke about while around the fires on the battlefield when they couldn't describe the specters who haunted the piles of the dead.

Fear raked his spine as he stood there transfixed, watching the woman's hands go up and down his Russian Imperial uniform jacket.

"I love red uniforms." She licked her lips and slowly looked him up and down.

Maxim would have called out for help, if there were any other soldiers nearby. Since the fighting began earlier in the evening, most had died… or run. He had stayed to guard the Imperial family only to find the Czar and Czarina dead. Then, he ran to find the children of the Czar so he could try to get them out, but he failed at every point. The only reason he had survived the night so far was because the monsters had caused even the Bolsheviks to run away screaming.

Once he realized that the entire Royal Family was dead, he began searching the palace for the Czar's royal advisors. It was the same everywhere he looked. The only person he did not find dead was another type of monster he wasn't sure he wanted to discover. The fact that Rasputin wasn't anywhere to be found didn't surprise Maxim, but it did have him wondering if the monsters on the loose weren't of his creation.

Surely, Rasputin wouldn't have done anything to hurt the royal family, would he? The tzar treated Rasputin as though he was family, giving him anything the scary man wanted.

Even though there was no reason for him to stay in the palace any longer, Maxim refused to run away. His job was to protect the royal family and he'd failed. Not only did he fail, but he had allowed the terrorists to completely destroy his country's leadership. As far as he could tell, everyone was dead. Either by the usurpers or by the monsters. He really wasn't sure which was worse.

If he couldn't protect the royal family, then he would do the one thing he could - stay at his post. Even if it meant death for him. Death would have been welcomed after his utter failure.

And so it was, a monster had found him as he was heading back to his post. A monster he couldn't hope to defeat.

There was no fighting these monsters. He'd seen a couple of his compatriots try... and fail miserably. No, Maxim knew it would be better to die defending his country than to die from some demon sucking his blood. He wished the Bolsheviks would have killed him. Then he could have died an honorable death.

Death at the hands of a vampire was anything but honorable. There was one thing he could do, and that was not to cry out or beg for his life. He would go out standing tall.

Maxim closed his eyes when the woman's nose ran up and down his neck. That basic instinct all humans had to either run or fight was beginning to kick in. Maxim had never run from a fight before, but now? His body was telling him to run. This was not a battle he could win.

With both sides of his heart dueling for action, one to run and the other to fight, Maxim stood still and waited for his fate to be decided.

"Mmmm, you smell delicious. I think I want a taste." Her tongue licked his neck and Maxim felt an involuntary shiver run down his spine, and not the kind that *other* women had given him. This was the sort that made him want to toss his piroshkies. It didn't stop until it got to his toes.

Would this be how he went out? After all of the horror stories he'd heard about the Czar's warlock Rasputin, would Maxim fall to a different monster?

The sharp pain only lasted a moment, but it felt like years. No, decades, before the pain vanished. When his eyes finally opened, he was in a bed. Silk sheets surrounded him and the beautiful woman from earlier. But he couldn't remember what happened. The only thing that stuck with him was the intense pain in his neck.

Then hunger.

A hunger like nothing he'd ever felt before. His throat had burned, and his body felt as though it would combust if he didn't get something to drink.

Maxim had no idea if he ever got that drink, but now? Now, he felt full. Well, maybe not full but satiated. His throat didn't burn any longer, either. All he wanted now was answers. Who was this woman and where were they? "Hello?"

"Mmm, my darling toy." The blonde woman turned lazily in bed and ran her hands through his hair. She seemed to like doing that, but Maxim couldn't understand why.

"What's going on?" He asked feeling as though he knew, but yet he didn't want to acknowledge it.

"You're mine now. I saved you from those bad men." Her lower lip pushed forward in a very cute pout.

It made Maxim's chest hurt with the need to reach out with his lips and capture hers. He cleared his throat. "What exactly does that mean?"

She leaned up on one elbow and her eyes focused on him. They went from a deep blue to a piercing red in the blink of an eye. "It means, you are my property now. We'll be together forever. You'll never die... unless I say so. And you'll never fear another revolution again." Her eyes softened and she leaned down to kiss him.

When the woman pulled back, Maxim felt a sharp pang in his mouth as his fangs came out. "What's happening?"

"Oh, darling. It just means you need to drink more. Come, I think I might have a light snack for you. Then tonight, we'll feast on the chaos of the city." She laughed as she got up out of bed and her blood red nightgown flowed down over her milky white legs.

"Wait, what's your name?" While Maxim wasn't sure how long it had been since they met, he was sure she'd never told him who she was.

Without missing a step, she looked back over her shoulders and pouted once more before her lips slid up in a sly grin. "Why, darling, I'm Tatiana. Queen Tatiana to you and everyone else in my household."

Chapter 2

Six Months Ago, Siberia

"Sofka, I can't do this." Anoushka Sidorov shook her light blonde hair. "I know, we're supposed to do as our Alpha says, but I can't." The beautiful young woman paced the length of her room while flailing her hands all around her head, and trying to keep her voice down.

"Shh." Sofia Federov, also known as Sofka, warned her friend. "KeeKee, if you aren't quiet, then Kirill will hear you. Or at the very least, one of his Betas will."

"I'm confused. I don't understand what's going on." Daria Ivanov, the third girl in the tightknit group turned furrowed brows to Sofka, their makeshift leader. "Why are we running away?"

Anoushka, KeeKee to her best friends, sighed and sat down on the edge of the bed in their little room. The three girls shared a room in the warehouse where their small pack lived and worked. "Ree, do you want to be free, or a slave for the rest of your life?"

"Well, that's just a stupid question. Of course, I want to be free. But Kirill said that we would be free to live a life in the real world. All we had to do was model. I don't get it." Daria, nicknamed Ree, rubbed her face. "Modeling could be fun. We'd get to travel the world and think of all of the clothes we would have." She sighed with a dreamy expression.

Sofka and KeeKee exchanged worried glances.

"Ah, Ree. I don't think it's that kind of modeling the humans want from us." While their Alpha, Kirill, had told them they would be the stars of runways all over the world, and most likely grace the covers of the best magazines, KeeKee had overheard something that didn't jive with what they were told.

"But, Kirill said so." Ree nodded and tried hard to understand. It wasn't that she was stupid, just too trusting of her leaders. Of the three girls, she was considered to be the prettiest among them. She had the high cheek bones most models would kill for. However, she was much shorter than the average runway model. At only five feet five inches, she wouldn't be able to work too many runways. She could do photoshoots, but not the major runways as Kirill had promised.

The only one tall enough to work a runway was Sofka. She was five feet, nine inches tall, with platinum blonde hair and ice blue eyes. If she had been the only one to be offered a modeling job, the girls might have believed it.

Even KeeKee, who was only five feet two inches tall, had supposedly been offered a modeling job. Of course, in her human form she was beautiful with light blonde hair and striking green eyes. But she was too short even for most photoshoots.

The biggest problem with the offer was that all three of them were arctic wolf shifters. No alpha in his right mind would allow any of his wolves to model in the human world. And certainly not in high fashion where their real identities might be discovered and revealed to the whole world.

KeeKee sat next to Ree on the bed and took her hand. "Ree, I know you want to believe this. In your human form, you attract a lot of attention and would be a smashing success as a model. But you have to know that we can't really be in the public eye like that, right?"

Ree sighed and nodded. "A part of me knows this." She put a hand to her heart. "But another part really wanted it to be real. Our lives here are...well...not nice." Which was an understatement.

The three girls had been treated as outcasts, even in their own packs. Their parents had been killed when they were very young. As they grew up, they were told it was a hunting accident, but Sofka had started to think otherwise.

"And that's exactly why we have to leave." Sofka stood up and put her hands on her hips. "Get your gear together, we're leaving tonight. Pack light, we will most likely need to make a run for it if they figure out what we're doing."

"Is there no other way?" KeeKee asked, hoping for a different answer than what was on her heart.

"I'm afraid not." Sofka turned to KeeKee. "Unless, of course, you want to be a slave in some man's harem?" She arched a brow to indicate what she really thought about the truth behind her alpha's story.

"I thought it was outlawed?" KeeKee bit her lower lip and looked down at the ground. "I mean, didn't Santa make it known to all packs that no one is allowed to sell their members?"

"Sell their members?" Ree blinked, then her eyes widened. "You don't mean..."

Sofka interrupted. "Yes, that's exactly what she means. Supernatural trafficking. The humans do it all the time, but when a supernatural does it..." She shook her head.

KeeKee jumped up and began pacing the room again. "If Santa finds out, this entire pack will be destroyed."

Ree gulped. "We aren't going to tell him, are we?"

"I don't think he'd believe us, even if we tried." Sofka shook her head. "Besides, if we went to Santa, he'd keep us in his pack and make us Omegas." She shivered.

"Oh, no. I don't think he would." Ree stood up and ran a hand down her face. "He'd be nicer than that, wouldn't he?"

"We'd be no better off than we are now. No possible chance of finding a mate. No way to have pups, and certainly never get a real chance at living a halfway decent life." The weight of what was coming suddenly caused Sofka to plop down on the edge of her bed.

"Then where will we go?" Ree asked.

"To the ends of the Earth."

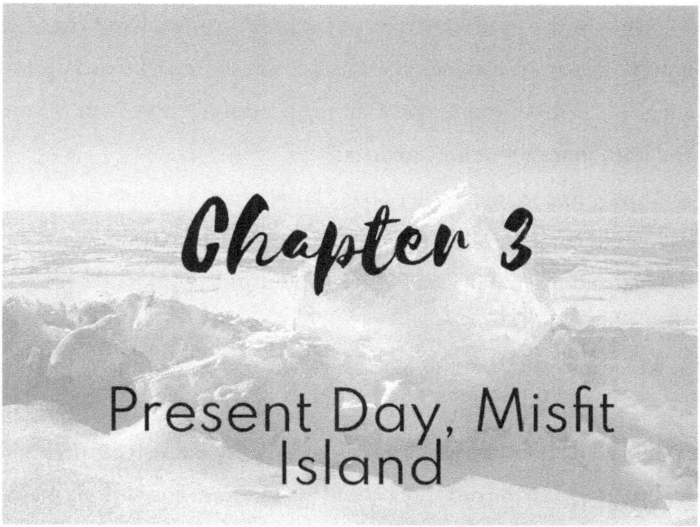

Chapter 3

Present Day, Misfit Island

"I vant to suck your blood. Blah, blah, blah." A tall handsome man who was built like a quarterback on steroids raised his hands in the air and came quickly at KeeKee.

"Horatio! Knock it off. You aren't funny at all." KeeKee rolled her eyes and waved her hand.

"But, I'm not trying to be funny, I'm scary. I'm a vampire." He stood tall with his hands on his hips and black cape flowing behind him. His fake fangs hung out over his lips and the eye makeup he wore looked more like he was starring in a Hollywood disaster film, than a vampire flick.

"Uh," Sofka tried hard not to laugh. She put a hand over her mouth. When she had herself calmed down, she straightened up and coughed. "I think you might want to spend some time with Maxim and learn more about how to dress."

"And," Ree scrunched her nose. "How to act."

Marcus Whitehead, a Fey prince in exile, came up behind Ree and put his arms around her waist. "Hiya, beautiful." He kissed her neck. "I've missed you."

Ree leaned back into his embrace. "Marcus, it's only been an hour since I said goodbye this morning."

"That's an hour too long." His nose ran up and down her neck and his lips settled on the soft spot behind her ear. "You know newly mated couples can't be away from each other very long."

Ree sighed and closed her eyes. "I know, but we have to work. And you know as well as I do that we can no longer work together."

Just two days ago they had been caught making out in a storage closet in the back of the clothing store Marcus managed. After that, Horatio said Ree needed a different job.

"Ree, you can work with me as we prepare for Halloween." Horatio took the fake fangs out of his mouth and waved at Marcus. Horatio ran the town's welcome center that doubled as Christmas Central all year long. Except, it seemed, for Halloween. The store that sat right in the middle of the tiny downtown shopping area on the island for misfit supernaturals, was now fully decorated for the spooky holiday with ghosts, goblins, and all sorts of ghouls everywhere one looked. In fact, just inside the front door was a tall, stacked, set of three pumpkins that laughed and yelled, "Boo!" Anytime someone walked by it.

"And you," Horatio pointed to Marcus, "need to get back to your store and get it decorated. Everyone else has theirs all done. But you have nothing yet. Not even a single pumpkin or ghoul. And why haven't you put up any Halloween lights?"

Marcus sighed. "You know, if we were back in Fairie, I'd have an entire Earth year of no responsibilities, other than getting to know my new mate." He pulled Ree tighter to him and closed his eyes, settled his chin on her shoulder, and turned his cheek into her hair.

Ree giggled. "I love being mated."

Sofka rolled her eyes and shook her head. "The entire island knows this." Then she turned to Horatio. "Do you think the island would allow them more time to get this," she waved a hand in the direction of the disgustingly sweet couple, "out of their system?"

Horatio, the unofficial mayor of Misfit Island, pursed his lips and took a moment to think.

On the back wall of the Information Center, where they had all gathered, a screen came to life. While electronics in general didn't work too well on the island just off of Antarctica, these special screens did. "*Give them two more weeks.*"

KeeKee sighed. "Thank you!"

Without a word, the couple ran home, with the plan to not be seen again for at least two weeks. Longer if they could manage more time alone.

Sofka chuckled and shook her head. "If I ever act like that, please just shoot me."

"Same here." KeeKee stuck her tongue out and gagged. "Those two are sweeter than an entire vat of cotton candy."

"Oh, speaking of sugary goodness." Horatio put a finger in the air. "I need someone to get the cotton candy machine out of storage and find the purple and black sugar crystals."

"Really? I thought this was like Christmas central all year long. Why are you going all out for Halloween?" When Sofka and her friends arrived a few weeks back, the information center had been decked out for Christmas, even though it was nowhere near Christmas in the human world.

Horatio, who not only ran the Info Center, but was also considered the leader of the island, had told them that he loved Christmas. They kept the season in their hearts all year long on the island.

As arctic wolf shifters, Sofka, Ree, and KeeKee thought it was a good idea. While they may not have been too keen on meeting the jolly ol' wolf in person, they did love the fantasy of Santa and everything the season stood for – good will toward men, and all that.

Horatio nodded. "Normally, yes. But we do love a good Halloween celebration as well. It's a chance for everyone to dress up as someone, or something else." He pointed to himself and grinned, showing that he had at some point put his fake fangs back in. "I vant to suck your blood."

Sofka shook her head. "If Maxim, or any of the other vampires on the island..." Her voice trailed off when Horatio quickly put his arms to his side and turned around. She felt, more than heard, that there was a presence behind her. With a sigh of resignation, she turned. "Well, speak of the devil."

Maxim Volkov put a hand to his chest and feigned pain. "Ouch, that hurts. You know I'm not the devil."

"No? You are undead and suck people's blood, right?" Sofka tilted her head, stuck her hip out, and put a hand on it.

"Should I dress up as an angel for Halloween, just to show you I'm not evil?" A half smile inched its way up Maxim's lips.

Ever since Ree and Marcus had succumbed to their mating bond, Maxim had been eyeing Sofka with a look that sent chills down her spine. She wasn't sure what he wanted with her. She was just an arctic wolf shifter, and not even a full-blooded one. She should be the last person on this island of misfits who Maxim would want. Which meant that he probably was up to no good. Sofka Federov wasn't going to allow anyone, no matter how sexy they were, to get close enough to break her heart.

She had had enough of alpha males wanting to dominate her and control her. Besides, whenever the other single females on the island caught sight of Maxim getting close to her, they all gave her the stink eye. Sofka wanted to make friends, not enemies. She already had enough of those.

Thoughts of her alpha entered her head, but she shook them away. There was no reason to think of Kirill anymore. He wouldn't find her, or her best friends, on this tiny island. Shoot, she doubted he even knew about it. They certainly hadn't before setting out on their adventure.

KeeKee laughed. "Well, the banter you two have going is fun, but I've got work to do. Since the island has decided to give Ree and Marcus two more weeks for their honeymoon, someone has to run the clothing store." She eyed Maxim.

He stepped back when he caught her eye. "What?"

"I think if you have time to constantly be hounding my friend," KeeKee glanced at Sofka, who's cheeks started turning pink. "Then you have time to help run that store."

"I already have a job." He took two more steps back, trying to get out of the information center before KeeKee could trap him.

The door closed and the lights dimmed.

Maxim sighed and looked down.

Sofka and KeeKee looked at each other, then to Horatio.

"I think the island has something to say." The unofficial mayor pointed to the back wall.

The screen had another message for the group. "*The new arrivals can manage the store for now.*"

"Huh. And here I thought those new arrivals were only visiting." Sofka shook her head. "I guess, the island knows better than we do."

"Doesn't it still freak you out a little bit? The island being sentient and all?" KeeKee shivered and ran a hand down her arm to warm herself up.

When the three wolf shifters arrived, they discovered that there was much more to the island at the end of the world that only certain supernaturals could find. If someone didn't fit with their kind, or with a pack, the island welcomed them with open arms. They did have to pull their weight, but somehow the island always seemed to know the best jobs for the different supes.

Most residents were there permanently, or at least long-term. But occasionally, the island did accept a tourist, or two. Or in this case, ten. The newcomers had pretty much kept to themselves so far, and hadn't been assigned any work – until now.

The island had paired up Marcus and Ree to work together. And on their first day of work, they had inadvertently begun a mating bond. While it was a different coupling than anyone had expected, considering the fact that Marcus was a Fae Prince in exile, it seemed to work. Maybe not at first, but the moment they gave in to their budding bond, it was as though they had been in love forever, instead of just meeting.

Horatio and Maxim both said, "no." At the same time.

Whenever the island wished, it could communicate with the residents via a roll down screen. While the island seemed to be sentient and full of magic that never ended, it couldn't actually vocalize its wishes. Instead, it used the screen to let the supes know what it wanted. The screens were the only electronics that consistently worked.

"Actually, I find it calming to know that the island is still in control." Maxim smiled and looked at Sofka. "I've been here more than fifty years, and I used to wonder when the island would run out of magic. It seems, that it never will." A slow smile crept up his lips and he took a few steps closer to Sofka. "How about dinner? Tonight?"

"Ah, I have plans." Sofka scrambled to come up with something. "I have to work the night shift." She had been assigned to the Sheriff's office as its first deputy. Sheriff Roscoe Coldtrain, the black bear shifter who had run the office for as long as anyone could remember, hated working nights.

Maxim ran a hand down her arm. "I could come by with dinner." He leaned closer. "We could have that talk you wanted."

Sofka had wanted to talk to him, but not alone. And not when he was thinking of eating. While Sofka knew that Maxim wouldn't try to drink her blood, at least not without her consent, she still felt a strange pull toward him that frightened her. Being alone with the sexiest man she'd ever seen wasn't something she was prepared to do. "I was actually thinking that we should have that talk with KeeKee present."

KeeKee's head popped up and she turned a confused gaze to her best friend. "What? Me? Why?" She put a hand to her chest.

Safety in numbers came to Sofka's mind, but she decided against voicing that concern. Instead, she said, "because I think we both need to know the answers. And in case I don't ask all the pertinent questions, you can fill in the missing ones."

With a nod, KeeKee agreed. "Yes, that's a good idea." She looked at Maxim and narrowed her eyes. "I do have a few questions of my own."

The three early twenties wolf shifters hadn't had much experience with other supernaturals. Sure, they'd heard about most of them, but other than polar bear shifters and various wolf shifters, there weren't many others in their neck of the woods. But here, on Misfit Island? They had come across supernaturals they had never even heard of before. Like Bart, the gargoyle who piloted the only way onto the island - a rickety old boat that must be held together with magic.

Speaking of wolf shifters...

"Oh, please. Tell me they aren't here to cause any trouble?" KeeKee blew out a breath and glared at the four troublemakers heading their way.

Since arriving on the island just over a month ago, all three girls had been hounded by what the locals dubbed as the Bully Boys. They were four tundra wolf shifters who wanted nothing more than to cause trouble for everyone.

"You know, I would have thought that the island would have kicked them off by now. I don't understand how this island maintains control and lets these four idiots stay." Sofka snarled when Tony Stanislav, the tall dark blonde tundra shifter who thought the sun rose and set on his every word, looked at her and winked.

Maxim had noticed the gesture and bristled at the audacity of Tony. Since he had already warned those boys that he was the protector of the girls, Maxim stood tall and narrowed his eyes before showing his fangs. Usually, when the Bully Boys saw Maxim, they went in the other direction. Sometimes, they even ran with their tails between their legs, literally. But not today.

Something had given Tony a backbone and Maxim didn't like it one bit.

Neither did Sofka. She glared at Tony when he stopped directly in front of her.

"Well, well, well, if it isn't the little girl," Tony turned and scoffed at Maxim, "and her little protector. Now, why aren't you in jail today where you belong?"

"Don't you mean where *you* belong?" Sofka scoffed and mentally cursed the island for letting these boys stay, even when they caused so much trouble. They had only gotten out of jail two days ago, thanks to their last round of rowdy behavior.

Tony raised his hands above his head. "Hey, now. I did my time. You can't touch me today."

Not that Sofka wanted to touch Tony, or any of his friends, but she did have an overwhelming desire to drag them by their scruffs back to jail and lose the key. However, even in the supernatural world, one couldn't just lock up an annoying tick. Tony would have to actually do something else deserving of lock-up. She smiled when she realized that it wouldn't be long. Maybe then, she'd get to lose the key to their cell.

Manny Smith, another of the Bully Boys, sauntered up to KeeKee. "'Sup?" He nodded once and winked.

Revulsion swept through KeeKee like a turbine on overdrive. She almost lost her breakfast. Words refused to come and she moved away from the disgusting little tundra wolf shifter.

Sofka laughed. "Well, I guess she told you."

Maxim almost snorted he laughed so hard. "Boys, why don't you go chase some cars on the freeway?"

Andrew MacKinzey snarled. "Hey, idiot. There aren't any freeways here on the island."

"Yeah," Johnny Appleton, the quietest of the tundra wolf shifters, scoffed.

Maxim raised a brow. "I know."

Sofka had to bite her lip when she realized that none of the Bully Boys got the joke. The nearest freeway was hours away by boat. It would have been nice if they would go and find it. If only to be rid of them for a day.

Lately, they had been making themselves known to the girls on a daily basis. And not just walking past them and whistling or calling out stupid things. They've actually been coming up to the girls and irritating them directly, face-to-face. Like this day.

Horatio finally stepped in. "Alright, it's time for everyone to get back to work." He turned to Tony. "I believe the island has assigned all four of you trash duty, is that correct?"

The four wolf shifters complained.

"You know, I don't think the island wanted us to actually do the trash pick-up. I believe our job was to supervise the pick-up. Which means that we can choose who does that job." Tony turned to Maxim. "I think you're the perfect candidate for the garbage."

The vampire crossed his thick, muscled arms over his chest. "Think again."

Three of the wolves backed up a couple of paces, but Tony stood his ground. And for the first time, too.

Sofka wondered where this backbone came from.

Maxim arched a brow and stared at Tony. Slowly, his fangs came out and his eyes changed to a deep, blood-red.

If Sofka didn't know any better, she'd be running away with her tail between her legs. Even knowing what she knew about Maxim, a little voice in the back of her head started to quiver with fear and told her to run. But she stood her ground and watched the stare-down continue.

Manny, Tony's would-be beta, cleared his throat. "Uh, Tony." He pointed to the screen on the back wall that had come down while everyone was too busy watching the two alpha's stare each other down.

The group all turned in unison to read the words the island had posted on the screen. *The four tundra wolves are to collect the garbage and dispose of it properly. They are not to supervise anyone else.* The screen rolled up, signaling it had finished.

"Well," KeeKee grinned. "I guess, it told you." She couldn't help herself, and a snicker escaped her lips. KeeKee didn't even try to cover it up.

Sofka tried to hold in her laugh, but gave up and let it go. "Alrighty, then. I guess we should all get to work." She had the days off, and worked nights. But felt as though she needed to get to the jail and check on Roscoe.

The bear shifter was the island's sheriff, but he tended to nap in his chair most of the time. It made sense, bears did nap the winters away. And living on an island at the bottom of the world that was covered in snow and ice all year long, did tend to make a body feel as though it was winter all year long.

"I'm heading to check in with Roscoe." Sofka waved but stopped at the door and took a lingering glance in Maxim's direction. He still had his eyes on the four tundra shifters who never did anything but cause trouble.

Chapter 5

Maxim questioned his decision to let Sofka walk away without his escort, but he didn't want her to feel as though he was stalking her. Only a few days earlier she had complained that his attentions were stifling, bordering on stalkerish. He didn't think so, but he could see why she thought that. All he wanted was to protect her, and her friends.

Instead of following her to the jail, he stepped into the street to keep a discreet eye on her progress. It wasn't as though she had far to walk, it was less than a five-minute walk down the road to where the Sheriff's office and jail sat, and that was with stopping to greet supes along the way. He could see the building from where he stood.

The island wasn't dangerous, per se, but those bully boys weren't exactly known to play by the rules. They seemed to have had a moment of stupidity that day and stood up to Maxim. Which was something they'd never done before. So, Maxim wasn't sure if Sofka was safe, or not.

Thankfully, Sofka was headed to the jail, where the sheriff would be. Sadly, the sheriff wasn't as much of a detraction to crime as he once had been. With life so easy on the island, Roscoe Coldtrain didn't have much to do other then put his boots up on the desk and nap. Maybe Roscoe's lack of attention was what had given the boys a bit of backbone lately.

If it weren't for Sofka, they wouldn't have been put in jail recently. They most likely would have gotten away with stealing from the Island Shack. Which could be why they seem even more intent on intimidating Sofka and harassing them all – they were angry.

And they certainly wouldn't have been ordered to do community service and take out the trash all over town, if not for Sofka arresting them. Maxim laughed out loud when he pictured those four little wolf shifters using the island's truck to load the trash and take it to their landfill.

The opposite side of the island was where their landfill was located. And with the frozen ground, digging holes wouldn't be easy. He used to think it sad that the island didn't magically dispose of the garbage from each trash can. Now, he realized why the island made someone dig holes and bury the trash before it magically dissolved. Nowhere else on Earth did all trash compost the way theirs did, at least not that Maxim knew.

Thanks to the island, they truly were self-sustaining and eco-friendly. Even plastics were magically dissolved.

"What's so funny?" Bart, the island's ship captain, asked after spitting on the ground by Maxim's feet. For some strange reason, the gargoyle always seemed to spit water. Even when he wasn't on the water. No one knew why he did it. But Maxim thought it was probably due to the fact that when he started out as a gargoyle over a century ago, he was on top of a building in Poland where they received an inordinate amount of rain. There had been a hole in the back of his head where rainwater drained in and then out through his mouth.

The architect of the building had built four gargoyles that perched out far enough over the corners of the building that the water would drain into the street, and not on the sidewalk where the people walked. It was a rather ingenious design. Too bad when the gargoyles became living creatures, the magic didn't put back stone replicas to keep the water off the walkway below.

"Just picturing those boys having to dig ditches." Maxim grinned.

After spitting out another mouth full of water, Bart's eyes rolled up to look at Maxim. The gargoyle was barely four feet and didn't really have a head that would move up and down too easily, but it did have the uncanny ability to turn ninety degrees to each side. "Dig ditches? Is that a euphemism for something?"

Maxim chuckled. "No. The island assigned them trash duty. They have to go around and pick up all the trash and deposit it in the land fill. With the frozen ground, that should keep them busy for a while."

"And out of trouble?" Bart asked.

"One can only hope." With a wave, Maxim headed to his favorite haunt – the Island Shack.

Maxim's hope of a peaceful afternoon was dashed when he heard a scream. He had just finished his bloody burger and sat back in his chair debating what to do next when a piercing scream, followed by a crashing sound, hit his ears.

Just because he heard screaming didn't mean that those pesky wolf shifters were up to no good, but it was a good bet. Too bad he hadn't put a hundred on it, he would have won.

The first thing out of Maxim's mouth was an expletive he rarely used. He shook his head, upset with not only himself for saying something so rude, but also with the tundra wolf shifters who had upset his day...again. "What?" Maxim shook his head and sighed. "There is no reason with these wolves, is there? So why do I even ask?"

The only real vehicles on the island were the truck that delivered supplies from the boat to the shops. And the snowplow that pulled a cart behind it for the trash pickup - Misfit Island's version of a trash truck. It looked to Maxim as though the boys had decided to use both vehicles and play crash test dummies. Only, instead of just injuring themselves, they had crashed into the side of the coffee shop, where multiple supes had been hit.

Using his superspeed, Maxim ran to the group of injured and helped to assess the damage. "Do we have any vehicle that can transport the injured to the medical clinic?"

One of the pixie's who worked at the coffee shop flew to Maxim. "We can fly them over if needed." She was flanked by three more flying pixies.

"I guess that'll have to work." Maxim knew that four of them could carry one person at a time. If the injured didn't seem to have a spine injury, he could also help carry them to the clinic, which was on the opposite side of Main Street from where they were.

"Out of the way, people step back and give the emergency workers room." Sofka's loud and commanding voice caused the throng of lookie loos to move out of the way. "What happened?"

"Don't you mean *who* happened?" Maxim looked over to the wolf shifters who stood by the vehicles more interested in the damage to the truck and snowplow than they were the injured supes. The ones they caused to be injured by their latest antics. "I think it's time the island did something about these four."

Sofka ran a hand down her face. "Will the island ever do something about them?"

"Oh, concrete whiskey!" Bart only swore like that when he was really mad, something Maxim had rarely heard since he met the gargoyle over five decades ago. "Those boys are menaces to the island. It's high time they get the boot." He snorted. "And I'd be happy to use mine." The gargoyle put his concrete foot up as far as it would go, which wasn't far.

Maxim almost smiled when he thought about how painful the concrete kick would be. "Let's worry about those ingrates later. Right now, we have injured to deal with."

With a supernatural's ability to heal quickly, most of those injured didn't need anything more than a bandage or cold compress. Only two supes needed actual medical attention.

"Ginger, can you get the other pixies to help take Micky to the infirmary? I'll carry Steve and meet you there." Maxim helped the djinn up and was about to carry him, when the man waved him off.

"I got this." Steve tried to stand on his injured leg, but fell right back down with a howl of pain.

"Alright, I know you don't want to appear weak, but please, let me carry you to the infirmary." Maxim understood male bravado, but this was taking it to the extreme.

"I can't even enter my bottle." The djinn bared his teeth and nodded once for Maxim.

Four hours later, Sofka, Maxim, Horatio, Bart, and the sheriff all met at the jail to discuss what happened that day.

Chapter 6

"I think it's high time the island boots those animals. They have no business being here if they can't contribute to the peaceful existence of this island." Maxim turned to glare at the sheriff, who had only put them in jail when Sofka demanded they be arrested for causing the destruction of a town building and hurting so many supes in the process.

The sheriff held up one hand. "I know, I know. Those boys are the bane of our existence here. But we can't make the island do anything it doesn't want to."

Sofka interrupted, "Look, I know I'm new here, but even I know that those, those," she bit her lip before letting what she really thought of the tundra shifters slip out of her mouth, "selfish, mean, cretins can't keep getting away with everything. We have to do something more than just a few days in the slammer."

Horatio sighed. "I know. If it were up to me, they would have been booted off the island months ago. But we don't make those decisions.

The island has a way of knowing exactly when someone needs to leave, even if we disagree." He turned to Maxim. "Remember last year when we were having trouble with that one vampire?"

"Yes," Maxim nodded. "Dimitri had been trying to bite just about any woman who crossed his path. Finally, after weeks of issues, the island booted him." He stopped and his mouth formed an O. "That's right. The moment he exited the boat on the mainland, he saw a group of vampires he knew. Vampires who had been trying to find this very island and attack us."

Horatio picked up the story. "Exactly. He told Bart before he left and when Bart returned with you, the sheriff, and a few others, you found that Dmitri had already tied them up nice and neatly."

Everyone in the room nodded and smiled.

Sofka looked between the males and waited for them to continue with the story. When they didn't, she threw her hands in the air and scoffed. "So, what happened next?"

Marcus laughed. "Dmitri was let back on the island and he's now one of the chefs at the Island Shack. I think he ended up mating with one of the waitresses, too."

"Eye, why do I even bother." Sofka stretched her neck. "I meant, what happened to the group of evil vamps? They were tied up, but where are they now?"

Bart snorted, then spit as usual. "The best part, in my opinion."

"Yeah." Horatio chuckled and nodded his head.

When they didn't go on, Sofka wondered to herself how they could be so daft. "The vampires? Since I wasn't here then, can you tell me what happened?" She tried her best to be polite, but by the end of her question, her teeth were gritted, and her hands were fisted at her sides.

The sheriff yawned and nodded. "Right, I s'pose you wouldn't know. We have a..." he tilted his head. "Well, not so much a prison, more like a long-term holding cell."

Bart snorted. "Don't you mean we have a popsicle locker?" He looked to Sofka. "There is a place where we can hold supes for very long periods of time. They get flash frozen with magic. The island decides when they can be awoken."

Sofka stood in place, not moving, except for the fluttering of her eyelids and the slow rise and fall of her chest. While she'd seen some pretty crazy stuff on this island, she had never heard of anything like this. Well, nothing outside of novels. Sure, in a novel a person, or supernatural creature, could be put into a sort of stasis and then revived without any issues. But, in real life? She'd never heard of anything that worked.

Even the rumor about Walt Disney himself being put into a sort of stasis was false. Cryogenics just wasn't a real possibility, at least not yet. But with magic? Was this island so powerful that it could put people in a sort of cryo-jail and bring them back without any issues? "Has anyone been awoken after being put into cryo-stasis?" Sofka had read about this, and she was pretty sure cryo-stasis was the correct term, not popsicle.

"Ah?" Bart rubbed his nose and stared at Sofka. "Cryo-stasis? What's that?"

With a little chuckle, Sofka went on to explain the term. "You see, popsicle isn't the right word. At least, I don't think it is. This isn't some version of supernatural soylent green, is it?" She shivered with the thought that all the food they had consumed on the island since arriving might actually be people, or other supes.

This time, an entire mouthful of water spurt from Bart's mouth. "Boy, am I glad I don't eat food."

The look on Maxim's face was almost comical. "That's disgusting. NO! We don't serve people up here."

Sofka raised a brow. "Funny, coming from a supe whose main source of sustenance is blood."

Sheriff Coldtrain raised his hands. "Alright, I think we've digressed enough. And no, we don't serve up humans or supernaturals as our food source. We actually have some farms and ranches on the island were most of our food comes from. The rest is supplemented from regular shipments from the mainland."

"Really?" Sofka tilted her head. "Why haven't I seen the farms and ranches?"

Horatio waved his hands to get everyone's attention. "That's for another day. I'll take you and your friends for a more detailed tour of the island. But for now, the cryo facilities are magical and none of us have access. And before you ask," he looked at Sofka, "yes, we do have residents that are released." He and the sheriff exchanged a strange glace.

It made Sofka wonder if she was in the presence of criminals. Or, were they called something else once they were released from cryo-jail? Cryo-parolee? She shook her head and realized it didn't matter. All that mattered now was how they were going to handle the Bully Boys. While the idea of putting them in cryo-jail appealed to Sofka, she knew they hadn't done anything deserving of that level of detainment. At least, not yet.

"Okay, so what constitutes deserving cryo-jail?" Sofka bit her lower lip and wondered if the supernatural prison was similar to what she'd read about for the humans. Well, minus the cryo-freeze.

Maxim winced. "Mostly, it's reserved for the worst of those who come our way, like murderers and rapists."

"Mostly?" Sofka raised a brow.

"Those vampires who were taken into custody last year hadn't actually committed crimes here on the island, or against any of our residents." Maxim looked from Sofka to the sheriff. "But, they had left a trail of dead humans and supernaturals across several continents."

"Oh." Not knowing what to say, Sofka just blinked.

"I don't see why the island froze them. I say we should stake them to the ground and let the sun take care of them." Bart spit on the ground and his strange water splattered against the sheriff's shoes.

"Hey, enough of that." The sheriff pointed to his shoes. "I don't need your gross phlegm hittin' my boots."

Bart grunted. "Next time, just stake the murderers and be done with it."

Roscoe sighed. "How many times do I have to tell you, I can't override the island."

Horatio jumped up. "Enough! It's done and over. I doubt those vampires will see the light of day for at least a century, maybe longer. So let's get back to the issue at hand, shall we?"

The entire time they had been chatting, and arguing, the island had remained quiet. But as soon as everyone shut up, they could hear the tell-tale sounds of a screen lowering. All eyes turned to the screen that hung above the sheriff's chair.

The four tundra wolves will spend the next week in jail. Then they will be assigned trash duty, without the use of the trash truck, until I decide they have learned their lesson.

The screen rolled up once everyone had time to read it. Sofka read it twice and shook her head. "Well, the island will get a week of peace."

"But we won't." The sheriff scoffed. "You and I will have to make sure we have the jail covered until they are released."

Sofka nodded. "It wasn't too tough when it was only a couple of days, but a week of working twelve-hour shifts without any breaks? Can you deputize a couple of supes to help us out?"

It wasn't that Sofka didn't want to work, she did. In fact, she had never enjoyed any job back in Siberia as much as she did being a sheriff's deputy. But without a television, it was going to be tough sitting in the small room with the four of those dingleberries. Hopefully, they will sleep most of her shifts away.

The sheriff grunted. "I s'pose we could get some help with the overnight shifts. We do have some supes who don't sleep at night." He eyed Maxim.

The vampire looked at Sofka and smirked. "I could help out a few nights."

She shook her head. "And what are you going to require for payment?"

Maxim grinned from ear to ear and looked her up and down. "Oh, I think we can come to some sort of mutually beneficial terms."

She put her hands on her hips and glared at him. "No way."

"What?" Maxim blinked and looked Sofka in the eyes. "I'm not going to ask for anything too difficult. Just dinner. With you."

Before Sofka could think of a scathing retort, the sheriff said, "Done. But dinner will have to wait until the week is up."

"What?" Sofka couldn't believe her ears. How could the sheriff make that decision for her? "I don't want to have dinner with *him*."

Horatio pursed his lips and stared at Sofka. "Really? Because I can't count how many times I've caught you checking him out as he walked away."

Heat seared up Sofka's neck and flared in her cheeks. "What? Uh, no." She shook her head. "I don't check him out."

A cheese eating grin spread across Maxim's face. "Is that so?"

She bristled with the idea that she was checking him out. "No, I don't. When I watch him walk away it's to make sure he really is leaving. The last thing I need is for some vampire to sneak up on me." She shivered at the idea of his fangs on her neck. But for the first time, she wasn't sure if it was revulsion, or something else she was feeling.

Maxim's soft chuckle permeated her entire being. Now, heat spread throughout her entire body as she looked him in the eye.

An idea began to germinate in Sofka's mind. "Has anyone spoken to them to find out why they are all of a sudden so fearless? I mean," she hitched her hip to the side and put a hand on it. "Until recently, they usually ran away from Maxim. But earlier they, well Tony, stood up to the vampire." She rolled her eyes at the memory.

"I had wondered that as well. In all the time they've been here, they've never once stood up to me like they have recently." Maxim scratched his chin. "What's changed?"

Chapter 7

"Well, that went faster than expected." Sofka looked to her boss, the sheriff. "Why do you think they didn't put up a fuss about being incarcerated again?"

Sheriff Roscoe Coldtrain rubbed the stubble on his chin. "I don't rightly know. Something's fishy in the state of Antarctica."

"I must agree." Sofka narrowed her eyes and looked at the four tundra wolfshifters sitting quietly in their individual cells. The holding cell area normally showed only one cell. But when they arrested more than one being, the magic of the island would create all the cells they needed. It still sent shivers down Sofka's spine every time she witnessed the magic of the island in action.

Instead of seeing the jail cells expand, they were already there and waiting with the doors open for the Bully Boys when they arrived after the decision was made to put them there. She had wanted to see the magic in action, but understood that the island could do anything it wanted in the blink of an eye. Even if she had been standing inside the sheriff's station when the cells expanded, she wouldn't have actually seen anything happen. It was that way every time they arrested the Bully Boys.

Sofka opened and closed her mouth a few times before she finally decided what to say. "Do you think someone has put them up to their latest antics?"

"Why would anyone want them to crash the only two vehicles we have on this island into the coffee shop? No one was hurt badly, and all the supes will heal quickly. Even Micky will be back to normal by tomorrow, the next day at the latest." Roscoe narrowed his eyes and waited for Sofka's response.

"I know, I know. But..." She shook her head. "Like you said, something isn't right. With Tony acting all tough and not backing down from Maxim earlier, and even his little buddies showing more backbone than normal. I gotta wonder what has given them their newfound confidence."

"Hmph," the sheriff scoffed. "I s'pose they are acting unnatural. Even for bullies."

"Especially for bullies. Normally, bullies back down when someone bigger and stronger get in their face. They almost never change overnight." Sofka tapped her index finger on her lower lip. "What happened since they were released from jail last week to now? Did they meet with someone?"

The scraping sound of Roscoe's hand rubbing across the stubble on his chin echoed around the room. It almost sounded like fingernails running down a chalkboard. "I think we need to find out what they've been up to."

"Agreed." Sofka nodded her head once. "I'll go and check with Bart to see if the boys left the island, and if he knows who they might have met up with."

"When Maxim comes to keep watch tonight, I'll check around town to see if anyone has noticed the boys talking to anyone new. We don't know anything about those latest arrivals." Roscoe turned his head and looked back to the door that separated the front office from the jail cells. On any given day, it wasn't there. The magic that expanded the cells would sometimes put up the partition, and sometimes it left the cells open to the room. This time, the island knew that the sheriff and his deputy would need some privacy to solve this mystery.

"I'll be back after I speak with Bart." And with a parting wave, Sofka left the sheriff to keep an eye on the vexing foursome.

It wasn't but a five-minute brisk walk to the docks where Bart usually spent most of the day, just waiting to head over to the mainland. But when Sofka arrived, it was to find Bart's boat tied to the moorings and no sign of the spitting gargoyle anywhere. In fact, the dock was eerily quiet. The sun had already set and the moon had begun casting shadows. Shadows that felt almost like they were alive. The island was alive. But were the shadows? Or was it someone hiding from her?

Sofka knew that the light from the sun was filtered and mostly artificial. It had to be. This close to the South Pole, it should be light all night long this time of year. In fact, from October to March, the sun never set on the South Pole. They shouldn't even have twilight this time of year. But they did. The sun and moon seemed to work for their little island just like it did in the Northern Hemisphere. Which was odd now that Sofka thought about it. If the island wanted to emulate the seasons where the most people were populated, she thought it would have taken its direction from the middle of Chile, where they were currently experiencing spring.

Since arriving on the island, Sofka had noticed that the time and the seasons were like that in North America or southern Canada. It was just about dinner time, and the sun had set on this island, but nowhere else in the region would it set yet.

The fact that vampires could walk without too much problem in the "daylight" on this island had caught her attention when she first arrived. Horatio had explained that it wouldn't be much of a safe place for vampires if they couldn't be out in the sunlight and mingling with the majority of the residents on the island. There were other nocturnal species, but none like the vampires who would die in real sunlight.

While Sofka hadn't seen all of the scary night creatures on their tiny island, she had heard enough to want to steer clear of them all. Especially the Snallygaster, a large chimera with bird and reptile features. That one scared her so much, that she refused to shift at night until Horatio finally got her to understand that no creature on the island would attack her, even in her wolf form.

The scary creatures that were there, had left the human world for good reason. And all they wanted was a quiet place to live out the rest of their very long lives. The island provided them with a sanctuary away from the rest of the population and they lived in relative peace.

Just as Sofka was about to turn away and head back to the middle of town, the hair on the back of her neck stood on end. She stiffened and scented the night air. A cinnamon spice scent was present, but that could have been because Maxim worked in the area when they were expecting supernaturals to arrive on the island at night. He was a sort of night watchman, when he wasn't being drafted to help the sheriff.

There was also a sulfur scent mixed with a bit of sewer stench for good measure. Sofka had smelled that before and was told it was their sewer when it backed up. It rarely happened, but when someone was pulling pranks, usually the Bully Boys, this happened. The rest of the scents were normal island and water scents. A bit of fishy odor floated on the air and she wondered if one of the infamous merfolk was nearby.

Since arriving, there were those supes Sofka and her friends wanted to avoid, but there were also supes she wanted to meet. Like the merfolk. Although, truth be told, she was most interested in meeting mermaids. From what she'd been told, the females of the species were the nice ones. The males were warriors and not always nice to new supes. The only one she was warned away from was the creature she feared might be creeping up behind her now.

A shifter's instincts were honed to almost a weapon in and of themselves. She could sense where a being was, even in the dark. And at that very moment, Sofka could tell that someone was coming up behind her. She was supposed to be safe on the island, especially now that Tony and his cronies were behind bars. But her instincts told her to be on guard.

There wasn't a sound coming from anywhere close by. She could hear the lapping of the waves in the water, the sounds of voices drifting over the air from town, and a single heartbeat. Which told her the creature near her wasn't a vampire, or any of the undead creatures that had sought safe haven on this island. But that didn't lower the possibilities by much. Most of the residents had a heartbeat.

Sofka did her best to keep her breathing even. She closed her eyes and pictured in her mind the surrounding area. Her mind filled in any blanks as it searched for what was coming towards her. She knew that if she moved too soon, she would lose the element of surprise. Whatever was stalking her couldn't know that she had been trained by her pack to sense when danger was close and how to defend against it.

One of the only good things her alpha did for them was to teach them stealth techniques and how to defend against any attackers. Probably because her alpha was one of the worst pack leaders she'd ever come across. He was into all sorts of shady dealings. The pack needed to know how to defend against anyone who wanted to seek retribution against Kirill and his pack.

Just when she felt the warm breath of her attacker, she quickly ducked and swept her leg out hitting her attacker and causing him to fall.

"Oomph." Was the only sound she heard as her attacker fell on his back.

Sofka pulled out a small pocket flashlight and shone it on the creature laying at her feet. What she saw baffled her. While his vampire fangs were kept at bay, his eyes had turned red with fury.

"Sofka, what was that about?" Maxim growled between clenched teeth.

She put her hands on her hips and glared down at the sneaky vampire. "You don't have a heartbeat. Why did I hear a heartbeat just behind me?"

"Ah, that would be me." A voice she didn't recognize hit her from the side and she whirled around with fists raised in anticipation of an attack.

The beautiful woman raised her hands in surrender. "Whoa, I'm not here to hurt anyone. I was just meeting Maxim."

Sofka raised a brow, then looked between the two. "You meet your conquests out in the dark, next to the water? What's wrong with bringing them back to your place, or going to theirs?" She scoffed and shook her head. "Never mind, I don't want to know where your fangs go."

Maxim jumped up and laughed. "Jealous?"

The woman who had long red hair that went all the way to her waste laughed. "What? You think him?" she pointed to Maxim. "And me? Please."

"Wait. What's wrong with me? Plenty of women on this island would love to go out on a date with me." His voice sounded hurt, as though he had hoped the beautiful woman was in to him and her obvious rejection hurt.

"You know what? I don't need to know what you two were doing out here." Sofka turned to leave but stopped when the pretty woman spoke.

"Wait, what are you doing out here after dark? You know it's not really safe to be out by the water after dark. Most of the merfolk won't bother you, but there are a couple who might not always follow the rules." The young woman winced and looked out to the sea. "Sorry."

Sofka wasn't sure if she was apologizing to the sea, or to her. It didn't really matter, she needed to find Bart, not these two...whatever they were. It didn't bother her in the least that Maxim was meeting one of the most beautiful women Sofka had ever seen outside of a fashion runway, here in the dark, with no one else around. Well, no one but her.

A splash sounded behind her, and Sofka craned her neck to see what made the sound.

"Oh, don't mind him. Haf is always swimming around here. This is his section to patrol." The red head waved a dismissive hand and looked back at Sofka. "Hi, since Maxim is going to be rude and not introduce us, I'll do it. I'm Luana, one of the resident mermaids."

Sofka's eyes widened so much, her brows shot up to her hairline. "A mermaid? Really?" She grinned, then giggled. "KeeKee and Ree are never going to believe this."

Luana smiled tentatively. "And you are?"

A hand hit Sofka's chest. "Please forgive me, I'm being rude. I'm Sofka. My two friends and I recently moved here. We've not met many supes before coming here. One of my dreams has been to meet merfolk." Her eyes looked down and she felt her cheeks flaming. "Sorry, that's rude. I'm not normally so rude."

Maxim scoffed. "Are you sure about that?"

Both women glared at him.

"Don't worry, I still remember my first-time meeting Bart. I swear, I screamed so loud my entire pod showed up with fangs and claws ready to tear apart whoever it was that had attacked me." Luana laughed a light, tinkling sound.

"Thanks. But what are you two doing here? Is a boat coming in?" Sofka didn't think there was more than one boat. And with Bart's tied to the dock, that meant that either someone was coming who shouldn't be, or something else was going on.

Luana looked away, almost as though she was embarrassed to be caught. Was she one of the females he fed on? Did merfolk have fishy blood? Was mermaid blood to vampires like lobster was to everyone else?

Maxim pointed his index finger at Sofka. "I can see where your mind is going. That's not what's happening here." He pursed his lips and stood taller. "The merfolk are responsible for monitoring our borders. I came to find out if anyone other than Bart has come to the island recently."

Sofka blinked. That had to be the most sense she'd heard from Maxim all day long, maybe even all week. "Good thinking." She turned to Luana. "Has anyone else come near the island?"

Luana sucked in her lips. "There have been no boats other than Bart's that have come anywhere near the island in a long time. But..." she looked to Maxim who nodded. "There are other ways to get on the island, with the right magic."

Chapter 8

Luana's statement sent a frisson of fear through Sofka's entire being. "If there are other ways to get on this island, then no one is truly safe here." Thoughts of her alpha plagued her the entire way back to town.

Maxim walked with her. He couldn't leave her alone after he saw the panic in her eyes. "I don't think you have anything to worry about."

She stopped in the middle of the road. "What do you mean? How can you say that? You heard Luana, there are other ways to get on this island."

She was right, but Maxim also knew that the island was in ultimate control. If there was a true danger to anyone, it would expel them. Or put them on ice for the next century, or two. "Look, I've been here over fifty years, and so far, no one has made it on the island outside of Bart's boat."

"And what about those mermaids and mermen? Did they arrive on the boat?" Sofka pointed back to where they left Luana.

He paused and thought about her question. "Actually, I think they did arrive on the boat in their human forms. While ocean wildlife can come and go freely in the waters, supernatural creatures cannot. There are limits to what can and can't get on the island, or even near it."

"Okay, then how are there other ways to get on the island?" Sofka raised a brow and waited for his response.

Maxim shrugged. "Magic."

As though that explained it all, Sofka scoffed. "Right. Seriously, how could someone get on the island without the island's permission?"

He rubbed his nose. "Ah, magic might be able to get someone on the island. It would have to be someone very strong, like a master wizard or witch. Or," he held up a hand when Sofka was about to interrupt. "There is a portal we don't know about."

"Would Luana know about it?" Sofka was about to turn and head back to the docks when she heard a very distinct whistling sound. It was almost like a kid without two front teeth trying to whistle with water in their mouth.

Maxim chuckled and turned to his right. "Bart, just the one we've been looking for."

Bart stopped right in front of the couple. "Who? Me? Why?" The small gargoyle tried to turn his head up enough to look at them in the face, but being under four feet tall, and unable to turn one's head back ninety degrees had its limitations.

"I'm conducting an official investigation on Tony and his cohorts. When was the last time you took them off the island or brought them back?" Sofka prayed it was as simple as the boys leaving the island to meet with someone who gave them a backbone, magically, or otherwise.

"I keep a log of all supes who come and go. Follow me to the office and I'll see. But I believe they left the island right after they were released from jail the last time you had them in there." Bart stopped and turned around to glare at Sofka. "If you would keep them in prison, then we wouldn't have all these problems on the island."

She held her hands up. "Trust me, if it were up to me, they would stay in jail, or be banished from the island."

Bart spit a huge amount of water next to her feet. Some of the water splashed on her boots.

"Hey, watch where you point that thing." Sofka pointed to Bart's mouth. "I don't care to have your icky saliva all over my new boots."

A cackle emanated from Bart that sounded more like concrete grating against more concrete. "Then tell the Sheriff those boys are a menace to society and be done with them."

"Now, Bart. You know as well as I do that the island makes the decision, not the sheriff or the deputy." Maxim's conciliatory voice rang true and both Bart and Sofka sighed.

"Okay, the book is in the drawer right there." Bart went to his locked filing cabinet and after he unlocked it, pulled a tattered looking hard bound journal that had to be at least two hundred years old. "Let me see. Tony Stanislav, Manny Smith, Andrew MacKinzey, and Johnny Appleton all went to the mainland and stayed overnight five days ago. I picked them up less than twenty-four hours later and brought them back here." He nodded and looked at a few more pages. "And from what I can see, they haven't left since."

"Wasn't that the day you picked up a case of supplies?" Maxim asked.

"Yes, it was." Bart answered.

Sofka perked up. "Does that mean you left the boat and saw them in town?"

"Eye and nay. I left the boat, but didn't see those boys in town. I would have remembered if I saw them." Bart looked back at the register before putting it away. "No one new has arrived on the island since then. In fact, the only new supes to arrive since you moved here are the ten that keep to themselves."

"I thought they were only going to be here for a vacation? They've been here for well over a month now. Who are they?" Sofka tried to remember meeting anyone of them, but she'd only seen them from afar.

"I met a few of them yesterday. I think they're shifters," Maxim stated.

"Shifters?" A chill went through Sofka. While she didn't recognize any of them, it was possible they were searching for her on Kirill's orders. Her alpha wouldn't give up on them too easily. Not when he was expecting a big payday for selling them on the supernatural black market.

Maxim looked at her funny and tilted his head to the side. "Are you hiding from someone?"

"Aren't we all?" Bart snorted and spit more water to the side.

Sofka stayed quiet.

"Let me rephrase that. Who are you hiding from, Sofka?" Maxim's eyes softened and his hand reached out to take hers. When she pulled back, he let his arm fall to his side.

"What sort of shifters are they?" Sofka directed her question to Bart.

The stone gargoyle snorted. "How should I know? I can tell if they're shifters, but not always what sort."

"But, you knew I was a wolf shifter." When Sofka first got on Bart's boat, he called her little wolfie. She had just assumed he was one of those types of supes who could discern what everyone was. Not all supernaturals had that gift.

"I did smell wolf on you, but I didn't know you were an arctic wolf shifter. Like I said back then, I can tell in general." Bart looked out to the distance and thought for a moment. "I think a few of them were wolf, one smelled of sulfur, and the rest were a variety. I know the island put them all together in one giant house, but something told me they weren't longtime friends. Maybe they all met up on the road and decided safety in numbers?"

"Sulfur? What creatures smell that way? Was it a demon?" Sofka didn't know about all creatures, but she'd never heard of any smelling like fire.

A slow smile spread across Maxim's face. "That can only be one creature, but I heard they had died off ages ago."

Bart snorted. "Well, if they had, she didn't get the memo. The supe who smelled of sulfur is a female. Pretty thing, too. But she stays close to home. I think she's hiding out from someone."

"Probably because she's the last of her kind. And a female, too?" Maxim whistled. "Her scales, and every part of her actually, would fetch a fortune on the black market. The sort that would set up anyone for many lifetimes."

Sofka inhaled sharply. "You don't mean..." she shook her head. "That's not possible, is it?"

"Dragon." Bart chortled and then spit more water when he started coughing.

"Wow!" Sofka reeled from the revelation. "They're real? I thought they went the wayside of the dinosaurs."

Maxim chuckled. "You really were kept out of the loop, weren't you? As an arctic wolf shifter I would have thought you knew their history."

She furrowed her brows. "Why would I know their history? What do they have to do with arctic wolf shifters?"

"Shoot, even I know their story." Bart chuckled. His head moved from side to side, but by centimeters, as though he was trying to shake his head.

With a deep sigh, Maxim began to regale Sofka with the history of the dragon. "You see, the dragons were dying off. That is until one mated with one of Santa's daughters. Not the current Santa, but his father-in-law. That was what? Twenty years ago?" He looked to Bart.

"Yup, and then another daughter mated with another one. After that, the dragon population had a growth spurt. They still keep to themselves, but there are now quite a few younglings. And even more hatchlings are born every year." Bart's mouth pursed, as though he was going to spit again, but held it back.

"Huh. I wonder what she's doing here then. I would think she'd be highly protected by her pack." Sofka tapped a finger to her chin. "Or are they called something else?"

"I think they might be called a clutch." Maxim stated.

"No, they're called a weyr. A clutch is a group of baby dragons." The gargoyle snorted, then changed his mind. "Or are they called a flight? I think the world has a lot of different names for a group of dragons."

Maxim interrupted, "I've heard them called a thunder before."

"Oh, I like that one. A thunder sounds so strong and formidable." Sofka laughed.

"I can see that. When their wings are all flapping, they probably do sound like thunder," Maxim added.

"And when they breathe fire, it's more like lightning." Bart chortled.

Sofka laughed heartily and the tension she had been carrying in her body eased as evidenced by her shoulders loosening and her laughter finally hitting her eyes. "Okay, so what do you think is really going on? Do you think anyone from that group is somehow doing something to the Bully Boys?"

"Ha!" Bart spit and this time it looked more like a fountain of water, it arched high and then landed several feet away from any of them. "If any of those newcomers are friendly with those rotten boys, I'll be a monkey's uncle."

"Do gargoyles reproduce?" Sofka thought all of them were created from the evil witch who tried to bring them to life only to suck their lifeforce away from them. And when she died, all of the gargoyles in Europe came to life. She'd never heard any stories of them having kids.

A look crossed Bart's face that might have been interpreted as longing, but Sofka couldn't be sure.

"No, we don't have kids. There will never be any more gargoyles than what we have now." Bart looked down at the ground and Sofka couldn't tell what he was thinking.

"Can a gargoyle die?" All she knew was that they weren't really alive like most supes were. They didn't have blood flowing through their veins, or even heartbeats. But they did have brains and if Bart was any indication, they were very intelligent.

This time, when Bart's eyes narrowed, Sofka knew he was mad. "Yes, we can. But it's not easy to kill us. That's all I'm going to say."

Sofka looked to Maxim who lightly shook his head once. She took that to mean to leave it alone. So she changed the subject. "Alright. If the boys have only been off the island once, no one new has arrived, and electronics don't work well in the south pole region, what changed?"

"That, my dear, is exactly what we have to find out." Muscly arms crossed over Maxim's chest and his eyes glared red.

Chapter 9

When no one had any clue as to what those boys had been up to, other than mischief, the three of them decided to start asking around. Maxim said he would try and get some info from them when he watched them overnight.

Since Sofka didn't have to do the night shift, she decided to search out her friend, KeeKee. They hadn't shared dinner in quite some time. When KeeKee couldn't be found on Main Street, Sofka headed home.

The second Sofka cracked the door to her house, she cringed. A sound she never expected to hear blared through the tiny crack in the door. The house was soundproof, so she had no clue what she was stepping into before she opened the door.

"What in the world?" Sofka put her fingers in her ears and winced at the pain of the sound coming from the speakers. She would have thought teenagers broke into her house if it wasn't for the fact that KeeKee was singing at the top of her lungs along with the latest boy-band song screeching throughout the entire house.

"KeeKee! What is going on?" Sofka tried to be heard over the loud sound, but it seemed her friend was in a world of her own.

She closed the door behind her and watched as her friend danced in time to the music as though she'd been doing this sort of thing for ages. Sofka wondered if this was what her friend did every night now that she had the house to herself. A laugh bubbled up and she didn't care to stop it.

Sure, they had all been into boybands when they were teens, but now? Sofka couldn't remember KeeKee, or even Ree, ever talking about boybands, except in the past tense when they laughed over their crazy antics growing up.

But K-Pop? They'd never even listened to the stuff, except for once. And all three scrunched their noses at the same time as though they'd smelled, or heard, something awful. All three of them had agreed to never listen to that stuff.

However, as Sofka stood there listening to the music, she started to feel her feet tap. Was she starting to get into the cheesy sound of the music? She'd never heard this song, and didn't think she knew who this band was. She stood there listening to the soft voices singing. The song was in Korean, so she didn't know what they were saying, but it sounded nice. The melody was sweet and upbeat at the same time, then it took a harder edge, almost like a rock song. Her hips began to sway and she smiled. This was a fun song.

It was too bad that KeeKee turned around.

"Ahhh!" Sofka's best friend screamed and ran to hide in her bedroom.

"KeeKee, don't run away. I actually liked it." She chuckled and followed her friend.

The house turned the music down to a low background sound and Sofka thought she could get used to this life. Somehow, the house seemed to sense what they needed, and when. It was like the human version of a smart home. Although, this house, and all of the houses on the island, were magically smart.

When the girls first arrived, it was nothing but a tiny shack on the outside. The moment they walked inside, it was a dream house. Each of the three girls had their own rooms, and the kitchen was exactly what she had dreamed it would be. The island had known what they needed, and wanted, before they even said anything. And poof, like magic the house inside was exactly what they wanted.

And the same day that Ree mated with Marcus, the house removed her room. Ree's personal items had been magically moved to the front room. No one understood how that happened, but they just accepted it.

The outside was another story. All of the homes Sofka had seen on this island looked like little old shacks. No one understood why the island didn't put its magic into the outside looks of the home. The magic only seemed to make the inside all pretty.

"KeeKee, it's alright. Don't feel bad. I kinda liked it." Sofka knocked on KeeKee's door since it had slammed shut before she got to it.

"Go away!" KeeKee's voice screamed through the door.

"Hey, don't worry. I won't judge you for liking K-pop. That song was actually good. Come on, let me in and we can talk about it." For a moment, Sofka worried her friend wouldn't let her in. But just as she was about to walk away, the door opened, and a light blonde head poked out.

"Really? You aren't just saying that?" The green eyes of the tiniest member the three-wolf pack glistened.

"Oh, KeeKee. I would never be upset that you liked something different than I did." Sofka chuckled, but stopped when she saw pain cross her friend's face. "Hey, I really did like that song. Who is this band?"

KeeKee opened the door and motioned for Sofka to enter. "They're called Monsta X."

Sofka nodded and smiled. "It's total dance music. But what I think I like the most is that they combine a lot of different styles. It's pop, hip-hop, and even a bit of rock in there. I like it. Why did you run?"

"You're going to laugh, but I was afraid you'd tease me. You know, like we used to do when we heard others listening to K-pop." KeeKee shrugged and looked down at her feet.

A frown took over Sofka's smile. "I'm sorry if you thought you couldn't share something you liked with me." She sat down on the bed next to KeeKee. "We were all just stupid kids when we hated K-pop. How long have you been into this music?"

KeeKee bit her lower lip. "What brings you home?"

It was obvious to Sofka that KeeKee wanted to change the topic. "Maxim is watching the jail tonight, and the cretins that are now in there." She sighed and told KeeKee everything that she'd learned since the crash earlier that day.

"So," KeeKee sat up straight and looked into Sofka's eyes, "you think that someone is putting them up to these shenanigans? But who and why?"

Sofka shook her head. "When you put it that way, it doesn't really make sense. But none of us understand why Tony and his minions all of a sudden are upping their antics, and why they stood up to Maxim. It doesn't make sense."

"So, what? You think they have some sort of evil employer who's gonna take over the island?" KeeKee laughed. "You know that's not possible."

"Well, I would have agreed with you only two days ago, but I've got a rotten feeling about this. Something happened to them the last time they went to the mainland, that's when their attitudes changed."

"Hold up, they've always been jerks." KeeKee pursed her lips. "Don't you think it's possible they are just getting bolder because the island isn't doing much to stop them?"

Sofka thought about that for a moment. "So, you think I'm overreacting?"

KeeKee winced and pinched her thumb and forefinger together. "Maybe just a smidge."

With a deep breath, Sofka nodded. "Alright, I'll consider that. But I think we should see if there is anything else going on. Haven't you noticed how brave they've been, compared to before?"

"Well," KeeKee paused and thought about it. "I guess they do seem to have a bit more backbone. But it could be like I said, they've gotten bolder just because the island hasn't really done much to punish them."

"Okay, okay. But they don't seem to be afraid of Maxim any longer. Do you think it's because the island hasn't punished them enough?" Many things could be behind the new attitude of the Bully Boys, but not enough punishment wasn't something Sofka could accept. If they had still cowered under the glare of the vampire, then maybe. But since Tony stood up to Maxim, Sofka had a feeling something wasn't right.

"Yeah, that is weird." KeeKee agreed. "I'll keep an eye out and see if I can find anything out. And tomorrow I'll even ask Horatio if he has any ideas."

"Good idea." Sofka stood up but paused before leaving the room. "Have you met those newcomers? You know, the ones who arrived after we did?"

KeeKee shook her head. "I wasn't working in the information center when they arrived, so I haven't met them yet. They do seem to keep to themselves." She scrunched her nose. "Do you think they might be involved somehow?"

Sofka moved her shoulders up and down. "I don't know. But I do know that they are now working in the clothing store. I think I might need a new pair of snow pants." She grinned and waved before leaving KeeKee's room.

It was later than Sofka realized by the time she finished speaking with KeeKee, so she went to her gourmet kitchen that the house had created for her and decided it was time to cook a nice meal. Since working nights, she hadn't had many opportunities to indulge her love of cooking.

The fridge had a few interesting ingredients, but none that she would have preferred for a gourmet meal. So instead, she decided on making something warm and filling – seafood fettuccine. They had plenty of seafood on hand, so she decided to mix a few different types into her sauce.

First, she started a pot of water to boil with some Himalayan sea salt to help it boil faster. Once the water had come to a boil, she added one package of fettuccine noodles.

Then she started on her sauce. She mixed heavy whipping cream, real butter, fresh minced garlic, grated Romano and Parmesan cheeses together in a saucepan. Then once it was all combined in the pan, she added shrimp, lobster that had been cut into small pieces, and some fresh crab meat. By the time the sauce was ready, her noodles had come to a boil, and she drained the water.

Sofka poured the noodles into the pan with the sauce and moved them all around, ensuring that each noodle would be coated with the creamy sauce.

"Dinner's ready!" She called, hoping that KeeKee would join her.

While the sauce was simmering, she had put in a few slices of Texas toast with butter and some grated mozzarella cheese and a dash of sharp cheddar to give it a zing.

By the time KeeKee made it to the table, Sofka had put everything out and her mouth was watering. For the past few weeks, she'd been eating diner food for dinner. Nothing wrong with diner food, but she missed cooking for herself, and her friends.

"Mmm," KeeKee sniffed the air and smiled from ear to ear. "I love it when you cook. Is that garlic I smell? And several different cheeses?"

"Yes, I made a quick and easy seafood fettuccine with cheesy Texas toast." Sofka grinned and licked her lips.

The moment her plate was practically licked clean, KeeKee put a hand on her stomach. "Oh, I don't think I'll be able to eat again for days. That was so good! Ree really is missing out."

Sofka laughed. "Somehow, I think she's happier having her mate than eating a good meal with us."

"Yeah, she always was the one who wanted a mate and family more than we did." KeeKee sighed and looked away, then a slow grin spread across her face and she looked directly at Sofka. "Soooo, Maxim?"

"No, don't even go there." Sofka pointed a finger at KeeKee and narrowed her eyes. "I get enough of that from others, I don't need you teasing me too. There's nothing going on, and there won't be."

"Oh, I don't know about that." KeeKee giggled. "I think once you get past the fact that he drinks blood, you'll find he's rather sexy, and sweet."

Sofka made gagging noises and put her hand over her mouth. "Sweet? Are you crazy? He's controlling and overbearing. I can't go anywhere without him being there. It's like he's stalking me."

"Uh, you do realize we are on a tiny island and the area we live in is really small? There are only a few places to hang out. He's not stalking you. Look around at the other people. How many of them do you see on a regular basis?"

"First," Sofka raised a finger. "I never see those new supes. So, there must be other places to go."

KeeKee interrupted. "Sofka, they stay inside their house. Horatio told me they were all pretty much hunkering down until he asked them to help with the clothing store. I bet now you'll see them out and about more."

"Hmm. That reminds me, I need to stop in for some new clothes tomorrow." Sofka grinned. "I think it's high time the deputy officially meets the newcomers. I mean, I've met everyone else on the island, but them."

"Really? You've met everyone?" KeeKee laughed. "I work in the welcome center and even I haven't met everyone."

Standing up, Sofka began clearing the table. "Okay, so maybe not everyone, but pretty close to it. I think there's only a couple hundred residents here."

KeeKee stood to help. "Actually, there's more than you know. There are a few places we don't go. It's not like they are off limits, but it's not exactly places we want to go."

"Really?" Sofka stopped in the middle of the kitchen holding the dirty dinner plates.

With Sofka's abrupt stop, KeeKee almost walked right into her back. "Hey, watch it." KeeKee walked around her friend and put the leftover seafood fettuccine on the counter. "Yeah, Horatio told me there are places for supes who don't generally walk on land." She turned quickly and her eyes widened. "Did you know that we have a pod of merfolk who live in the water surrounding the island?"

Guilt crept into Sofka when she realized something huge she'd left out earlier. "Ah, yeah. I discovered that myself today."

"Oh, you didn't!" KeeKee slapped Sofka's arm lightly. "Tell me everything."

They made coffee and sat down, after they cleaned the kitchen, and discussed the merfolk Sofka met and then KeeKee told her about the other creatures on the island.

"Did you know that there's an entire area devoted to the darker species?" KeeKee, thinking she knew something Sofka didn't arched a brow.

Sofka put her hands up in front of her. "Okay, don't get mad, but I had heard something about that. However, I have not met anyone in that group. Not yet, at least."

"Ha!" KeeKee pointed at her friend. "I met one the other day."

"And you didn't tell me about it?" Sofka pouted, but she really wasn't upset. It wasn't like they sat down each and every day sharing all the things they had learned about the island.

KeeKee snorted. "It's not like we've had much time to chat lately. I think I like that Maxim is covering for you tonight. I hope this happens more."

"Me, too." Sofka hugged her best friend. "Let's try to make more time to hang out."

"I think that's a wonderful idea. But first, I have to tell you who I met!" KeeKee bounced in her seat like a little kid who had too much sugar and couldn't sit still.

"I met the bride of Frankenstein." KeeKee sat back and waited to see her friend's reaction.

"Shut up! You didn't! But isn't Frankenstein a novel?" Sofka wondered aloud.

"That's what I thought, too. It seems that the novel was loosely based on a real supernatural creature. She wasn't actually created from multiple body parts. She's more of a wraith than a humanoid. Her name is Annie, if you can believe that." KeeKee chuckled. "She's really nice. After Mary Shelley's Frankenstein novel came out, she had to disappear. She found herself here and hasn't left in over two hundred years. Can you imagine?"

A shiver went down Sofka's spine. "Please, don't let me end up like that. I don't want to spend the rest of my life here. I mean, don't get me wrong, this place is awesome. I can't imagine leaving any time soon, but over two hundred years here? And it sounds like she doesn't get involved in the village life."

KeeKee shook her head. "Not really. She comes into town once in a while to get supplies and check in with Horatio, but that's pretty much it."

"Does she have the big black hair with a lightning bolt in it?" Sofka knew she was being silly, but still wondered.

After KeeKee finished laughing, she nodded. "She does. It seems that she was born with really long, thick black hair. Did you know she was born a dhampir?"

"What? Those are real?" Sofka put a hand over her mouth. "You mean to tell me that vampires can have kids with humans?"

"It's extremely rare, but it happens. But yeah, when she was hit with lightening, a long silver line appeared in her hair. It's not really a lightning bolt, it's just a long silver line of hair." Thinking about it caused KeeKee to run her hand down her hair. "She really does have beautiful hair."

"Hm, I wonder if any of those supes who live on the edge of our society know anything about the Bully Boys and what they've been up to lately?" Sofka couldn't get the idea out of her head that they were up to something. "I wonder if I shouldn't take a trip around the island meeting everyone and ask a few questions."

KeeKee shook her head. "I wouldn't do that without Horatio and Maxim. Some of those outsiders are very dangerous. And I heard they don't like strangers, at all."

"But I'm not a stranger, not really. I'm the deputy sheriff. They should respect the badge, right?" Once the words were out of Sofka's mouth, she realized how bad they sounded. "Okay, so maybe they won't."

The idea of touring the island was a good one, she knew it was. But doing it alone wouldn't be smart, no matter how well Sofka could defend herself.

The next day Sofka headed to the Sheriff's office to speak with her boss about her idea. All night long it kept coming back to her. If she was going to be a great deputy, she needed to know the island better. It seemed there was a lot she didn't know about the place she now called home. And if it would help her figure out what those boys were up to, all the better.

"Roscoe? You in?" Sofka walked inside the sheriff's office building and looked around. The door to the cells in the back was closed, but there wasn't anyone in the front office. Usually, Roscoe sat around sipping coffee and shooting the breeze with anyone who came to visit. Or he took a nap if there was nothing going on.

It was eerily quiet in the building that should house four criminals and have at least one supe guarding them. The building sat at one end of the main street and it did have space between it and the shop next door, which allowed for more quiet. But still, there should have been some noise at least from the dingleberries in the cells.

The fact that the prisoners were very quiet pricked at her nerves. Did they still have prisoners? Or did something happen overnight to break them out? Before heading to the back to check on the boys, Sofka looked around the front office.

Usually, the Sheriff was a pretty messy guy. But today, his desk was clean. There wasn't even a used coffee cup sitting on top, which meant he probably hadn't come in yet.

Sofka moved to her desk, and found a mess that she hadn't left on her desk the last time she used it – Maxim. He must have used her desk all night. On the top was a used coffee mug. Her hand reached out to pick it up and see if he had spiked it with something, but decided she didn't want to know what a vampire put in their coffee. If he put blood in there, she had no desire to know it. Instead, she pulled her hand back and decided she'd clean that mug later. For now, she needed to know what happened.

The daily log was sitting on her desk, closed. That she did feel comfortable picking up. But nothing interesting was logged. She noted the lines about the boys being in processed, but nothing after that. "That's no help."

She sighed and put the logbook back on her desk. Slowly, she scanned the room and listened for any sounds. There was nothing that stood out. Then she decided to see if Maxim left her a note on her desk. She pulled the drawers open, but there was nothing out of the ordinary. She pulled her chair back and looked at the ground when something caught her attention. Underneath her desk lay a flat piece of paper.

Her eyes bulged when she read the words on the paper.

You can't keep us locked up any longer.

"No, no, no. This can't be happening." Sofka ran to the closed door and yanked it open. When her eyes took in the scene before her, her shoulders sagged and she knew she had been right. Those Bully Boys had someone powerful helping them.

If the situation wasn't so dreadful, she would have laughed. There were still four cells in the back, but only two were currently in use. The one on her right held a large man with his hands tied behind him and a large piece of duct tape covering his mouth.

Across from him, was a tall, dark, and handsome man in the same position.

Sofka's nose itched, and her lips cracked a smile. From the scowls on their faces, they weren't hurt. "So, I take it they had some pretty powerful help getting out?"

It was too much; she couldn't keep the laughter from bubbling up and she tried to hide it by putting her hand over her mouth. Although, she knew they couldn't miss her shoulders bouncing up and down. "I guess it's a good thing I have my own keys, and keep them on me. Something tells me those boys took the cell keys with them. Am I correct?"

Both caged men nodded.

Sofka pulled the keys off her belt and headed toward the Sheriff first. He was her boss, after all. "I wonder why the island didn't warn me this was going down." She shook her head and reached out to touch the cell door, but yanked her hand back when she felt a bolt of electricity pulse through her hand. "Ouch. What did they do?"

When the sheriff's eyes widened, Sofka wondered if they didn't know the bars had been electrocuted. She looked around for the source of the shock. "Did they plug it in to the wall? Or to a generator?"

Both men shrugged.

Maxim tried to say something, but it just came out as a muffled yelp.

"Alright, until I can get the tape off your mouth, I see neither of you will be of any help. I really wish cell phones worked here." She sighed and wondered how she was going to get the sheriff out.

Key in hand, she moved over to Maxim's cell and put the key in the lock. Nothing hurt, so she thought if she turned it, the door might open. Maybe they had only one electrical outlet to plug into a cell so they chose the sheriff's? As a bearshifter, he might have the strength to knock the door down in his bear form. But with the electricity running through the bars, that might not work so well.

A vampire was strong, but she knew the bars would be strong enough to keep a vampire in. Maybe the Bully Boys understood that as well and didn't bother electrocuting his cell? It was a long shot, but she had to try.

However, when she turned the key, an even stronger bolt shot up her arm. This time, the pain was excruciating, and she screamed out.

Maxim jumped to his feet and moved toward her. The moment his body touched the cell bars, he flew back and crashed against the back wall. He lay there lifeless for a moment.

"Maxim?" Sofka forgot about her pain and took a step closer to the bars but halted when she remembered what they were. "Are you alright?"

A light moan came from around the tape surrounding the vampire's mouth.

She sighed in relief and closed her eyes for a moment. "Thank candy cane goodness you're alright." She turned around and noticed Roscoe was standing up, but kept his distance from the bars.

When their eyes met, she saw the anguish he felt at being held prisoner in his own cell.

"Roscoe, can you shift? Would that break the restraints holding your hands behind you? And get rid of the tape covering your mouth?" Sofka needed to understand what happened, but unless they were able to take the tape off, she'd never get the story out of them.

He nodded. One second a man with his arms cuffed behind his back stood in front of her, the next there was a giant black bear standing on four legs staring at her. He didn't roar, and he didn't move, either.

Sofka realized he was doing is best to steer clear of the cell doors. "Good, now change back into a man. Let's see if those restraints are gone."

Normally, when a shifter shifted to their animal form, their clothes stayed in a sort of magical statis. And when they shifted back into their humanoid form, their clothes came back just as they were before the shift.

It was nothing like the movies where when they shifted, their clothes would tear into a million pieces.

Unfortunately, the handcuffs and tape came back just as they were before.

"Well," she rubbed her neck. "At least we tried."

"Do you know how they got out?" Even if they couldn't talk, she could ask them yes or no questions to get some details.

The sheriff nodded.

"Did they have help?"

The sheriff nodded again.

"Did you recognize the supes who helped?" Since the sheriff did know everyone on the island, Sofka hoped to find a way to get their descriptions, at least, if not their names.

He shook his head.

She wasn't done, not by a long shot. Sofka turned to Maxim, but before she could even ask her questions, he shook his head. "So, you don't know who helped, either?"

Maxim began moving his mouth, she wasn't sure what he was trying to do, but all of a sudden, fangs pierced the duct tape. Guess the old adage about duct tape working on everything wasn't exactly true.

While Maxim worked on biting the tape off, Sofka looked to the wall at the end of the walkway. "Island, why didn't you stop them?"

She waited for a response. The island didn't always answer questions, she knew that. But this was a serious situation, surely it would speak up now, wouldn't it? A few heartbeats passed and no response. "Can you hear me?" Still nothing.

"What good is a magical island if it doesn't work when its help is needed most?" Sofka rolled her eyes when the wall stayed blank.

"Sofka," A soft voice called.

She whirled around to see the tape was mostly off of Maxim's mouth. At least enough that he could get some sounds to come out. "Maxim, are you alright?"

He nodded. "You need to get help. Get Marcus."

"Really?" Sofka couldn't believe her ears. "You want me to get the supe you hate, to come and help you get out? Marcus, the fae who mated with my best friend, Ree?"

Again, he nodded. "This is serious. I think they had help from a fae creature. Only Marcus can tell for sure."

"Not another fae on the island could tell?" The idea of disturbing Marcus on his honeymoon made her sick to her stomach.

"No, I'll explain later. Please, go get him and have Ree round up all of the supes you trust. Starting with Horatio." Maxim had more of the tape off of his mouth, allowing him to speak easier now.

Torn between staying to protect them, in case anyone came back, and needing help, Sofka took a deep breath and nodded. "I'll be back as soon as I can."

While Marcus' house wasn't far, Sofka knew that she could travel much faster in her wolf form. So the moment she exited the sheriff's station, she shifted. The feeling of power that always thrummed through her veins during a shift propelled her first jump and she howled. If any wolf shifters were within hearing distance, they would hear her call for help and find her.

Only two found her by the time she reached Marcus and Ree. Not wanting to tell the tale twice, she knocked on Marcus's door after she shifted back into her human form. "Marcus! I need your help, right now! Hurry up!"

The two wolves shifted back into their human form. Both were females Sofka had seen around town, but she didn't really know them. The one thing she did know was that they hated the Bully Boys.

"Tony and his gang escaped from jail, with outside help." Sofka turned back to the door and pounded again. "If you don't open this door, I'm going to pull out my sheriff's deputy key and open it."

"Hold your horses." Marcus' voice came over a speaker by the door. "I'll be out in a minute."

She turned back to the wolves. "Have you seen Tony, or his buddies?"

Marna, a gray wolf from Alaska, shook her head. "I've not seen them since you arrested them yesterday. How'd they get out?"

The door opened, and a handsome man who only wore a bathrobe and a frown glared at her. "Sofka, this had better be good."

"Marcus, the Bully Boys broke out of jail with some very powerful help. Possibly fae."

He interrupted her. "I'm not a deputy, so what does this have to do with me?"

Sofka's nostrils flared. "Let me finish. Whoever helped them escape used very powerful magic and now both the sheriff and Maxim are locked in the cells." She held her hand up. "Wait, before you say anything, I do have a key."

Marcus tried to interrupt, but Ree showed up in a pink, fuzzy bathrobe. "Sofka, I love you, but please. Let us have this time."

"Ree, I'm so sorry. I wish I could. Fae magic was used to lock the cells. I can't get Maxim or the sheriff out. It's really strong and painful." Sofka winced with the memory.

Ree shoved past Marcus. "Oh, no. Are you alright?"

"I'm fine, but I need Marcus' help to get the cells open to get them out. Then we have to start a search party to find the escapees." Sofka waved for them to come out, but stopped when she realized what they were wearing. "Hurry, go get dressed. Marcus, I'll meet you at the jail. Ree, can you go get Horatio and meet us?"

They both nodded and shut the door.

The two wolves had stood behind her listening in the entire time.

Solana, the other gray wolf, asked, "How can we help?"

"Honestly, I don't know how this could have happened. Can you ask around if anyone has seen the boys, or anyone new? The sheriff didn't recognize the supes who helped Tony and his minions escape." Sofka needed to get back to the jail, and see if there was anything new. She prayed that the magic holding them in the cells wasn't doing anything else to harm them.

"Yes, we can start searching the docks and find Bart. If anyone new came on the island, he'll know," Marna suggested.

Another idea popped into Sofka's head. "Do you know the merfolk? If you do, see if they can help."

"Oh, yes. That's a great idea." Solana smiled. "I should have thought about that. Luana is a friend of ours, she joins us for bunco each month. You should join us next time. It's a great way to meet the other females on the island."

Last week, Sofka was going to attend, but got put on the night shifts. "When this is all over, and we have those Bully Boys on ice, I'll be happy to join you. But for now, let's focus. I'm going to have Horatio be the point person, if anyone has any information, they should go see him at the information center. Got it?"

Both girls nodded before they shifted back into their gray wolf forms.

Sofka shifted as well after only a few paces from the house then she heard the door open again. When she turned her head to see who was exiting, it was just Marcus. Made sense, men could dress faster. But Sofka knew that Ree would only be a few paces behind them. The knowledge propelled her, and she made good time getting back to the jail.

Chapter 11

"I see nothing's changed since I left. I don't know if that's good or bad." Sofka propped open the door that led from the front office to the cells. If they were gonna be coming and going, it would be easier to have the entry left open.

"Not exactly. I got all of the tape off of my mouth. I think someone needs to invent a better tasting glue." Maxim stuck his tongue out. Other than the tape no longer being an issue, everything else was the same. He sat on the bed in his cell with his arms pulled behind his back.

Sofka looked to the sheriff. "You alright?"

Roscoe nodded.

"What about Marcus?" Maxim asked.

"What about Marcus?" A smooth, deep voice asked as the fae himself walked into the cell room.

"Do you know the magic coating these cells?" Maxim gave Marcus a knowing look.

Sofka looked between the two supernatural alpha males and realized that there was another conversation going on between them that she wasn't picking up on. "What's going on? Why would Marcus recognize the magic?"

Marcus cleared his throat.

Sofka bit her lower lip waiting for someone to tell her what was going on.

"I'm not sure how much Ree has told you about me." Marcus ran his hand through his messy hair. It appeared that he only took the time to put on clothes, and didn't bother with running a comb through his hair. Although, it probably took him an hour to get the perfect messy hair look that men loved to sport.

She twisted her mouth and answered, "I know you're a fae prince who doesn't get along with his family." She knew a bit more, but not a lot. However, what she did know, wasn't exactly something to discuss at this point in time. "Wait, do you think this is your family? All color drained from her face and her jaw dropped.

If the Unseelie court was after him, the entire island would be in danger.

A quick chuckle escaped his lips before he schooled his features. "No, it's nothing like that. This magic," he pointed to the cell bars, "is fae, but I don't recognize the person who cast it."

"What about the supe? Do you know what sort did it?" Maxim asked.

Marcus pursed his lips. "This isn't magic from my court. It's from the Seelie Court. But the creature who wielded this magic is very low. King Oberon probably has no clue that it came here."

"What sort of supernatural is it? But more importantly, can you break its magic?" While Sofka loved learning about all of the different types of supes, she didn't have time to indulge her inner geek.

With a nod, Marcus stepped forward, then looked to Sofka. "Who should I break out first?"

"The sheriff." A twinge of guilt caused Sofka to wince. She felt bad about leaving Maxim behind, but he could speak. The Sheriff still had the tape over his mouth. And he was her boss, so he was higher on her list of priorities.

The sheriff shook his head and motioned to Maxim.

Maxim's eyes widened. "Does it really matter? You can get us both out, right?"

Marcus shook his head. "I can, but it will take time to get the magic down off the second cell. I'll need to recharge."

"I thought this was a low-level Seelie fae? Shouldn't it be easy for the Unseelie Prince to break his spell?" Sofka chuckled. Never in a million years did she think she'd be saying something like that. Even though she knew Marcus was a fae prince, she never really thought of it. Besides, they hadn't spent much time together, so there wasn't really an opportunity to talk about his talents, or rank.

"Normally, yes. But I've used up most of my power over the last few weeks. And I've not taken the time to recharge." He hitched his brows and gave Sofka a sly smile.

"Oh, gross!" Sofka put her hands in the air and shook her head. "Look, I'm glad you and Ree are mated, but there is absolutely no need to share the details." She shivered with the thought of what they must do behind closed doors.

"Enough, get the sheriff out and then recharge and come back for me." Maxim growled and narrowed his eyes at Marcus.

"Chill, dude. The sheriff wants you out first." Marcus looked between the two magically sealed inside the cells. "And while I prefer Roscoe to you, I can see why he'd want you out first."

Maxim sat there seething with anger. His eyes turned red and his fangs elongated. "Then get on with it. I have four little mice to squish."

"Ah," Sofka held up a finger. "Before you squish, maim, eat, or whatever you plan on doing to Tony and his friends, I need to question them first. We have to know who they are working with and how they are getting past the island's defenses."

Maxim slowly cleared the anger from his face.

Marcus put his hands up above the space in front of the cell door. Then he closed his eyes and began chanting incoherent words. The strain of using what little magic he had left was evident on his face in the way it tensed up and his mouth puckered like he'd just tasted something extremely sour.

Maybe he had.

Sofka had heard tales of magic that had rotten tastes. While the arctic wolf shifters had their own magic, it was mostly related to shifting. They did have a flavor when they shifted. All wolves did. The arctic wolves were lucky in that that would taste peppermint – like a candy cane. The more pure the bloodline, the more magic they had within them. And the more magic, the stronger the flavor. Some even had the scent of candy canes.

Originally, Sofka thought that Marcus would come in and wave his hands, or something simple like that, and the spell protecting the doors would vanish. She hadn't thought it would be difficult for Marcus to do this.

After what must have been at least ten minutes of sweating, Marcus lowered his hands and swayed on his feet. "There, it should be done."

A tiny spark shone over the lock, then it went poof, like a magic act. No one said a thing. They all looked at the door and waited as though they thought it would open on its own.

"Well, don't just stand there, unlock it with your key." Maxim stood against the bars with no ill effects.

"Okay. That was intense." Sofka turned her head to Marcus, who was wobbling out of the room. "Are you going to be alright?"

He waved and then plopped down in the nearest chair.

Before Sofka could open the cell door, she heard a scream come from the front office. She whirled around to see Ree kneeling in front of Marcus.

"Marcus, sweetie. Talk to me." Ree's shoulders shook.

Sofka knew that her friend was crying. Her first instinct was to run to her best friend, but she knew she needed to care for Maxim first. It wouldn't take but a minute or two to get him out and uncuff him.

She turned back to the cell door and put her key back in. "So far, so good." She turned the key and when nothing happened, she breathed a sigh of relief. Then she pulled the door open for Maxim to exit.

"Thank you." Maxim exhaled his relief at finally being free. "Do you have the keys for this?" He turned his back to her and lifted his cuffed hands as best he could.

"If they took our set, then yes." Sofka looked at her key ring and found the key that would fit the supernatural restraining bands that were wrapped around Maxim's wrists. These looked like regular handcuffs, but they were magically spelled to hold strong supernatural creatures. It was extremely rare that anyone got out of them without a key, or using a special magical incantation.

With a click, one cuff was released. Then Sofka used the key on his other wrist, and both of his hands were free.

Maxim rubbed at his wrists. "Thank you. I can't believe those four did this. And what was that little creature? Was it a hobgoblin? Or something else?"

A loud mumble came from the other room and Sofka moved closer to the door. "What was that?"

Ree turned to look at Sofka, and the deputy noticed tears streaming down her friend's cheeks. "He said it was a killmoulis. A distant relative to the brownies, but not a brownie. Certainly not as helpful. Well," she tilted her head, "unless you think using magic to hold the innocent as prisoners is helpful."

Sofka nodded. "Okay, so it's a small supe. Will it be easy to find? Or do we need something to entice it?"

Horatio had just given Marcus a glass of water. He downed the entire drink in one gulp. When he was done he handed the glass back to Horatio. "I'm going to need food, lots of it."

"Not a problem. I'll see that the Island Shack sends over a dozen. Do you want fries, too?" Horatio asked as though this was just a regular request. There was a sense of urgency in his voice, but no fear or anguish.

Marcus nodded then turned to look at Sofka. "I doubt it's still here. Usually, they are tied to someone else. Unless one of the boys recently met this Killmoulis, and somehow tricked it, I doubt it's sticking close to them." He shook his head. "No, I think it's more likely that someone else has the killmoulis as his or her servant. And had it come here to get the boys out."

"Do you think the boys are still on the island?" Sofka wasn't sure if that was a good thing, or a bad thing. Sure, it would be nice to be rid of them, but would it be fair to unleash them on the world?

Marcus drank another full glass of water. "It's hard to know, but my guess would be that they are here on the island still. If whoever they are working with wanted them off the island, then they wouldn't have come back the last time they left. I think whatever is going on has to do with someone on this island." He paused, "or something."

"You know, now would be a good time for the sentient, magical island to speak up and let us know what's going on. Or at the very least, give us a clue." Sofka glared at the back wall that was normally used by the island to communicate with the sheriff's office. But nothing showed up.

"How long will it take you to recharge?" Maxim interrupted the conversation, not really caring about where the boys were at that second. "We need to get the sheriff out as soon as possible."

"I'm sorry, Marcus, but Maxim is right." Sofka looked back into the holding cell area. "I need to get out there and find those boys and discover their plan. Hopefully, in time to stop them from doing anything that will hurt someone, or worse."

Chapter 12

After coming up with a temporary plan, Sofka took Maxim and left everyone else back at the jail. Horatio said after he got Marcus some food, he would man the Information Center, and everyone should coordinate through him.

Even the sheriff nodded his agreement with the plan, knowing he was going to be stuck in that magical cell until Marcus got his strength back.

"Maxim, I'm not sure who all we can trust. So far, I don't think anyone we've brought in on this is going to work against us, but who knows? I mean, those tundra wolves had to have some pretty powerful help to do what they've done so far." Sofka was leading Maxim to the other end of town, towards the coffee shop. That was one of the places that supes tended to hang out when in town.

There weren't many options, and the Frozen Bean Coffee Shop made any and all types of drinks a supernatural could want. The vampires enjoyed a shot of blood with their coffee, the pixies tended to like a green concoction that smelled like daisies and even the gargoyle found a drink there that was to his liking. Not that he needed anything to drink - or eat.

The information center where Horatio worked was also a place the supes tended to congregate when in town. Most of the houses were only a short walk away, but some had longer walks and therefore stayed in town for a while chatting with their friends, or making new ones.

He shook his head. "I think those four only have help from the outside. I highly doubt anyone living on this island would help them. I can't even imagine someone from the dark side helping them. They are pariahs here."

"True, but could anyone be tempted to help them? If their outside help is powerful, and they must be to do what they've done today, then who's to say supes on the island wouldn't agree to help the Bully Boys?" Sofka hated to think that any of their friends would work against them, but if KeeKee was correct about the number of residents on the island, then there were still a lot of people she didn't know. Which meant there were a lot of people who wouldn't be loyal to her. And probably wouldn't be loyal to Maxim, either.

"Who should we question first?" Sofka stood outside the coffee shop looking through the glass wall that separated at least twenty residents from her and Maxim. When she first thought about questioning everyone, it didn't seem like it would be a big deal. But now? Now that she knew there were hundreds more than she realized on this island, it seemed daunting, to say the very least.

"Look," Maxim pointed to a pretty supe inside the shop who was smiling at them. "Micky is already back at work."

Sofka smiled at the barista who waved them inside. While Sofka couldn't call Micky a close friend, they had spent many hours chatting and laughing over coffee. The first thing Sofka noticed about the female, was that she had very long purple hair. It went all the way to her waist when it wasn't up in a ponytail.

Maxim opened the door, waving Sofka inside before him.

"Micky? Should you be back at work already? You looked pretty injured yesterday." Sofka hugged her new friend and looked her over from top to bottom, which wasn't too easy to do since the supe was just over six feet tall. But, most polar bear shifters were very tall.

The barista waved her hand as though it was nothing. "I'm fine. Even my bruises are healed."

"You could have taken some time off to recharge." Even though Sofka probably would have done the same thing, she knew that Micky worked six days a week. She'd asked why last week when she realized how many days the supe worked. Micky had told her that there wasn't much to do on the island, and with the coffee shop being one of the centers of everything, it was fun.

Micky shook her head and chuckled. "You know I hate to sit around doing nothing. And even if I had the day off, I'd be here with everyone. So I thought I might as well work." She shrugged.

"That might work to our advantage." Maxim looked around and noticed that he recognized everyone in the place. "Have you heard about the Bully Boys escaping?"

Micky's nostrils flared. "Yes, and if I see them I'm going to pummel them. How could they get out?"

"That's what we'd like to know." Sofka touched the barista's elbow and led her to the only quiet corner in the place. "We need to know if you've seen anyone new lately."

Micky looked outside and seemed to be off in another universe as she thought. "No. Only one group has arrived since you and your two friends. That group of ten who keep to themselves."

Both Sofka and Maxim nodded.

"Have you seen anyone talking with Tony, or his buddies? Is there a chance he's working with anyone who lives here?" Maxim asked.

"Pft. Are you kidding me?" Micky practically growled. "Not a single resident on this island likes those boys. Everyone comes in here complaining about them and wondering why the island lets them stay."

"Yeah, I have wondered the same thing." While Sofka agreed with Micky, she still thought it would be good to ask around. "We've got to get going, but do you think you can ask around and see if anyone knows anything?"

"Ohh, you mean like a detective?" Micky's eyes gleamed with the excitement of running an investigation.

Sofka chuckled. "Not exactly. But maybe you can find out what they've been up to. Maxim and I have to go around and see if we can find anyone who might have seen something. But with everyone coming through here, you could help us, a lot."

Micky stood straight and grinned. "I'll do anything to help get those guys back in jail where they belong. After what they did yesterday, I doubt anyone will sit by and let them get away with this."

"Thank you! Be sure to let Horatio know if you find out anything, even if it seems insignificant." Maxim then asked for a coffee, the vampire special.

"Oh, can I get a PSL?" Sofka loved the way the coffee shop made their foam.

When Micky came back with their drinks, Sofka smiled. She looked at the foam before putting the lid on her to-go cup and noticed a smiling jack-o-lantern on top made from the pumpkin pie spice they sprinkled on top.

Once they were both outside, Sofka looked to Maxim. "Where to first? Who do you think might know something?"

He sighed and looked toward the Northeast. "There is only one place where those boys might find protection."

Sofka looked out where Maxim was glaring and shivered. The Northeast had a little mountain, more like a tall hill. But she had heard there were caves up there. And that was where the darkest creatures who came to the island tended to congregate.

"I really wish those boys hadn't destroyed both vehicles. It's at least a two-hour walk, even with our enhanced speed." Maxim snarled and took off toward the Dark Hills.

The tell-tale sound of a screen rolling down caught Sofka's attention. She looked around until she found the communication device the island preferred to use when communicating with its inhabitants. "Look, the island has a message for us."

The side of the clothing shop had a screen rolled down. *There's a snowmobile in the city shed.* Then the screen rolled up.

"I would have thought the island would have given us more help. Why do you think it's being so quiet and not doing anything about this?" While Sofka hadn't been there long, she did know enough about the sentient island to know that it protected itself just as much as it did the residents.

"The island did inform us about the snowmobile, which I hadn't heard of before. My guess is that its sudden appearance is a way the island is helping us." Maxim turned around and headed to the east of Main Street, where the city shed was located.

"I didn't even know there was a city shed. But, I am new to the island." Sofka shrugged and followed quickly behind the vampire. "Maxim, do you think there's a reason the island hasn't stopped the bully boys yet? Or why it allowed you and the Sheriff to be locked up?"

Maxim looked back over his shoulder when Sofka asked her question. He didn't stop walking, but he did slow down. "I think the island knows exactly what its doing. We may not understand why things are developing as they are, and why the island hasn't stopped those boys. But rest assured, the island is still in control." He pointed to the maintenance shed. "This here is evidence enough for me to believe."

She didn't respond, just followed the vampire to the shed and internally filed all of this information away about the island.

Once inside the shed, they found a large snowmobile that looked as though it had never been used. Maxim looked over his shoulder and grinned. Sitting on top of the seat that was clearly designed for two, were a pair of shiny, black helmets with snow goggles.

"What do you know? The island has prepared a nice, safe, way for us to travel today." Sofka picked up the first helmet, but before putting it on, she sat in the driver's spot and gave Maxim a cheesy smile. "Get on, I'll drive."

The vampire shook his head and chuckled. "Do you have any idea how to get there?"

Without even pausing, she put her helmet on, then replied, "No, but I'm sure you can guide me."

"That won't work." Maxim held his helmet in his hands.

Sofka tilted her head to the side. "Why not? Afraid a little she-wolf will do a better job at riding the snowmobile than you can?" While it was a bit of a jab, Sofka did have years of experience on snowmobiles. An arctic wolf shifter grew up riding these things before they could even walk.

He shook his head. "No, I'm pretty sure you would outride me in a contest. But, here on the island? I know the way to where we are heading."

"Okay, then just tell me when I need to make turns." She shrugged.

"Turn on the motor." Maxim put his helmet on and waited for her to comply. Once the engine was purring, he tried talking to her.

Sofka shook her head and put a hand to the side of her helmet, where her ear would be, signaling that she couldn't hear.

Maxim took his helmet off and waited for Sofka to turn off the engine. Once it was off, he smirked.

That smirk was going to be the death of Sofka. On the one hand, he was totally arrogant, but on the other, the way his lips moved was sexy. And to make matters worse, she couldn't keep her eyes off his mouth whenever he smiled. Even if it was a sexy smirk. She sighed. "Fine, you can drive. But on the way home, I get to drive."

"Deal." He put his helmet on and waited for Sofka to move back.

Once he was positioned in front of her, Sofka hesitated for a moment before wrapping her arms around his waist. Then she had to hold her breath as she almost sighed in contentment. The one thing Sofka knew for sure was that if she let him know how much she enjoyed sitting behind him, he would take advantage of her feelings.

And the last thing she needed was a vampire thinking she wanted anything more than friendship.

Chapter 13

Misfit Island was a safe harbor for the misfits of the supernatural world. Sofka and her friends knew this because they were misfits and the island called to them before they even knew of its existence. But when they first arrived, they assumed that most of the residents were like them, they just didn't fit in with their pack.

Now that Sofka was heading to the Dark Hills, she realized that everyone had a story of their own. And not all of them were as simple as hers. Maxim had said that the darkest creatures lived in the caves within the Dark Hills. But he hadn't expounded on what he meant by *darkest creatures*. Were they evil? Or did they just prefer to live in areas that the sun didn't reach?

Well, there wasn't much sun on the island. The light they had was magically created, for the most part. While Sofka didn't understand the science, or magic, behind it all, she did know that some real sunlight came through the magical barrier that protected the island from the human satellites. For anyone looking at the island, they would see clouds or ice. It was something similar to what Santa had done with the North Pole. But this barrier also provided a type of light that allowed the vampires to walk around in it, without too much difficulty.

It also had nutrients that natural sunlight afforded. Which seemed strange to Sofka. She had learned from Horatio that it was the UV rays in the sunlight that was deadly to a vampire. And almost zero UV rays made their way through the magical barrier, hence the vampire's ability to day walk.

But what about the *dark creatures*? Did light hurt their eyes? Or was it something else that gave them that moniker? Sofka wondered how much Maxim knew, and how much he would tell her before they entered the caves.

Her mind quickly changed when she noticed the beauty of the island as they drove through the little forest. No one had informed her that trees would grow in Antarctica. She had been taught that it was similar to the Arctic Circle, with a few tundra bushes but not much else. In fact, when she learned about Antarctica, she was told that they didn't even have tundra. It was all ice and snow with a few small lakes and rivers. Most of those were because of climate change.

Now that she was here, at least on Misfit Island, she wondered if the nature around her was natural or magical. There were trees like one would expect to see in the mountains – evergreens with needles. But she also noticed there were some Aspen trees in a grove not too far from the side of the pathway they were driving along.

"How is there a pathway here if the island didn't have but two vehicles?" The moment she asked her question, Sofka realized that Maxim wouldn't hear her. Or if he did, he wouldn't be able to answer her in a way she could hear. The engine was too loud to hear over. That and the fact they were both wearing helmets, would make communication difficult. Which was why he was driving and not her.

She told herself to remember the question for when they stopped. And she wanted to take a proper tour of the island once the current danger was settled. If they had trees right here, what else did they have?

Thoughts of winter wonderland possibilities flooded her imagination. Did they have a ski resort on this island? Were there hot springs to take dips in that was close enough to do the polar plunges so many humans loved to try? While she'd never done that back home in the Arctic Circle, she'd like to try it here. If it was possible.

Before she realized it, they were at the base of a small set of hills. They were covered in ice and snow, with the occasional pine tree growing tall and large.

When they came to a stop, Maxim took his helmet off. "Are you alright back there?"

Sofka removed her helmet and jumped off the snowmobile. "I'm good. I had no idea we had trees here. What else is here that I don't know about?"

Maxim stopped halfway through standing up on the snowmobile. "You know, the island is always changing. Every few months I take a vehicle and tour the place to see what's what, but I haven't done that in a while now."

Sofka didn't have to ask why. She knew he didn't like leaving her, or her friends, in town without him nearby. "And why is there a track in the snow and ice going from town to here?"

"Oh, that's simple. It's for deliveries. The tiny community here has a large snow truck. They come into town monthly to get supplies." Maxim pointed to the distance. "See that shed?"

The first thing she noted was a large opening in one of the hills. Then next to it stood a large, red shed that looked more like a barn. It even had white wood frames around what would normally be windows. But in this building, there weren't any windows, just a large door that slid to the side like a barn door.

"Is that where they keep their snow truck?" Sofka pointed to the red building and almost asked what else they kept in there.

"Yup. And there are some tools and other supplies. Since the residents live within all three hills, they keep the community supplies in that shed." Maxim jumped off the snowmobile and laid his helmet on the seat, then took hers and put it down as well. "Come on, let's see who's out and about."

Without a word, Sofka followed the vampire into what she knew not.

"Hello? Anyone here?" Maxim called out when he entered the mouth of the closest hill.

"Um, Maxim? Who, exactly, lives in these hills?" She had forgotten to ask him about the residents before they ventured into the hillside.

He turned around and furrowed his brows. "Didn't anyone tell you about the dark creatures?"

"No." She put her hands on her hips and arched a brow. "I didn't even know about this place until today."

"We used to have a bridge troll, but once he left the island, the bridge was removed. It was never used by anyone except for the troll."

Maxim walked into the hill more and turned to the right, then the left looking for anyone.

"A bridge troll? Really? And he never hurt anyone?" Sofka had heard of them, of course, everyone had. The Seattle Bridge Troll was world-famous, but she'd never seen any.

Maxim stopped and looked up. "No, I don't think so. Horatio was the only one brave enough to get near his bridge, and he only did that once a month when he delivered the troll's food."

"Ah, yes. No one messes with the food delivery guy." Sofka chuckled and remembered when her alpha, a hideous excuse for a leader, tried to stiff the pizza delivery man. They never got pizza delivered again from that place. And word got out about how cheap Kirill was. It took months of leaving good tips, when they had to go and pick up food, before anyone would deliver to their compound again.

"You got that right." A harsh voice called out, then cackled. "But you aren't here to deliver food, are you?" The voice moved from one side of the cave to the other in a matter of seconds. It wasn't like an echo, it was more like the creature had moved quickly enough that his voice could be heard all over the cave.

Sofka felt her throat constrict and silently prayed for safety. She knew that Maxim would protect her, but were there creatures there that were stronger than Maxim?

"Walter? Is that you?" Maxim called out and then laughed when the mysterious voice made a gargled noise.

"Really? You had to mess up my fun?" Walter made a raspberry sound and then hoofbeats sounded off the walls.

"How is he making those sounds?" Sofka turned in a circle looking to see who they were talking to.

"What sounds?" A growl sounded behind her and Sofka whirled to see who, or what, had snuck up behind her.

"Oh." She wasn't sure if she should be afraid, or excited. With so many different creatures crossing her path recently, Sofka didn't know what she should be feeling anymore. "Hi."

Without even realizing it, Sofka scooted closer to Maxim as her head rolled back to look at the creature before her. It must have stood at least nine feet tall, maybe taller.

Dark eyes glared down at her, and its mouth formed a tight, straight line before opening. "Take a picture, it might last longer. Well, that is if you can get a camera to work here."

A squeak exited Sofka's mouth, and she jumped back to hide behind Maxim.

Maxim chuckled. "That's a good one, Walter."

A whinny escaped the creature's mouth. "Thanks."

"How long have you been waiting to use it?" Maxim asked.

A large, toothy grin spread across Walter's face. "At least a year. We don't get many visitors here." He paused and turned his head. "Although, I thought I might get to use it when those little wolves visited the other day." He shook his head.

"Wha...what?" Was all Sofka could get out. Her ears, nor her eyes, could get the sights and sounds to make any sense to her brain.

Maxim chuckled. "I take it you've never seen a centaur before?"

Sofka shook her head, dumbfounded. She had heard about them, but they were mostly in the land of fairie, not on Earth. And from what she'd heard, they weren't very nice. But this one, tried to crack a joke. He even planned them in advance, if what Maxim said was true.

Then, his words hit her. "You said wolves visited the other day?" Could that be who Tony and his friends were working with? Then her eyes bugged out and she put a hand over her mouth and shook her head violently. "No, it can't be."

"It's alright. Walter won't hurt you." Maxim turned to the giant centaur – half man and half horse. "Go on, tell her."

His teeth, more like a horse's mouth than a man's, shined in the dim light of the cave. "Well..." his shoulders shook with suppressed laughter. Then he waved a hand. "Nah, Maxim's right. I won't hurt you. In fact, I can't. The island would boot me, and anyone else, off its magical soil if we hurt another creature here."

"No, that's not what I meant." Sofka took in a long, shaky breath. "You said there were wolves here. Who was it? A regular resident of the island? Or someone new?"

The little wolf girl sent up a silent request to anyone listening that it be a resident, and not someone new. The last thing she and her little pack needed was her old pack finding them. And with everything going on lately, Sofka wasn't so sure that the island was looking out for any of them anymore, shiny new snowmobile notwithstanding.

"Ah, I don't think so." Walter shrugged. "I think they were just visiting. But, I'd stay clear of them. Anyone new coming here and looking for what they were, isn't going to be someone you want to be friends with."

"What do you mean?" Maxim asked. His head turned and his nose sniffed out in different directions.

A deep, hearty chuckle that felt more like a small earthquake, rumbled from the giant centaur in front of them. "My friend, you won't be able to smell them now. Too many have come through here lately to pick out certain scents."

The vampire's eyes darkened with a red closer to burgundy, and his teeth elongated. "Someone is messing with my m..., friends. And I won't stand for it."

Walter slowly looked from Maxim, to Sofka, who still stood close enough to Maxim for their arms to touch. Maxim put a protective arm around Sofka and Walter smiled. The look was so startingly different from before. The face went from scary to sexy.

Sofka wasn't sure if he was about to flirt with her, or if something else wasn't going on that she didn't understand.

"I see. Your *friends*," Walter put air quotes around the word *friends* and lightly chuckled, "are in trouble, and you're here to find out who's out to hurt her, I mean them?"

Maxim shuffled his feet and cleared his throat. "Um, yes. There have been some things happening in town lately that are a bit unusual."

Sofka snorted. "Unusual? I'd say." She turned to look at Walter. "Do you know the pack of four tundra wolf shifters? I think they have been nicknamed..."

Walter cut her off with a growl. "The Bully Boys. Yes, I know them. Unfortunately. If they're the ones hassling you, it's nothing to be too worried about. They are more bark than bite." The centaur smiled when he realized what he said. "Pun totally intended."

Tension left Sofka's shoulders and she sagged just a bit. "Yes, them. But something happened this past week and their antics have ratcheted up a notch, or two."

"More like they got a backbone and are working toward an actual goal," Maxim added.

Walter rubbed his clean-shaven chin. "You know, I didn't see them here with the newcomers the other day, but one of them did mention Tony."

"You met the newcomers?" Sofka took a step forward and waited to see if Walter could tell her more about them.

He shook his head. "No, they weren't here for me." He cleared his throat. "I saw the newcomers head into the black cave. And I tend to steer clear of those folks, if you know what I mean."

Sofka didn't and regretted letting them know as much.

Chapter 14

"Who lives in the black cave?" Sofka furrowed her brow and looked between the two supernatural male creatures who were so different from one another, and yet she did pick up on similarities. Besides them both having nice facial features.

Both of them stood tall and proud, as though they were alpha males and had nothing to worry about. Vampires generally only worried about the sun. But since there wasn't real sunlight on this island, Sofka knew Maxim didn't have much to worry about.

And Walter was a centaur. She thought that fact was enough to keep anyone away from him. These two males had to be at the top of the food chain on this island.

But it seemed she was wrong. There were other creatures on the island who held positions much scarier than these two.

"Basically, your worst nightmares," Walter said with a straight face.

If that was meant as a joke, Sofka didn't think he was funny. Her worst nightmares were pretty heinous. "You might be surprised by my worst nightmares. Give me a better description."

After running a hand down his face, Maxim turned his head to look into Sofka's eyes. "These are the types of creatures who never wonder into town. I doubt you'll ever have reason to see any of them."

"Yeah," Walter interrupted, "they don't like light. Not even the light provided by the island. Hence the name, black cave."

She nodded. "Okay, but what creatures live there? Who were those wolves going to see?" As she thought about what she just said, it dawned on her that it might not be a who, but a what. If nightmares lived in that cave, it was possible the *what* would be a real monster.

Before saying anything, Walter looked to Maxim who gave a slight nod. "Have you heard of redcaps?"

Eyes wide, Sofka grabbed Maxim's arm and squeezed with all her might. "What? Redcaps are here? On this island? How is that possible?"

Maxim put his hand on hers and tried to remove her vicelike grip from his arm. "It's alright. They know better than to harm anyone. And there's only one pair of them."

"Yeah, they're retired," Walter scrunched his nose. "Sort of." He held up a hand to stop Sofka's response. "They only go after indigenous animals. And they keep their hunts on the downlow. Everyone knows to steer clear of them when they're on the prowl."

"Is that who those wolves came to see?" Sofka shivered. She'd seen pictures of the little fae creatures. Until she saw their eyes and mouths, she had thought they looked like garden gnomes. But when she looked at the face of one, she knew nothing but blackness filled their souls. They were the spitting image of Freddie Krueger, just shorter.

Walter looked away from Sofka, and she realized he was trying to hide something.

"Who did they come to see?" Even if it was something worse than Freddie, she had to know.

"If it has to do with your, ah, *friends*, then I'd say they tried to see Sigurd. But you know him, he would have turned them away." Walter stared at Maxim, not even glancing at Sofka.

"What's a Sigurd?" Now Sofka was just confused. She'd never heard of a creature called a Sigurd before. But, then again, she hadn't heard about most of the creatures living on this island. It seemed as though every single paranormal creature known to man, and a few unknown, were hiding out on the island.

Maxim rubbed the back of his neck with one hand, and the other he used to pull Sofka closer to him. "Sigurd is the name of a Nixie. He's, well...he's a sort of male siren. His kind lure women and children to water to drown them all the while they are smiling and looking happy."

"Ah. I see." Sofka looked around and noticed that they had an audience. She straightened up and cleared her throat. It was one thing if Maxim and Walter thought she was weak, but if Sigurd was in the crowd, or one of his friends, she didn't want anyone thinking she was weak. In fact, she needed to display strength in public if a male siren had been hired to kill her.

Walter put up a finger. "Wait. Sigurd would never hurt you or your friends."

"He's right." A new voice said from the crowd growing around them.

Sofka turned to see who was speaking to them. A male creature that looked more like a Viking, than anything else, stepped up next to them. He wore a fur pelt around his body and had on fur trimmed boots as well as a fur hat. She almost blurted out that she hoped he was wearing faux fur, but thought better of it. While she wasn't sure what type of fur it was, if the male in front of her only used the fur from animals he hunted for dinner, then she could accept that.

"Sigurd, it's good to see you again." Maxim nodded, but didn't put his hand out for the tall, blonde male who could have easily been cast in one of those Viking shows so many humans loved to watch.

The Viking nodded at him. "Walter, what tales have you been spinning?" While his voice wasn't harsh, it wasn't friendly, either.

Not wanting to be the center of attention or grab the attention of someone who might have been hired to kill her, Sofka stood next to Maxim and kept her mouth shut.

"My friend, I haven't been telling any tales. Just shooting the breeze." The centaur shuffled all four of his hooves.

Even Sofka could tell Walter was nervous now that Sigurd was standing so near.

He turned his emerald, green eyes on Sofka, and she wanted to shrink behind Maxim. But she also knew that she was the island's deputy sheriff. No one was going to mess with her if she stood her ground. "Sigurd, nice to meet you. I'm Sofka, the deputy sheriff here on the island. I have a few questions for you."

One beautifully trimmed brow arched and a half smile crossed Sigurd's lips. "What can I do for the sheriff's office?"

The almost perfect male specimen standing near her, dwarfed her. He had to be close to seven feet tall. His blonde hair was pulled back and held in place with a leather cord. Nothing on him said twenty-first century at all. He could have just walked through a portal from an age where Leif Erikson lived and ruled the high seas.

Not wanting to appear afraid of the strong supe in front of her, Sofka raised her chin and looked him in the face. "I hear you had visitors the other day. Please tell me who they were and what they wanted."

Sigurd chuckled. "I didn't realize we had to tell the sheriff's office anything about our visitors. Is this a new policy?"

She narrowed her eyes. "So, you did have visitors."

His head jerked back, and he realized what she had done. "Nicely played, little wolf." He cocked his head to one side. "You seem familiar. Have we met?"

Sofka knew she would remember him if they had met before. And if what Maxim said was true, then there was no way Sigurd could have ever seen her. Unless...

"Let me guess, you've seen a photo of me recently?" It was her turn to arch a brow and wait for him to answer.

A light growl emanated from him and he took two steps closer to her.

Maxim jumped between them and a deep growl sounded loudly throughout the entire cave. "She is under my protection, nixie. You'd be wise to keep that in mind."

Sigurd stopped and scoffed. "I have no plans to hurt anyone. Especially the island's deputy sheriff."

"Then what made you upset? The fact that I knew someone had approached you to hurt me? Or the fact that you don't scare me?" Inside, Sofka was totally quaking in her boots. But on the outside, she seemed cool as the icy snow around her. In fact, she crossed her arms over her chest and glared back at the Viking Adonis who stared her down.

"No, the fact that you thought I would have taken that contract at all. No one on this island would do anything to hurt another resident. We all know the deal." Sigurd looked at Maxim. "None of us want to become the island's next popsicles."

Heat surrounded Maxim, which was extremely difficult for an undead creature on an island in Antarctica. Shoot, it was difficult for heat to emanate from anyone on an icy island. "Then tell us what happened, and who those wolves were that visited you."

Sigurd turned bored eyes on their audience. "Maybe we should take this elsewhere?"

Maxim, Walter, and Sofka all looked around and noted the prying eyes and ears.

"Is there anywhere around here we can have privacy?" Since Sofka had never been to this part of the island, and in fact, hadn't even heard of it until just a little while before, she had no clue if there were any offices that could afford them some privacy. And with supernatural hearing, it would have to be soundproofed.

Sigurd looked like he was about to puke, his face turned red and his lips pursed tight. "No. We don't have secrets here. Or at least, not for long."

"What about the storage shed? Where we parked our snowmobile?" Sofka asked.

Walter grunted. "That's probably the best place to go."

Everyone headed out. A few members of the audience even tried to follow them.

A loud roar emanated from Sigurd and Sofka jumped. “No one is to follow us. Don’t you all have anything better to do than listen in and gossip?”

Sofka’s shoulders shook with the laughter she was trying hard to keep inside. A few of those listening in would have been scary, if she hadn’t just met a real-life centaur and a Viking. Okay, okay, so Sigurd wasn’t a Viking, but he sure looked like one. And he had the hard, scary expressions of one, too. The only thing that would have scared her more was if those redcaps had made an appearance. Just the thought of them sent chills down Sofka’s spine.

Chapter 15

Maxim never let Sofka get more than two steps away from him on the short walk to the storage shed. While she was grateful for his protection, she also felt odd. A warmth infused her body when he was near and she couldn't get his lips out of her mind. Of course, it was probably the fact that behind those lips hid fangs that could elongate at any moment. And those teeth could kill her.

That was it. She kept telling herself that the only reason she kept looking at his mouth, and those luscious lips of his, was to make sure his killer fangs didn't come out to play. While she knew that Maxim wouldn't kill her, or even try to hurt her, he liked her too much. That much she could tell on her own. Still, the idea that he might want to sink his teeth into her neck bothered her.

Walter sat down like a horse would, folding his legs underneath himself. Sigurd took a chair and turned it around so that the back was facing his stomach before he took a seat.

Maxim motioned for Sofka to sit on a loveseat in the corner and he sat down next to her. With his height, and the small seating, their sides melded and folded like a book spine. She didn't mind so much, as his warmth felt nice.

Sofka cleared her throat and decided she needed to think about something else. Maxim wasn't warm, he was dead for Frosty's sake. No warmth came from him, it was just her imagination.

Sofka cleared her throat again and focused back on the topic at hand. "Alright, please tell me who came to visit and why?"

Sigurd rolled his eyes and sighed. "I don't feel right telling the cops about my visitors. This is a free island, isn't it?"

Before Sofka could come back with something snarky, Maxim growled. She put her hand on his arm. "Look, Sigurd. This is a free island. But something nasty is preparing to go down. If you help us, maybe we can stop it."

"How do you know something nasty is about to go down?" Sigurd asked.

The sheriff's deputy took a moment to think about his question. She really didn't know, not for sure. But, with the way things have been going the past few days, and now with how these supes were acting, Sofka's senses were in overdrive. And a wolf's senses were always spot on.

"This is exactly what we are trying to discover." Sofka thought it best to keep it vague, then maybe if they knew something, their subconscious would fill in the blanks and think she was on to them. And, if they had any conscience whatsoever, they would tell her. Or, if that failed, they could just plain mess up. That would help her to find out almost as much as if they told her the truth.

"Well," Walter piped in, "I don't know what's going on. Just that there were a few wolf shifter visitors to the black hill." He looked straight at Sofka, and his eyes never darted away. That was either a sign of honesty, or of a psychopath.

Sofka prayed it was the former. She turned to look at Sigurd. "Did you meet with these visitors?"

Sigurd shrugged. "I might have seen some new supes. Since I don't get into town, I can't really say."

It was Sofka's turn to roll her eyes. After a long sigh, she pursed her lips and glared at the Nixie. "Really? Just be straight with me. I don't have time to play games."

Under his breath, Sigurd whispered, "We shall see."

"What was that?" Even with supernatural hearing, Sofka wasn't sure she heard correctly.

Sigurd waved a hand. "Nothing. Look, everyone here knows that I hate hurting anyone. That's why I'm here, because I refuse to use my gifts. Nothing has changed."

Maxim leaned forward and rested his arms on his knees. "So, you're saying that you didn't talk to a couple of wolf shifters this week?"

A smirk crossed the nixie's face. "I didn't say that."

Sofka stood. "No, you just said that you don't want to harm anyone."

Maxim pulled her back down on the loveseat.

"Fine, what can you tell me about those wolf shifters?" She knew she needed to relax and play the game, no matter how much it irked her.

Sigurd leaned back a little bit in his chair and smiled slowly. "Now you're getting it."

Sofka motioned her hands for him to get on with it.

"Fine, just be impatient." The nixie looked to the centaur. "Cops, they're all alike, aren't they?"

The laugh that escaped Walter was more of a whinny. He put a hand up and shook his head. "Keep me out of this."

Sigurd looked back at Sofka and his back straightened. "Yes, a few shifters visited the other day. They wanted to know if I was still in the business. And I said no."

Sofka felt her eyes widen. If wolf shifters were here trying to start something, it was most likely due to her and her friends. "Did they say what they wanted?"

"No." Sigurd looked Sofka up and down. "Did you cross someone before arriving?"

A growl sounded next to Sofka and she turned her head. Maxim jumped up and had his hands clenched at his side. The fangs that she had feared, were out on display. They sent shivers down her spine.

When his eyes turned red, Maxim barked, "So, it's true. Someone is after Sofka and her friends."

Sigurd stood so quickly, he tipped his chair over. He put his arms up in front of him as if to prepare for an attack. "Hey, man. I told you, I'm no longer in the killing game."

"I didn't ask if you were. I asked if there's someone after Sofka." Maxim appeared to be growing taller as his anger became more evident.

Or was it just that Sofka was shrinking back in her seat?

"They asked if I could be convinced to kill a few females, and I said no. They left after asking a couple more times. What they did after that, I don't know." Sigurd took two steps back.

Maxim glared between the two dark supes. "If either of you see anyone else that's new, or something out of the ordinary, I expect you'll notify Sofka, or myself, right away."

Walter and Sigurd nodded.

Sofka stood and took in a deep breath. She had been holding her breath without even realizing it. "Right. Okay. Thank you for your help."

Neither said a word until they made it back to town and put the snowmobile away.

Sofka was the first to break the silence. "Do you think they were being honest?"

Maxim shook his head. "I don't know. Probably. But it's difficult to know for sure."

Sofka bit the inside of her cheek. "I think there was more they knew, but for some reason they held back." She tilted her head. "Well, Walter was probably being honest. But there's something about Sigurd that I don't trust."

Maxim snorted. "That's because he's a nixie. They like to lure women and children to their death."

"Yeah," Sofka chuckled. "There's that." She sighed.

"But you think there's more to it?" Maxim took her hand and squeezed it. "Don't worry, I will protect you and your friends."

"I know you will. But why should you? We aren't your responsibility," Sofka asked softly.

He put his finger under her chin and tilted her head to look at him. "Because I want to. I want..." Instead of finishing his sentence, Maxim moved his head closer to Sofka's when she looked at his mouth, her breath hitched.

Sofka wasn't sure what she wanted. The only thing she knew was that she didn't want Maxim to bite her. But kiss her? With his lips moving closer to hers, she thought she might like it. Her lashes fluttered in time with her heartbeat and her lips parted in anticipation of what was to come.

"Sofka?" Maxim's soft voice feathered her face.

"Yes?" She barely breathed.

"Hey, what...whoa, sorry. I uh..." The voice that interrupted their almost kiss worked like a bucket of water.

Sofka jumped back. "Horatio? What's going on?" She felt her cheeks heating up and all Sofka wanted was to jump into a pile of snow and hide forever. What was she thinking? She almost kissed a vampire, for Frosty's sake.

Horatio turned around. "I can come back later."

Maxim chuckled. "No, you had something you wanted to say. Go ahead."

When Horatio turned back around and looked at them, his cheeks were flaming red. He rubbed the back of his neck and looked at Maxim's feet. "I, uh..." He cleared his throat. "How'd it go? Did you find out anything?"

"We did, but it wasn't much." Maxim proceeded to tell Horatio the Cliff's Notes version of what they discovered.

"So, you think Sigurd knows more than he's letting on?" Horatio nodded. "Possibly. But I do know that he wouldn't hurt you, Sofka, or anyone else on this island. He swore off his talents when he sought refuge here. I think the island even told him that if he hurt anyone he'd be put on ice."

Maxim and Sofka exchanged a look.

"I see. But, would he be safe if he knew something and didn't tell us?" That would be the sort of loophole that Sofka thought anyone could get away with on this island. While Sigurd wasn't actually doing anything to hurt anyone, it also meant he wasn't doing anything to help, either.

However, that was assuming Sigurd actually knew something about what was going on lately with the Bully Boys. While Sofka figured he did know something, it might not have anything to do with her. It was very possible he was into something else. What that was? She had no clue.

Horatio scratched his chin. "Well, I do think there is a big difference between hiding information and actively participating in something against the rules." He shook his head. "No, I don't think the island would step in if Sigurd was just holding back some little bit he might have gleaned."

"Right, so we need to figure out who got on the island, and how," Maxim added.

"I really wish electronics worked properly on this island." Sofka sighed.

"Why?" Maxim wasn't big on electronics. He had spent the past fifty years on the island, so he wasn't really up on technology. Nor did he really care about any of it.

She pursed her lips. "Because, if we had cameras watching the island entry points, we could see who came on the island, and which way they went."

"Right, but we have Bart. He's the only way on and off the island." Confusion filled Maxim's eyes when he looked at Sofka.

She sighed. "What about the unknown ways onto the island? There's got to be backdoors of some sort, right?"

Horatio and Maxim exchanged a look that said a million words, without actually saying anything at all.

Maxim rubbed his chin. "Well, since you're the deputy, you might as well know." He looked to Horatio.

The unofficial mayor of the island cleared his throat. "You see, there are a couple of ways off the island. In case of emergency."

"So, that means there are ways on the island as well, right?" Sofka interrupted Horatio before he could say more.

The polar bear shifter shook his head. "Actually, there is only one way on the island besides via Bart's boat – swimming."

So far, no one had actually said how one could get onto the island if the boat wasn't an option. The other day, when Sofka met Luana, she had told Sofka there were ways onto the island that bypassed the boat, but nothing specific. She may have been upset about the various ways onto the island, but it was a relief to finally be getting some details about this little glitch in island safety.

"Right, so basically anyone who could withstand the freezing waters could make it on the island." Sofka shook her head. "That's not a good safety system. We really do need to find a way to get electronics to work."

Maxim snorted. "Or get the witch to put up a protection spell that alerts her when someone comes ashore."

Horatio's head whipped around. "NO. We've discussed this already. We don't bother her, and she doesn't bother us."

"What witch?" Witches weren't friends to supernaturals, or even to their own kind. They pretty much kept to their own covens and that was it. Sofka knew there was a witch on the island, but surely that wasn't the one they were talking about.

"Sherrie. She offered to put up a protection spell on the island. A sort of supernatural alarm system." Horatio chuckled. "The only problem was that every time a merperson came ashore, it went off."

"Ah, I see. Couldn't she do a sort of password? You know, tag the merpeople who live here so that they can get through without issue? That's how Bart's boat came and went, right?" Even though Sofka didn't know a lot about magic, she had read enough fantasy books to have an idea of how magic worked. Or how it could work.

"That would require all the merfolk to meet the witch and submit blood. None wanted to do that." Horatio's nose flared and his fists clenched at his sides.

Sofka wasn't sure what had Horatio so upset. He was always the happy-go-lucky one. Nothing ever seemed to get under his fur.

Maxim noticed her confusion and explained, "Sofka, this witch. She's not normal. In fact, she's quite powerful."

Horatio interrupted. "She's the sister to the witch who almost destroyed the entire world."

Chapter 16

Sofka had a lot on her mind. After the bombshell that Horatio dropped, she and Maxim headed out. If he hadn't suggested they head back to the jail to check on things, she would have asked Horatio for more details. But when she looked at Maxim, he shook his head.

Something funky had happened, and she didn't understand it. Not one single bit.

Once they were far enough away from Horatio, Sofka put a hand on Maxim's arm. "What's going on with this witch?"

"Most witches are sketchy, you know this, right?" Maxim asked.

Sofka nodded. "Yes, from the moment we can understand, we are taught to stay clear of witches."

"And you know about our island witch. She was given asylum here with the stipulation that the first time she hurt anyone she'd be put on ice." Maxim pursed his lips. "I really don't like that practice, but in this case, I have to agree with the island."

Maxim began to walk again, but Sofka yanked on his arm to stop him. "Are you saying that this witch helped the one who created the gargoyles? The witch who tried to create a species just so she could harness their magic?"

"Yes. Sherrie, that's our witch as you call her." Maxim's nostrils flared. "I really hate that description. We just call her the island witch, or Sherrie."

"Okay, sorry about that. So, this Sherrie, she's the sister of the witch who created the gargoyles and turned herself into a gargoyle in the process?" All supernatural children are told about this. In fact, it's the largest fairy tale that supernatural children are told about, besides Santa. There are many different books written about that witch. But as far as Sofka knew, there wasn't anything about a sister. "How is it none of the tales talk about this sister?"

He shrugged. "I don't really know. All I know is that Sherrie was part of a coven. They were always besieged by other covens who wanted their power. In the world of witches, they were the third most powerful on Earth. Legend has it that the second most powerful coven was jealous of the Woodburn Coven, they were the top witches at that time. Lilliana, the leader of the second seed coven, wanted to be number one. So they tried to get Sherrie's coven to join them. Of course, they refused. Like I said before, witches don't play well with each other."

"Yes, I remember. But why wouldn't Lilliana just get some lower-level covens to join with them if they just needed more power?" As far as Sofka knew, the only way to move up a spot was to have more powerful witches. Numbers didn't matter, just overall power.

“No one really knows. Lilliana died before the war was over. But, back to Sherrie and her coven. They wanted more power to protect themselves from Lilliana.” Maxim paused and Sofka interrupted.

“Kind of like a hostile takeover?”

Maxim chuckled. “That’s a great analogy. And yes, a lot like that. Sherrie’s sister, Sonya, thought if she could just make their coven more powerful, they wouldn’t have to worry about anyone trying to take them over. So she created the gargoyle race. More by accident than actual design. She was just trying to find innate magic that she and her sisters could tap into.”

Sofka had heard the magic behind what Sonya had done. A witch could steal a supe’s magic and that would boost their power. Not by a lot, but if they kept it up, they could have seriously increased their power so much, that no one could have defeated Sonya.

However, Sonya pushed it too far. She ended up turning all of the European gargoyles at that time into live supernatural creatures. All of her magic infused them and they came to life. While she turned to stone right where she was.

“Okay, so then why is Sherrie the only one left? Did the rest just die out over time? Or something worse? Villagers with pitchforks and so forth?” It might have been a cliché, but that sort of thing did happen. Quite a bit until the turn of the twentieth century. Then, supes got smarter and started to hide better.

“Sofka, sometimes you can be so sweet and naive. No. Sherrie was the only one of her coven who wasn’t actively participating in the spell.” Maxim’s voice was soft and tinged with sadness as he spoke. “They were all turned to stone with Sonya.”

Sofka's mouth dropped open and she stood there transfixed as she took in Maxim's words. After a moment, her brain finally clicked back into motion. "You mean her entire coven was helping to drain the few gargoyles they had created of magic? And it backfired on them?"

"Haven't you heard the tales? Surely, as someone who grew up in a pack of wolf shifters, you would have heard it all." Maxim shook his head not understanding how anyone in the supernatural world didn't know all of this already.

"I." Sofka closed her mouth and shook her head. "I grew up on tales of Sonya and her evil deeds, but no one had ever mentioned the coven. I had actually thought she was a loner. In fact," she rubbed her temples as she thought about the stories from her childhood. "We were told this was the sort of thing that happened when we left our packs. Supes would go power crazy and have no one to help them back to reality."

"Боже мой." Maxim rolled his eyes and tsk'd. "I see why you and your friends don't know much. I take it your Alpha made sure to tell you only what he wanted you to know."

Sofka shrugged. "I guess." Her eyes widened. "No, it couldn't be."

"What?" Maxim took a step closer to Sofka and took her hand in his. "Tell me what's going on?"

With her free hand, Sofka put her fingers to her lips and crushed her eyes closed. "This is all my fault. I just know it is."

"What? What's the matter?" Maxim implored.

Tears leaked out of Sofka's closed eyes. "It can't be. I...It just...no. It's not possible." She opened her eyes and looked up into Maxim's. "Could it be that my alpha is trying to get us back?"

Maxim's hand tightened around Sofka's. His eyes glowed red and his fangs hung down lower than Sofka had seen before. "If he comes anywhere near you, I will end him."

"No, you don't understand. He sold us! We technically belong to some supernatural trafficking group. It's either Kirill who is doing this, or the guys he sold us to." Sofka pulled away from Maxim. "I have to warn KeeKee and Ree."

She started to turn away from Maxim but he reached back out and held her in place. "Sofka, don't worry. You are going to be safe. If it is your alpha doing this, then we know who to look for and can protect you."

"How? The Bully Boys escaped a magical jail and almost killed you and the sheriff in the process." Sofka pulled back and threw her hands in the air. "They are nothing compared to those we ran from. If Tony and his buddies could do that, how much damage can Kirill do here on the island?"

Maxim pulled her close to his chest and held her tight. "Shhh, I promise I will protect you. Now we have a lead. And this island is so small, those boys won't be able to hide for very long."

"What if they're already off the island?" Fear edged Sofka's words and she clenched her fists against Maxim's chest. She knew she had to keep it all together for the sake of her packmates. Ree and KeeKee needed her to be the leader they all knew her to be – strong and fearless.

After a few shaky breaths, she got herself together. "Kirill and his buddies will *not* get us. I will fight to the death if I must, to protect Ree and KeeKee."

"That's my girl." Maxim smiled and rubbed her arm. "And besides, we now have an Unseelie prince on our side. Those wolves have no idea what they're in for when Marcus finds out his mate is in danger."

The stress must have been too much for Sofka to keep inside any longer. She couldn't stop it, a full belly laugh erupted from her. It started deep down, in her gut, and made its way out of her mouth so loudly, they caught the attention of passersby.

"Sorry, I couldn't stop it," Sofka said between gasping laughs.

They say laughter is contagious, and Maxim proved the old adage to be true. Once he finished with his laughter, he wiped the tears from Sofka's face. "I think laughing is better than crying."

She nodded. "I agree." Then she took a deep sigh. "Okay, where do we go from here?"

"Back to the jail. And then to the information center so we can update everyone." Maxim led them away.

Chapter 17

"You're free. Thank Frosty!" Sofka sighed when she caught sight of the Sheriff sitting at his desk.

"Yes, and the jail is put back to rights, too." Sheriff Roscoe Coldtrain stood up with a coffee mug in one hand and pointed to the door that led to the jail cells. It was gone. In its place was one set of bars with a cot sitting ready and waiting for a criminal.

"I don't know if I'll ever get used to the way this place changes as needs change." Sofka winced. "But why did the island let them get away? What could the island want with the Bully Boys free?"

Roscoe shook his head. "I don't think the island *let* them get away. I think that someone with some very powerful magic interfered. There's a difference."

"Sofka, you have to understand that while the island is extremely powerful, it isn't all-powerful. It's not a god, or anything like that. There are supes who are more powerful and can defeat the island's magic." While Maxim's words were said with a solemnity usually reserved for church, his eyes were the intense red that could send anyone running for their life.

"But, earlier, what you said led me to believe that the island was in control and in time we'd understand why everything was happening." Sofka couldn't believe the change in opinion from Maxim and confusion etched her features.

He shrugged. "That was before we spoke to Walter and Sigurd. Now, I'm starting to think that something more powerful than the island is behind all of this and the Bully Boys are just a distraction."

"So, then we aren't truly safe here on this island. Are we?" The entire time Sofka and her friends traveled to the island, they thought it would be their protector. They were led to believe that no one was stronger than the island. And that no one would be able to hurt them on the island. That day had proved everything they knew to be wrong.

She plopped down on the chair at her desk and put her head in her hands. "How can we fight something that's stronger than even the island?"

Maxim leaned down next to her. "Sweetheart, we can do anything if we put our minds to it."

"And if we all work together, we will be unstoppable," Roscoe added.

Sofka snorted. "What? Are we supposed to be like the Musketeers? Or something?"

Maxim stood up and put his hand in the air as though he was holding a sword, and his other fist on his hip. "All for one, and one for all!"

Roscoe laughed, and Sofka joined him.

"Thanks, I think I needed that." Sofka sighed. "But really, how do we battle something we can't see?"

"Oh, we can see them," Roscoe interjected. "I saw the Bully Boys when they attacked us and shoved us in the jail. The problem is the magic that was loaned to them. That's," he put his hand in the air and pointed at the air above them, "what we need to discover."

Discovering the magic that was used was much easier said than done. After a little pow-wow with the team over at the information center, everyone decided that they should split up and check with their various friends.

"What about me? I don't really know too many supes yet." KeeKee asked.

"What? Of course, you do. You work in one of the most visited shops on the island." Horatio scoffed.

"I wouldn't say I know any of the supes who come through our doors. I may know their name and say hi, but I wouldn't call any of them friends." KeeKee always had trouble making friends. Thanks to the way she grew up, she never learned to trust anyone outside of Sofka and Ree. So calling someone a friend was almost unheard of. Even calling someone an acquaintance wasn't really her thing.

"KeeKee, you know a lot of people. They may not be friends yet, but I bet some of them would like a chance to get to know you better. Use your connections and see what you can find out." Sofka encouraged her friend to step out on a limb and take a chance with others.

"I don't know." KeeKee shrunk back into herself.

Horatio, the one who knew absolutely everyone on the island stood next to her. "Hey, how about we team up and I introduce you to those you don't know yet?"

It was a great idea. And Sofka hoped that maybe the two would find they had a lot in common. Who knew, by the end of the day they could be on their way to mated bliss.

That idea stopped Sofka short. She shook her head. She didn't want KeeKee to leave her all alone as Ree had done. When they all decided to split up and check everything out, Ree didn't even ask if she could team up with Sofka or KeeKee, she just left with Marcus without so much as a backward glance.

Sofka internally chided herself. The pair were mated now, and she'd have to get used to the fact that Ree would always choose Marcus over them. But nothing said she had to like it. The thought of losing her other best friend to a male almost made her cry. When her nose burned and her eyes itched, she turned away from them and walked outside.

Once clear of the door, the crisp air dried up the tears that had begun to well in Sofka's eyes. She let loose a long, slow sigh, then ran a hand over her face. She noted the supernaturals that walked down the main road without a care in the world.

Even though everyone knew about the attack on the coffee shop, and the subsequent jailbreak, some of the residents didn't seem to be worried. Sofka couldn't understand how they were able to put it all aside and live in bliss. A part of her envied them that ability.

But maybe they knew they weren't the targets and were relatively safe.

She hadn't realized it, but Maxim had come up directly behind her.

"Sofka, what's wrong?" Maxim asked.

She startled and the air around her misted and for just a second her eyesight was sharper, and her nose began to elongate. But she caught herself and stopped the transformation. When startled, some wolf shifters would instinctively shift into their other form. Sofka was one who could do that, but she could also stop it just as quickly.

"Don't ever sneak up on me like that. I almost shifted." Her eyes rolled upward in exasperation, and she took two steps away from the vampire who had the uncanny ability to unsettle her whenever he got too close.

"Sofka, I'm sorry. Sometimes I forget to make a noise when coming up behind someone." Maxim waved a hand in the air. "It's just my instincts. All that time as a vampire on the prowl instilled the need to be as quiet as a mouse."

Sofka arched a brow. "Really? You think you need to sneak up on me?"

"No, no. That's not it." Maxim shook his head emphatically. "I don't want to sneak up on you. It's just my training just has me naturally...Oh, never mind." He waved his hand to dismiss the rambling sentence.

"What did you want, Maxim?" Sofka realized too late that she worded her question wrong. She should have asked him what he needed, not wanted. She had a pretty good idea of what he wanted. And she wasn't about to give it to him.

He smirked, obviously catching the double meaning in her words. "I came out here to see if you wanted to team up with me again. We did really well earlier, and I think we can keep up the good work."

It was on the tip of her tongue to deny his request. But the moment she realized that both of her best friends were already teamed up with other males, she decided that Maxim would be a good partner. But not in the relationship sense, just as a working partner. He did know a lot of supes on the island. And he was strong.

Sofka could take care of herself. That was something she'd been doing ever since her parents died when she was little.

All Sofka could remember of her parents were their smiles. Her mom and dad loved her and always said or did things to make her smile. And until recently, she had believed the stories about their death. That it was an accident. But the way her alpha had been behaving lately, had Sofka and her two best friends doubting the stories they had heard.

Even KeeKee and Ree's parents had died when they were young. The three wolf shifters had been kept on the periphery of the pack ever since they lost their parents. Sure, none of them were full-blooded arctic wolf shifters, but neither were any of the others in their pack. Some were closer than others, but that didn't matter for the rest of the pack.

It only seemed to be an issue for the three of them. Which made Sofka wonder about the deaths. Were they really accidents? Or was something worse at play here? All three of the girls had been put at the bottom of the pecking order. They were omegas. Which meant that they were treated poorly. And they'd never be allowed to mate and continue their line. In essence, their lines ended when each of their parents died.

The three had always wondered how it was that each of their parents died as pairs. It never seemed to happen that one died, and then the other. Although all three pairs died at different times, they weren't too far behind each other.

Within eighteen months, all three girls had become orphans. Of course, the pack helped to raise them, but they never let the girls forget they were at the bottom of the pile.

"Sofka? What's wrong?" Maxim stared into her eyes and had his hands on her shoulders.

She was shivering, even though she had her winter parka on and wasn't really cold, at least not for an arctic wolf shifter. "Sorry, I was lost in thought. What did you say?"

Maxim's brows furrowed and he looked her up and down. "Are you sure you're alright?"

With a nod, Sofka took a step back, again. Lately, she had noticed that Maxim was always finding ways to touch her or step within her personal space. They seemed to be doing a dance. One that Sofka didn't enjoy. "No, I'm fine. Just thinking about my parents."

"They died when you were young, right?" Maxim asked. They had spoken about it, but only once when they both shared about their family, or lack thereof.

Maxim's family had all died out. That was common for vampires. But Sofka's parents died in a snowmobile accident when she was only eight years old. Or, at least, that was the story she was told.

Not wanting to talk, or even think, about her parents, Sofka asked if he was ready to leave. "Where do we start?"

The vampire looked at her and his face softened. "You know, you can talk to me about anything at all. I'd like to think I'm your friend."

Sofka sucked her lips in before she could come back with a rude remark. She didn't really think of him as a friend. But as she stood there thinking about all of the help he'd offered since they arrived, she realized that he really did want to be their friend. He might want more from her, but he had helped Ree and KeeKee just as much as her.

When Marcus started the mating bond with Ree, without her knowledge, it was Maxim who had looked into how it was possible. He even threatened to get rid of the Unseelie prince if they wanted Marcus gone.

Which would have caused a lot of problems for them, and most likely the island. Marcus Whitehead was the Unseelie prince, but second born. Which was why he was on the island. His brother, the crowned prince and Queen Mab's successor, had tried repeatedly to kill Marcus, despite the no-kill order from Queen Mab. Somehow, Sofka doubted Marcus's brother would take too kindly to anyone else killing him. The Unseelie were ruthless, and prideful.

But Marcus was starting to grow on them all. All three of the wolf shifters were glad that Maxim didn't hurt, or kill, Marcus. In the end, it all worked out for the best. True love did find a way.

Sofka pulled her thoughts back to the present situation. It seemed Maxim was still trying to be her friend. Not that she had sought out his friendship, or done anything to deserve it, but it might be something good.

Good wasn't exactly a word she could use to describe her life since her parents died. It had just been the three of them for so long that Sofka wasn't sure how to bring Maxim into her little pack. But maybe she didn't have to let him into their pack, she just needed to accept his help. And maybe the friendship would develop naturally from there.

"What do you say we start this search? I think we should keep our focus on the present issues." It wasn't easy for Sofka to open up to anyone. Ree and KeeKee were the only ones she shared her thoughts and feelings with. However, having Maxim as an ally, at the very least, was a smart move. One that she would pursue.

"Great, I know just where to start." Maxim led her away from the center of town and toward a small grouping of homes in an area Sofka hadn't been to yet.

Chapter 18

The walk only took about ten minutes. But the tiny neighborhood was as different from the center of town as night was from day. First thing she noticed was the small playground. There were three swings, a small slide, and one of those teeter-totter things with a colorful snail on one end and a Christmas gnome on the other.

A smile crossed her face when she realized that kids lived in this area. The homes were nothing like hers. They reminded Sofka of a street of houses one might see on a sitcom. They had little yards with toys out front, chimneys with billowing smoke, and Halloween lights all over the front of each house. It was a suburb of sorts.

"I know there are kids here, but I guess I hadn't really thought about it before. Are they all born here? Do supes really live here that long?" Sofka noticed the drapes on one window swooshing as though she had just caught someone spying on them.

Maxim chuckled. “Of course, there are families here. Some kids are born here, while others move here with their parents. It’s just like any other place on Earth.”

“Yeah, I guess I just never really thought about it. I have seen some teens hanging out at the coffee shop, but not too many.” Sofka knew that Horatio had conducted a census of sorts the previous year. But she couldn’t remember the details of the count.

“Since the island only has about five hundred residents, you wouldn’t see too many kids. I think most are in this general area. They kinda stick to themselves, for safety.” Maxim pointed to a large house on the end of the cul-de-sac they went down. “That’s a house full of polar bear shifters.”

“Really? Any relation to Horatio?” Sofka hadn’t heard him talking about family, but one never knew with Horatio, he seemed to keep his private life just that – private.

“Nah.” Maxim chuckled. “I don’t think he has any real family on the island. But he does have a lot of supes who look upon him as family.”

Sofka nodded. “Makes sense. He’s the outgoing and friendly type. I’m sure he could make friends with a troll.” She laughed thinking about the stories she’d heard about trolls. Those guys stunk to high heaven and were meaner than a pit of vipers. She’d never want to befriend one, but Horatio would.

“He has made friends with a bridge troll. Did I ever tell you about that?” Maxim grinned.

“Maxim!” A loud male voice interrupted what was sure to be a good story. He waved at them and motioned for them to join him on his porch.

"Elias, good to see you again. How's the family?" Maxim led them both to the house that looked like a New England style home with a slanted roof, and covered porch, but the coloring was more like something one would expect to see in Santa Fe. The fascia board was painted a bright red and the walls of the house were a deep teal. While the windows were trimmed in sunset orange. And of course, Halloween lights decorated the house. Horatio would be proud of all of the lights and yard ornaments.

Sofka had never seen a house like it before. As she stepped up on the patio, she looked around the other homes and noticed each one was the same frame, but all of the colors were different.

"Everyone is great." Elias eyed Sofka up and down. "Who's your friend?"

Maxim put a hand out motioning for Sofka to join them on the orange patio. There were thick cushioned seats flanking a roaring fireplace. It was actually warm and inviting. "This is Sofka, she's the new deputy sheriff."

"Howdy, Ma'am. Nice to meet ya." Elias put his hand out to shake. "I'm Elias."

Sofka's genuine smile lit up her face. "So nice to meet you, too. How long have you and your family been here?"

Elias laughed and his belly shook, almost like a bowl full of jelly. Sofka wondered if that was what Santa looked like when he laughed.

"I've been here almost as long as Maxim. But I didn't meet my mate until about ten years ago." Elias motioned for them all to take a seat near the fire.

"I must say, this is a very nice patio. Do you sit out here often?" Sofka looked around and made note of how it was set up and decided to ask her house about making them a nice back patio. Somewhere she could sit and be alone with her thoughts while still warm. Maybe even read a few books out there.

Elias chuckled. "We have four pups all under the age of five. I come out here as much as possible."

Sofka imagined that Elias' house would be similar to the nursery back at her old pack. "If it's anything like what I've experienced in a wolfpack, then your house must be crazy loud at times."

"You've no idea what four black bear pups can be like when lunch or dinner is late." A feminine voice said from behind where Sofka sat.

Sofka startled and turned around. "Oh."

Elias stood. "This is my mate, Melanie." He motioned for Melanie to sit next to him. "Where are the kids?"

Melanie sank down into the seat with a cup of coffee in her hands. "Sleeping." She sighed.

"Really? All four?" Elias asked with a hint of incredulity in his voice.

She nodded as she brought the mug of coffee to her lips. After she took a long sip, she looked at her guests.

"Mel, let me introduce Sofka to you." Elias made the introductions and Sofka noted that his mate already knew Maxim.

"Maxim, it's good to see you again. It's been way too long since you've been over for dinner. You really should come and visit soon." Melanie smiled from ear to ear and her soft brown eyes crinkled at the edges.

Sofka noticed the black bear shifter's long, silky black hair and wished she could get hers to grow out that long. Melanie's hair went down to her waist.

When Melanie looked at Sofka she added, "And of course, you're invited as well. It would be nice to get to know Maxim's girlfriend."

"Oh, no." Sofka waved her hands in front of her.

Maxim chuckled, but said nothing.

"I don't think Maxim has dated anyone since I've known him." Melanie noticed Sofka's pink cheeks. "What? Did I say something wrong?"

Maxim cleared his throat. "It's alright Melanie. Sofka isn't my girlfriend, at least not yet." He winked at Sofka, who only shrunk down in her seat.

Sofka could feel her cheeks getting hotter and hotter.

Elias laughed his huge Santa-like laugh, which helped to ease the situation a bit.

Sofka sat up straight and took in a deep breath. Once her face cooled down, she remembered what they were there for. "Ah, Maxim and I are actually on a case. I assume you've heard about the issues in town this week?"

The smiling Melanie disappeared and a stern, almost scary-looking woman sat across from her. "Yes. I've told Horatio several times that we needed to get rid of those good-for-nothing wolf shifters."

Sofka's hackles rose, but Maxim put a hand on her arm.

"I take it you're specifically referring to the Bully Boys? Tony, Manny, Andrew, and Johnny?" Maxim asked.

"Yes, those four are nothing but trouble. You know they actually tried to kick my little Tobias?" Melanie huffed and crossed her arms over her chest. "If I ever get them alone..." A harsh growl emanated from the woman who had seemed like a very sweet lady until only moments before.

Elias's nostrils flared. "If you're here looking for them, I can tell you that no one in this neighborhood would help them. Every one of us has had run-ins with them, and all of us are hoping the island sends them packing."

"Okay, do you know who might be helping them?" Sofka asked.

Maxim added, "Someone is helping them. There is no way they have the magic required to break out of our jail."

"Or to overpower you, right?" Elias asked.

"Exactly," Sofka answered for Maxim.

Melanie shook her head. "I'm sorry, but I haven't seen them since the incident at the coffee shop."

"You were there?" Sofka's brow furrowed. She didn't remember seeing Melanie, and she'd even looked at the list of witnesses. There wasn't a Melanie on the list. Doubt crept in and she wondered if they were helping out somehow and using this story to try and move suspicion elsewhere.

"Oops." Melanie chuckled nervously and jumped up.

Sofka jumped up and put her hands on her belt. She didn't carry a weapon, but she did have cuffs that could hold just about any supernatural. "What are you doing?"

"Sorry." Melanie waved a hand in front of her. "I'm nervous."

Elias pulled on his mate's hand. "Honey, sit down. You didn't do anything wrong." He glared at Sofka. "See what you've done? You've upset her."

"I've upset her?" Sofka put a hand on her chest. "Your mate left the scene of a crime without letting anyone know she was a witness. She shouldn't have done that." Sofka looked at Melanie and arched a brow. "It makes you look guilty."

Finally, Melanie plopped down and a lung full of air escaped her mouth. "I know, but I had the kids with me. They were already so hyper. And when that truck crashed through the wall, they all started crying and howling. I had to get them out of there. They're just babies."

Sofka had heard someone say they thought a family with little kids left right away, but no one knew for sure. Several patrons had heard wailing and just assumed it was little kids. "I can understand wanting to get your children away from a scene like that, but you should have contacted the Sheriff's department and told us what you saw."

"I know, I know. I was going to head back there once the kids were settled, but…" Melanie shrugged.

Sofka struggled to get her anger in check. For all she knew, this family had seen something material. Something that could have broken the case wide open. Maybe even something that would have stopped the boys from escaping.

Elias looked at Sofka's hands, and then into her eyes. "You aren't going to arrest my mate, are you?"

The situation didn't warrant arresting a mother of little pups, but Sofka sure did want to instill some fear in the supernatural family. "I don't know. Why don't you run me through what you saw that day."

Elias put a comforting arm around his mate. Melanie leaned into his warmth. When she visibly relaxed, Sofka wondered if that was normal for a mate. Did mates really help each other relax? Did they help them feel safe and protected? Or was it just this couple?

Melanie shut her eyes and took a couple of deep breaths. "Alright. It was just me and the kids. We had gone to the coffee shop as a treat. The boys had been really good for their sitter the day before."

When Sofka furrowed her brows and was about to ask what happened the day before, Elias answered her unspoken question.

"It was date night. We try to go out at least once a month just the two of us." Elias leaned toward his wife and kissed her forehead.

Melanie smiled and sighed. "Usually, the boys act up for their sitter, but this time they were pretty good."

"Anna did warn them the Bully Boys would get them if they were bad." Elias chuckled.

"What?" Sofka couldn't believe the tundra wolves were already being used to scare kids into submission.

Melanie winced. "Yeah, I wasn't too happy about that either. But, Anna said if they acted up, the tundra wolves would come and get them. Kinda like the boogeyman."

"I bet after the crash at the coffee shop, the boys were extra upset." Maxim rubbed his hand down his face and shook his head. "This is the trouble with using current bad guys as the boogeyman."

"Right. I've already spoken with Anna. And she feels awful." Elias pulled his wife in closer.

Sofka put a hand in the air. "Alright. Let's move on from the local boogeyman. What did you see or hear at the coffee shop?"

After a few more questions, and Melanie recounted everything she could remember, Sofka realized that there was nothing Melanie could have added to that investigation. She sagged with dejection and wondered, not for the first time, if the island really was safe.

"Can you think of anyone on this island, or off, who might help them?" It was a standard question. And Sofka doubted they'd know anything about the boys, but she wouldn't be doing her job if she didn't ask.

Melanie and Elias exchanged glances.

"I don't know who it was, but a couple of days ago I did see someone new on the island," Elias offered.

"Can you describe this supe?" Sofka asked.

Elias nodded. "Of course. There were two of them. One female and one male. I got the feeling that they were shifters, but I couldn't tell you what sort."

Sofka nodded for him to continue. She had a small notepad that she kept in her pocket and had pulled it out when she first sat down. Now, she was writing furiously everything the couple had been telling her.

Maxim interrupted, "Where were you when you saw them?"

"I was at the end of our little street. The pair was walking from town out toward the Dark Hills." Elias' little neighborhood sat between town and the Dark Hills, but not on the same track that Sofka and Maxim had taken when they went out there earlier.

Sofka looked out toward the only hills on the island. "What's between here and the hills?"

Melanie jumped in, "Two small communities like ours. One is for those with kids, and the other is mostly older supes who don't like to go into town much."

"Do you think they were headed to the hills? Or to one of those little communities?" Sofka didn't recognize the supes based on the little description Elias had given. He'd only said they were average height and both had brown hair. That could be so many supes, too many to narrow down with that little description.

"I really couldn't tell you." Elias shook his head. "I noticed them because we don't get too many visitors, but it's not like I know who all of the new arrivals are. Until today, I didn't know who you were."

"True. I don't know everyone either." Sofka nodded and made a few notes in her book. "Do you think they could be the small group who arrived after me and my friends did? Or do you think they were only here for the day?"

Melanie nodded. "I had heard news about those ten supes who came in after you, and now that you mention it, several of them are shifters." She looked at her husband. "Do you think they're part of that group? I hear they've been assigned jobs in the past few days."

Elias' eyes widened and it looked as though he was remembering something; or putting two and two together. "You know, there is a home in that direction," he pointed to where the two new people had walked. "It's older supes who can't get out as easily. We all take turns bringing them food and news, or anything they might need. If it's those who came right after you, then that would make sense."

"So, you think those new supes were just out here helping those who couldn't get out?" Sofka deflated. If that was what they were doing, it was a good thing. But it also meant another dead end for her investigation.

Elias shrugged. "I don't know. You'll have to go and check it out. But my guess is that's what they were doing. The island is always trying to find supes to help those who need it."

"The island will only do so much for us, and then it's up to us to do the rest. I think it's nice that new supernaturals are already on the list to help the elderly." Melanie smiled and sighed. "One day, we are going to be too old to do much for ourselves, and it will be nice to know that there is a system here to help us, that works."

Sofka felt like she'd been prodded by the tip of a gnome's hat. And it hurt. She was so focused on her current problems, that she'd never even known there was a group home here for the elderly who needed help. Supernaturals lived a very long time. And since they all healed up quickly, it was extremely rare that a supe wasn't able to take care of themselves. At least not until they got up there in age.

All supernaturals had different lifespans. The vampires, for example, would continue to exist until someone killed them. They could live a thousand years, or longer, if they were smart. Arctic wolf shifters generally lived closer to two hundred years, but they could die of other things than murder. Illness was very rare for a shifter of any sort.

Even bird shifters didn't get sick from the avian flu that hits humans every so often. Never mind colds or fevers, those just didn't affect the supernatural community like they did the humans.

Sofka stood to leave. "Thank you for the information. If you think of something else, or see anything, be sure to let me or Sheriff Roscoe know right away. We have to catch these guys before they can hurt anyone else."

"Of course." Elias stood up and walked Sofka and Maxim to the edge of the patio. "Maxim, when this mess is wrapped up, let's grab a burger together."

"You got it, man." Maxim put a hand on his friend's shoulder and squeezed. "It's been too long since we last had a night out with the guys."

"Agreed." Elias waved as the two investigators walked away.

Chapter 19

"Well, that was a bust." Sofka plopped down on the couch in her house.

Maxim sat next to her. "No, it wasn't. No news is actually data we can process. We know where the boys are not, which will help us to focus more on a different area tomorrow."

"True. Thank you for a long day of work. I know you generally don't stay out all day long, but I appreciate your help." While Sofka didn't know Maxim's exact schedule, she did know that he preferred to nap in the afternoons. Vampires didn't need as much sleep as everyone else did. Normally, they'd sleep for a few hours a day. Then once a month they slept for over twelve hours in one night, or day, depending on their schedule.

He waved her comment off. "No worries, I can sleep when I'm dead." Maxim grinned.

Seeing as how vampires were technically dead, the comment didn't make a lot of sense. "Aren't you already dead?" A small smile crossed Sofka's features and the edges of her eyes crinkled.

"Too true. How about I make you some dinner before you call it a night?" Maxim stood and headed to the kitchen.

"You can cook?" Incredulity laced Sofka's words, and she stood to join him.

"Of course, I can. Vampires may not eat a lot of regular food, but we do enjoy it. Anything with meat can help us maintain our strength between feedings." Maxim hadn't said much to Sofka about his eating habits, before now.

"So, you eat a bloody burger at the Island Shack. And I assume you have a few females who, uh," Sofka felt her face heat.

"Go on, you can say it." Maxim tried hard to keep the smile off his lips, but he failed. When he grinned at Sofka, she chuckled.

"Right, I guess you have females here on the island who volunteer their necks?" Sofka would have said bodies, but she didn't get the feeling that Maxim used females that way. She didn't think he was a saint, not by any stretch of the imagination. But she doubted he floated from bed to bed.

He shook his head. "No, not really. In a pinch, there are a few supes on the island who would volunteer their blood, but usually, I stick to animals. It's not as appetizing, but I can't rely on the island coughing up donors for me."

This was all new information for Sofka. "You mean you can survive off the blood of animals? Really?" She hoped he meant real animals, the wild sort. And he wasn't using that as a way to classify supernaturals whom he killed.

Although, if supes went missing, she'd know about it. As would the sheriff, and the island. In a small place such as Misfit Island, gossip was everywhere. And privacy wasn't guaranteed for anyone.

Maxim nodded. "I can. It's not the best, but after a while, I got used to it. And adding red meat into my diet has really helped."

"Except, you prefer your meat bloody." Sofka squirmed and stuck her tongue out. The idea of eating bloody meat always grossed her out.

"Wait, you're a wolf shifter. Don't you eat raw animals in your wolf form?" The imperious brow arched and he stared her down.

Maxim had gotten her there. When in her wolf form, she did chase the occasional rabbit and eat it raw. "Don't judge. Wolves don't have opposable thumbs. It's not like I can stop and skin the rabbit before putting it on a stick over a fire." She knew she could shift back into her human form and cook it without issue, but her wolf enjoyed the hunt. And she enjoyed eating the fruits of her labor. It would just be mean to shift after her wolf caught the rabbit, and before she could eat it.

Sofka didn't usually think about what her animal form did when it was in charge. It was all part of nature and she just let it be. "But, it's different for you. You don't shift into another creature."

"I don't know if I agree with you on that. Right now, I'm a calm man, almost human again. When the vampire instinct kicks in, then I do change in a way. You've seen my fangs and my red eyes." Maxim shrugged. "I'd say I do shift when I vamp out."

Sofka squirmed. She didn't like that he spoke about his vampire side like it was a wild animal that took over instinctively. At least her animal form hunted wild animals, and not humans, or other supes.

Maxim put up a placating hand. "Alright, how about we focus on dinner in our humanoid forms? What do you have?"

She motioned for him to enter the kitchen. "Take a look and help yourself. Just make sure my meat is medium-rare, at least."

After only a moment or two perusing her refrigerator, Maxim closed the door and smiled. "How about surf and turf?"

"Mmm, my favorite. Steak with shrimp sauce over a bed of fettuccine? I can make the noodles." Sofka pulled out a large pan and started to put water in it.

"I was thinking more along the lines of steak and lobster. With a butter and garlic herb sauce." Maxim put the items on the counter he had pulled from the fridge.

"Oh, that sounds wonderful. But garlic?" Even though it was an old wives' tale, Sofka wasn't sure that vampires could eat garlic.

The vampire chuckled. "Really? You think I can't eat garlic?' He stepped into her personal space. "Or, are you hoping for a goodnight kiss?" He leaned down slowly, giving her a chance to pull away.

When she did, he smirked. Sofka pulled back, but he could see the desire in her eyes before she turned them down. The way her soft lips parted in an O shape was almost more than he could handle, but he was a gentleman and would never kiss her if she didn't want it enough to say so.

When KeeKee cleared her throat, both Sofka and Maxim turned. Maxim looked like the cat who caught the canary. But Sofka's cheeks were flaming hot and she couldn't look her friend in the eyes.

"So, what's for dinner? Or is this a romantic dinner for two?" KeeKee giggled and walked further into the kitchen. She stood behind the island and grinned at her friends.

Sofka knew that once Maxim left, she'd be getting grilled to death by her best friend. "Knock it off, or no dinner for you." She arched a brow and knew that KeeKee would go nuts when she found out what they were having.

"Sorry, too late. I already ate dinner in town with Horatio." KeeKee turned to Maxim. "We stopped in at the Island Shack." She grinned, knowing how much Maxim loved that place.

He returned her grin. "Good for you. We're going to have steak and lobster. My steak will be even bloodier than what the Island Shack serves." Maxim winked at Sofka.

That act alone sent shivers through Sofka's knees. His confidence was one of the vampire's attributes she liked best. Well, next to his striking good looks, of course. She knew she should have thought about his personality, but wasn't confidence a part of a man's personality? Okay, so she did like his personality.

But, whenever she thought about him, it was his eyes that got her every time. Not the red ones of the vampire, but the warm brown eyes with flecks of green and gold that sparkled when he looked at her. That was what she thought about the most. His personality was just icing on the handsome cake.

She had to turn away from his gaze when she felt her cheeks flame. He had to know she was into him. And if she was honest with herself, even she knew it. But there was a difference between thinking him handsome and wanting to date him. Sofka couldn't get her head wrapped around the concept of dating a vampire. It was true she was a bit naïve and didn't know much about vampires and dating. But, that didn't mean she had no clue at all.

No one had ever described the leader of the tiny pack as clueless. Even Sofka knew that Vampires had voracious appetites for more than just blood. She'd seen plenty of human movies that always showed vampires in bed with their lovers. Not that Sofka was a prude, but the arctic wolf shifter didn't have casual sex.

They mated for life.

Chapter 20

“What’s with the newbs?” Sofka couldn’t get them off her mind, she decided they must be up to something with their hiding out and steering clear of every one since they arrived.

“Newbs?” Horatio asked with furrowed brows.

“Yeah, you know. New supes?” Sofka answered.

Horatio shook his head.

“New visitors who all of a sudden are now residents? You know, the ones who have stuck to themselves and not socialized at all. Newbs.” Sofka shrugged.

“Ah, yes. Well, they are now working all over town. Four of them are working at the clothing store. I think one is working at the coffee shop now, and another is serving at the Island Shack.” Horatio counted them off on his fingers.

Sofka nodded. “Okay, but that’s only six. What about the rest?”

Horatio chuckled. “The rest volunteered to collect trash.”

Maxim arched a brow. "That's the worst assignment, usually reserved for punishment. What did they do to deserve being volunteered for trash pickup?"

"I know, right? I wondered the same thing. Turns out, their trash hadn't been picked up in almost two weeks so when I spoke to them about jobs, they decided to do something about the trash issues." Horatio walked over to the bookshelf that held some Christmas books. Somehow, the island knew what books the supes would want to read and always stocked the shelf with the books readers came in looking for.

Before they knew it, one of the mystery supes walked in as they were talking about them. Everyone shut up and smiled at her.

A beautiful female who was close to six feet tall with long auburn hair and green sparkling eyes grinned from ear to ear. "I see you were all speaking about me." She arched a perfectly manicured brow at Horatio, who went all week-kneed and blushed.

"Ah, well." He had a Christmas book in his hand about wolf shifters up at the North Pole. He held it up. "I have the book you wanted, Aelita."

The beautiful female made a face and shook her head. "I don't want to read about Santa's pack. I asked for a book about a group of women singers in New Orleans."

Horatio looked down at the book in his hands and felt his ears heat up. "Oh, yeah. This was for someone else. Sorry. I do have that book." He reached down one shelf and grabbed New Orleans Magic. "Here you go."

Aelita slowly walked toward him with her hips swaying. She kept her eyes on Horatio, but noted who all was in the shop. She stopped when she was right inside Horatio's personal space. "Thank you. This is exactly what I wanted." She plucked the book out of his hands.

Then when she turned, she smiled coyly and waved a little. "Are you going to introduce me to your friends?"

He nodded. "Yes, of course. Aelita, this is Sofka, she's the new deputy sheriff. She and her friends arrived only a few days before you and yours." He waved toward Sofka, who smiled.

"Hi, it's nice to meet you. Aelita? That's a beautiful name. Very different." Sofka made a mental note to remember that name and look her up. All she could tell was the female was a shifter. But she wasn't sure what sort of shifter. Possibly a bear with her height. But she could be a larger wolf. There was a scent of wolf on her, but that could easily be from her housemates.

Sofka did know that some wolf shifters had moved into the house Aelita shared with nine others. But she didn't know what sort of wolf shifters they were, or what everyone else was.

Usually, shifters didn't mix well with non-shifters. The fact that Ree had mated with a fey was very strange. It's probably because he's a prince. She knew that she and KeeKee would one day mate with other wolf shifters, hopefully they would meet some nice arctic wolf shifters who didn't mind the fact that they weren't purebred. But for either of them to mate with a male who was anything but a wolfshifter, would be very odd.

So, the ten newcomers were most likely all shifters. Maybe some were wolves, and some bears, and some could even be cat shifters, like a jaguar or lion. Although, the feline forms rarely mixed with anyone else. They were what was known as elitist shifters.

But, since Sofka had arrived on this island, she had seen so many different types of supernatural creatures all getting along, and mating. The island sure did attract the strangest of them all.

Or, maybe it was just the most open to differences who showed up here?

Well, with the exception of Tony and his cronies. Those Tundra wolves weren't good at accepting others. Talk about elitist shifters, but they weren't even from a high-level species. They ranked along with the hyenas, groups that were considered very low on the pecking order.

Which was something Sofka had to rethink. Supes shouldn't be categorized just on their species. If one was going to be judged, it should be on who they were on the inside and how they treated others.

Since arriving on the island, Sofka had met some of the nicest supes from species that her Alpha would have scoffed at. Kirill would have kicked the brownies aside, literally, if they crossed his path. And she didn't even want to think about what he would have done if he met Annie, the bride of Frankenstein.

Kirill probably would have made an alliance with any of the darker creatures from the Dark Hills region. Which only made her think that it was very possible he was the one they were looking for. Sofka could see him using Tundra wolves to do his bidding, and then kicking them to the curb once they had served their purpose. They would make the perfect lackeys for someone like her alpha.

Horatio had introduced Aelita to the rest of the gang in the Information Center by the time Sofka got her mind back on the female shifter standing near her.

"Aelita, how do you like the island so far?" If Sofka was going to try and get some information from this supe, or any of her roommates, then it would be a good idea to play nice. She knew Maxim liked to flex his muscles, but she was a bit more subtle in the way she gathered intelligence.

The beauty turned her smile to Sofka. "I like it. It's quiet and no one bothers me here."

"Is it loud where you're from?" Sofka wanted to come right out and ask her where she was from, but one of the first things she learned here on the island was to be subtle and not ask directly where the supes were from. Since most were on the run, they didn't like to let anyone know where home once was.

Aelita frowned. "Sometimes it could be. Lots of screeching and yelling." She shivered but didn't say any more.

Screeching would indicate bird shifters, but Aelita was too tall for that. Most bird shifters of any sort were quite short, even the eagle shifters generally weren't taller than five feet.

"Well, I can't imagine that living with nine other supes would be quiet." Sofka chuckled. Then she remembered how her house could dampen sounds from other parts of the house and keep her in a quiet bubble. Something she did like to experience when KeeKee had the TV up too loud.

Aelita smiled. "It's actually nice living with so many different supes." She tilted her head. "Does your house put up sound walls, too?"

They spent a few minutes talking about their homes and what the island could do, and did do for them. But Sofka knew it was time to refocus and see if Aelita knew anything about the tundra wolves.

"Say, have you heard of the Bully Boys?" Sofka watched Aelita's face for any recognition of the nickname given to Tony and his crew.

Aelita's eyes narrowed, her mouth puckered, and her nostrils flared. "Yes, and I hope they leave this place, and soon."

Sofka knew there was a story there, but she didn't have time for more. The boys had been missing for two days now, and she had no idea where they were, or what they were up to, other than a general need to cause havoc. Although, there did seem to be someone looking to hurt people on this island, possibly Sofka and her little pack.

Maxim jumped into the conversation, "Have you seen them lately?"

"No, and I'm glad of it, too. You know they tried to intimidate me on my first day here?" Aelita snorted and shook her head.

For just one moment, Sofka could have sworn smoke wafted up from Aelita's neck, but that couldn't be right. She blinked a couple of times and the smoke had disappeared. "Yeah, that seems to be their M.O. They enjoy ganging up on females they think are weak and won't fight back."

Aelita's face brightened. "I know. They won't be bugging me any time soon." Then her features darkened once again. "But, they seem to have it out for one of my roommates, Carmin. She's a sweet thing and so timid. I'm glad she's working at the coffee shop, it's the perfect environment for her."

Sofka tilted her head. "How so?"

Aelita chuckled. "No one messes with the baristas. They make the coffee and other drinks that all of the supes on this island crave. If any of them are hurt, or harassed, the customers stand up for them. Carmin already has a posse who walk her home each day."

It made sense everyone would want their baristas protected. After Tony ran into the coffee shop the other day and hurt a couple of them, the residents who witnessed the attack were rather angry with the tundra wolves. And they all expressed their concern for the two who were injured.

"I'm glad she has already begun to make friends. It's really important to have a close group here on this island, as we have noticed." Sofka rolled her eyes. The Bully Boys had tried to intimidate Sofka and her two friends from the very beginning. And it was Maxim and Marcus who always came to their rescue. Which had kept Tony at bay, until recently.

"Then you know what happened with Tony and his little group? They trashed the only vehicles we have on this island when they crashed them into the coffee shop?" Maxim asked.

Sofka could tell that Maxim was getting a bit antsy and wanted to move this questioning along. He couldn't even stand in one place, he was moving back and forth from one foot to the other.

Aelita put the book she held in her backpack and then when it was securely on her back, she crossed her arms over her chest and glared at Maxim. "If I knew where those criminals were, I would have gone and picked them up by their scruff. They wouldn't still be loose, or be able to hurt anyone else."

The shifter's answer was enough to convince Sofka she wasn't involved, unless Aelita was a fantastic actress. "Thanks, we are looking everywhere for them. And asking anyone we see if they have any idea where the boys could be hiding."

Aelita nodded. "Yeah, they must be hiding somewhere. If you've been looking, and asking everyone, then they aren't out in the open. This is a small island with only one set of hills. Did you check there?"

"Yeah, no one is saying much over there." Sofka bristled at the memory of their time in the Dark Hills. Someone over there knew something, but they were the sort to not share. She was going to have to find a way to infiltrate them and get the info she needed. But, she doubted Tony and his gang would be hiding out there. No, that would have been too easy.

"I'll keep my eyes, and ears, open for anything. If I get any information I'll be sure to share it with you. The sooner those guys are caught and put back in jail, the better everyone on this island will be." Aelita said her goodbyes and left.

Sofka still wondered what sort of shifter she was. Once the female in question was far enough away, she turned to Horatio. "What type of shifter is she?"

Horatio was still looking out the door with a funny expression on his face. Which made Sofka wonder if Horatio had a thing for the pretty female with long auburn hair, and not interested in KeeKee.

Suddenly, a guilty feeling attacked Sofka's gut. She had wanted KeeKee to stay single, but for selfish reasons. If KeeKee was interested in Horatio, and he was interested in Aelita, that might hurt KeeKee. Now, Sofka wanted to slap that silly look off of Horatio's face and tell him he had to fall in love with her best friend. She never would do such a thing, but she did think about it for like two seconds.

When Horatio didn't answer, Sofka poked his arm. "Hey, Earth to Horatio. Horatio, can you hear me?"

"Huh?" The polar bear shifter shook himself and looked at Sofka. "What was that?"

Everyone in the room chuckled, including KeeKee. Which made Sofka wonder about the relationship between the two. She had seen

KeeKee checking Horatio out only the previous day. Was there something romantic between the two? Or was her friend just appreciating a handsome male?

Not that Horatio was her type, but it was obvious that he was a good-looking shifter. Horatio was tall, well-built, and always had a smile on his face. He liked to crack jokes, too. Many times Sofka had walked in on the two of them laughing over a joke Horatio had said. So, if KeeKee didn't seem upset about Horatio going all gaga-goo-goo over the new female, then what was going on? Friendship?

"Dude, what sort of shifter is she?" Sofka pointed in the direction Aelita had walked.

He shrugged. "I'm not really sure. If she had been blonde I would have thought she was a polar bear shifter." He looked out the front window again. "Maybe she's a brown bear shifter? I know she's tough, like really tough. Tony and his gang only tried to intimidate her once. They learned very quickly that she wasn't to be messed with."

Maxim laughed. "What? Did she shift and sit on them in her bear form?"

Horatio chuckled. "I wish I would have seen what she did. All I know is that when they walk near her, they always give her a wide birth."

"Now that's a story I'd like to hear." KeeKee grinned from ear to ear. She'd stayed quiet for the entire encounter with Aelita, but now she wanted to know more.

"I'm sure we'll see her later. She's one of the newbs," Horatio looked to Sofka. "I like that term. Anyway, she works at the clothing store."

"Well, now that they are all getting out and about, I say we start inviting them to dinner." KeeKee nodded once, as though she was agreeing with herself.

"Actually, that's a great idea. What do you think Maxim?" The deputy sheriff was coming to the forefront of Sofka's demeanor, and she put a hand on her waste. Almost like she was trying to rest her hand on the butt of a service gun, which she did not carry. Neither she, nor Roscoe, needed a gun to do their job. She did have a belt that held a flashlight and handcuffs, but that was really all that anyone needed in order to police this island. Usually.

"Not a bad idea. We could invite several different supes to dinner and that way we could ask questions without seeming like we're interrogating them," Maxim agreed.

"Do you think we could have a dinner party tomorrow night? Or is that too soon?" Sofka gnawed on the inside of her lip. If it were up to her, she'd gather anyone and everyone she thought might know something and have them over right then and there. However, she knew one must give time for supes to make plans. If she called everyone up now, most would probably have other plans. Even tomorrow would probably be too soon.

Maxim thought for a moment before answering, "I think you should give at least three days' notice. And in the meantime, we can go out and question others. It's not like you can invite the entire island over for dinner." He chuckled.

But Sofka furrowed her brow and tilted her head. "You know, we could do that."

"What? Even if the house expanded enough to hold everyone, there would be no way they'd all come. And I can't imagine that you could cook enough to feed everyone, either. Even if I helped."

"But, that's the beauty of a potluck." Sofka put a finger in the air. "If everyone brings a dish to share, then we could get the entire island together."

"While I love the idea, I don't think you're going to get any answers out of anyone if the entire island is all together in one place." Horatio lifted a shoulder. "Where would you find privacy to ask questions?"

"I know, once this is all over, we can do an island potluck! And in the meantime, we can have a small dinner in a few days. We can use the idea of holding an island potluck as a way to go around the entire island and speak to everyone. Be sure to mention the potluck and see if they would be interested in joining us. Then, you could put something in about Tony and his gang." KeeKee wiped her hands in the air as if to say it was easy peasy.

"Let's do it." Excitement rippled through Sofka as she figured she would have those evil tundra wolves in custody again.

Chapter 21

"Sofka, I want to be out there searching for those rotten, stinking, no good, sorry excuses for wolf shifters!" The anger in KeeKee's countenance was so strong, everyone could see a shimmer surrounding her body. If KeeKee wasn't careful, she would shift into her wolf form right there, in the middle of the information center. With all of the Halloween decorations, and everything.

Some of those decorations were breakable, too. Like the standing ghost that held a bowl full of candy. Anytime someone walked by it, it yelled out "boo!" It was cute, but also could break if a wolf broke out of a human body at the wrong time.

"KeeKee, I know you want to help. And you are helping." Sofka put an arm around her best friend and spoke in a soothing voice, hoping to keep the wolf at bay. "We need you here, helping Horatio to be the reporting point. We have a lot of supes out looking now for Tony and his little gang of mutts."

KeeKee pulled free from Sofka. "I know, but I can't stand sitting around doing nothing." She held up her hands. "Excuse me, manning the telephone so to speak. I really wish we could use cell phones here." The island did have a phone system, but it was the old-fashioned wired kind. One couldn't just send a group text to update anyone.

"Just think," Sofka tried to console her friend. "If anyone finds out information, you'll be the first to know. Then you can call me, and everyone else, then meet us wherever we need to be."

KeeKee sighed dramatically and threw her arms in the air. "Fine." She growled but kept her human form the entire time. "But, as soon as we know where they are I'm joining you. With or without Horatio. Got it?"

Sofka nodded. "Of course."

"Okay, now that we all know who's staying and who's going, I have something to show you." Horatio pulled a large sheet of paper out from under the counter and put it on top. "I found this old map of the island. Not all of the houses are shown on here, but I highly doubt the Bully Boys are hiding out inside someone's house. Especially since we are fully booked right now."

"Agreed." Maxim moved to the counter to get a better look.

Sofka stood next to the vampire and took her time taking in all of the details of the map. She pointed to a spot she hadn't noticed before. "What's that?" Her finger tapped an elevated spot on the map. It wasn't a hill or mountain, but it did look to be elevated above the majority of the land.

Horatio grinned. "That's our dump."

Sofka arched a brow. "I thought the trash was magically recycled once it was dumped there. Why does the map show an elevation?"

"That's because this is an old map, maybe one hundred years old? I'm not really sure. Back then, the trash was just dumped in large piles. Since then, we've become more green, so to speak. The island now recycles." The polar bear shifter shrugged.

"Do you think there's a chance the boys are hiding out there? They did have trash duty, so they'd know what was over there." Sofka thought about it and wondered why they would want to hide out in trash. Those boys thought they were too good for working at the dump. There would be no way they'd want to sleep there, would they?

Maxim took a moment to consider it, and then nodded. "I doubt they are there, but we've checked so many other places. Unless someone in the Black Hills is helping to hide them there, the dump really is the last place on the island where they could be."

"Alright, then let's head over there now to check it out." Sofka looked to Maxim, who nodded his agreement.

"Hold up now. I think that as the Sheriff, I should go, too." Until that point, Roscoe had been happy to stay quiet and let Sofka take the lead. But now that they had a good idea of where the boys were hiding out, he seemed interested in doing his job.

Sofka almost laughed. The old bear shifter was nothing if not predictable. The idea of Roscoe waiting until the last moment to swoop in and take the credit for arresting those guys almost ticked her off. But, he was the sheriff. It really was his job to take them down. And, since they had attacked him and locked him up in a magical cell, she could understand why he'd want to be a part of the arrest.

The more she thought about it, the more she realized that Roscoe wasn't trying to take the credit for getting those guys, he'd said nothing about taking them down. No, he wanted to make sure they didn't get away. "The more the merrier, I always say."

"Does that mean I can go, too?" KeeKee's eyes glowed with anticipation.

"Um." While it wasn't really Sofka's decision now that the sheriff was involved, she figured it wouldn't hurt. This really was the best opportunity they had for catching the Bully Boys. "As long as the Sheriff is alright with it."

Sheriff Roscoe Coldtrain shrugged. "I don't see why not."

"Great, now how are we all going to get there?" KeeKee asked.

The screen at the back of the shop rolled down and the island communicated with the group. *All of the vehicles are now fixed*. Then it rolled back up. Since the boys had used some sort of extra-powerful magic to break out of jail, the island had been pretty quiet.

As far as Sofka knew, the communication the previous day regarding the snowmobile, that had to be brand new, was the only thing the island had done, until now. "Huh, do you think the island has been so silent because it was working overtime on fixing those vehicles?"

"No, that's not it. They should have been fixed within a few hours of the destruction. The coffee shop was, but the vehicles weren't. And the island has been awfully quiet. Even that one message was brief, even for the island." Horatio narrowed his eyes and looked outside the front window.

He didn't say anything more, but Sofka wondered if she was thinking the same thing he was, that the island was somehow injured. Or maybe it was using up too much magic lately? There had to be a reason for the island's lack of response to everything going on.

"Well, we won't know what's going on if we don't get going." Roscoe waved for everyone to follow him. "Come on, let's get a move on."

For someone who typically laid about and napped at his desk so much, the sheriff sure was being active. He still had a calm demeanor, but he was displaying more energy than she'd seen out of him since she'd arrived.

All three vehicles were needed to transport them all to the island's dumpsite. Sofka and Maxim took the same snowmobile they used the previous day. KeeKee used the snowmobile that worked as a mule to transport the sled that usually hauled the trash to the site, while the Sheriff used the delivery truck that typically hauled groceries or supplies to and fro.

The ride wasn't long, but the wind whipped so harshly that Sofka's knees felt as though she'd been pelted with rocks by the time they arrived at the site. She could only imagine how Maxim must have felt, since he drove there.

All three vehicles stopped far enough away that the sound shouldn't travel to the dump site. The last thing they needed was for the Tundra Wolves to hear them coming. It was bad enough that the Bully Boys would most likely scent them before seeing them. But they couldn't help that. If they were lucky, the island's dumpsite smell would mask their scent right up until they were upon the Bully Boys. Then they wouldn't stand a chance to escape.

"Alright, listen up." Sofka waited until she had everyone's attention. We need to stay in pairs. KeeKee, you work with the Sheriff. If you find them, howl for me and I'll come running. With the four of us, they shouldn't be able to overpower us."

The sheriff chortled. "Right. Unless of course, they have more of that weird magic they used on Maxim and me the other day."

"Right." Sofka sighed. "Let's not borrow trouble if it isn't needed. We don't know if they still have that, or if that magic was used by someone else on their behalf. Keep that in mind."

"So, basically, watch your back. There might be more than four wolves here," Maxim added.

He and Sofka headed to their right while the sheriff and KeeKee headed left. It was a toss-up as to where they might be located if they were even there. Although, it would be poetic if Sofka and her team apprehended the jailbreakers in the dump. Too bad she couldn't have the island set up a jail cell right there in the middle of the piles of trash and debris.

The hairs on the back of Sofka's neck began to stand on end. She got that funny feeling when she was being watched, the sort that made her think someone was walking all over her grave. Even though she wasn't dead. Her head pivoted around as she looked to see if someone was indeed watching her every move.

She couldn't pick up any scents above those from the trash dump. One more sign something fishy was going on with the island – the trash was all still there. There had to be several weeks' worth of trash sitting in heaps upon heaps. While Sofka didn't like the idea of cleaning up a literal dump, she did know that they needed to get that trash buried, or recycled, before it began attracting whatever wildlife and bugs lived on the island.

She got the eebie jeebies just thinking about what might be crawling through those piles of trash at that very moment. As she continued to walk further and further from her best friend, her mind continued to wander.

That was until she heard a muffled cry. Sofka's head whipped around in all directions in an effort to locate the sound's author. She wanted to ask Maxim if he heard it too, but she knew they needed to keep quiet if they wanted to find out what was going on.

Maxim must have known what was going through her head because not five seconds after she thought about it, his hand pointed up toward a section of the dump they hadn't come close to yet. He tapped her shoulder and indicated his desire to move in that direction.

She led and he followed close on her heels. Both were quieter than a church mouse as they walked toward one pile in particular. The sound was growing louder and louder, and Sofka had no idea what it was. They didn't have any machinery that she knew of, in this part of the island. The trash recycling was done magically once pits were dug manually and filled – manually.

The sound was more of a muffled growl than anything else. Sofka's first thought was that KeeKee had been taken and muffled the moment they separated. But that couldn't be right. She would have heard a struggle. And even though KeeKee wasn't much of a fighter, she could still fight a little bit. She wouldn't go down easily.

Then there was the sheriff. He's a bear shifter. Those guys might be slower than molasses, but they were strong. He would have still been fighting if they'd been ambushed.

She looked at Maxim, who seemed just as confused as she was. Did something happen to the bully boys already? Did someone else find them and restrain them? If so, she'd like to shake their hand.

For a shifter, the stench was already acrid. Sofka's eyes were beginning to water and her nose itched. This garbage had to be sitting around for weeks for it to be this rank. But the problems only began a couple of weeks ago. That wasn't enough time for this level of stench.

Unless...the idea had Sofka's stomach roiling. As far as she knew, there wasn't anyone missing since she'd arrived. Could this smell be from someone from before? But that couldn't be possible, either. The sheriff was lazy, but he wouldn't ignore a missing person's report. But, with the residents of the black hills, would a report be filed if one of them was the victim?

There was only one way to know for sure, she had to round that last pile of stench and see what was waiting for her. Was it a trap? Or something worse?

Chapter 22

Sofka rounded the pile and almost gagged from the intensity of the stench. She put a hand up to cover her nose and tried to breathe out of her mouth. Something dead was most definitely close by, and it wasn't a church mouse.

"I'm so glad I don't actually need to breathe." Maxim rubbed his nose and stopped the inhalation he had begun. As a vampire, breathing wasn't necessary, it was just something he did to fit in with the living. But there were times when he shut off his lungs. Usually, it was an olfactory response, like today.

A sound caught Sofka's attention, and she turned her head to the left. She almost jumped back when she saw a live supe laying tied up to a body. She ran to the female who had tears running down her cheeks and immediately ripped the tape off her mouth.

"Get me out of here. Now." The female began sobbing and closed her eyes tightly.

Maxim ripped the rope from the bodies, but Sofka would need to try her keys to get the handcuffs off the supernatural's hands and feet.

Sofka didn't recognize the female, but introductions could wait. First, she needed to get the female away from the body. She didn't doubt that the acrid scent was coming from it. She pulled her key ring off her belt and tried the two different handcuff keys she had. The first one didn't work. "Oh, for Frosty's sake!"

Finally, after almost dropping her key ring in the pile of trash, Sofka was able to get the second key into the lock. The satisfying sound of a click and a swoosh caused her stomach to jump in excitement. "Come on, let's get away from the body." She helped the female up, but the supe couldn't stand on her own two feet.

"Here, let me carry you to a safe distance." Maxim leaned down and picked up the female who felt no heavier than a feather in Maxim's arms.

As they walked away, Sofka remembered she was to call out when she found something. She'd say she did. But, what if the boys were still there, hiding out somewhere in the debris piles? She couldn't give their location away. No, she'd have to keep quiet until they knew more.

Maxim led them back toward the vehicles. And once they were far enough away, he stopped and helped the female to sit. "What happened?"

The girl shook her head. "I'm not really sure. I think I was jumped from behind and drugged." She shook her head and coughed. "Thank you. I woke up a few minutes ago tied to a dead body."

"Do you know the supernatural?" Sofka interrupted and asked.

"No, I'd never seen him before. He's been dead for a while now. Do you know who he is?" The female turned shining eyes up to Sofka, who towered over her.

"Sofka, take a seat. The poor woman has to crane her neck to look at you." Maxim, who had sat down next to the female, scowled.

Sofka returned his scowl but sat down across from them. "I'm Sofka, the sheriff's deputy." She pointed to her chest. "That there is Maxim." She indicated the vampire.

The woman's brows lifted. Either in confusion, or surprise. "Hi, I'm Sienna. A group of us moved in a few weeks ago and I don't really know anyone here. Is it always like this?"

Sofka's chuckle held no mirth. "I don't know. Me and my two best friends moved in only a couple of weeks before you did. But, I can say that there have been issues ever since we arrived."

"So, you don't know who the man was that you were tied to?" Sofka asked, in an effort to get things back on track.

Sienna shook her head. "Sadly, no. We have all kept to ourselves since arriving as much as possible. Those Bully Boys haven't made it easy for any of us, even those who have a gift for fighting."

"I see. So you know who the Bully Boys are." Sofka didn't so much ask the question, she just restated what Sienna had said.

"No, not really. We've just had a few run-ins with them. And of course, now that we are working in town, we have all heard stories about them." Sienna winced and looked down at her hands folded in her lap.

Sofka bit her lower lip. Instead of saying something rash, she decided to take her time. This was the most intense case she'd seen up close and personal before. "I heard that some of your group were working trash duty, is that how you ended up here?"

Sienna nodded. "I was one of the volunteers." She sighed long and heavy as she looked out across the dump. "I came out here today to see what supplies we were going to need." All of a sudden, she began searching her pockets. "I had a pen and paper to take notes. Where'd they go?"

This interrogation was getting off-track, and Sofka still didn't know if Tony and his gang were somewhere onsite, or if they'd left already. Shoot, Sofka didn't even know for sure if Tony and his buddies had done this to Sienna. Or if they had even killed that male. She needed to get the Sheriff over there so they could do a proper investigation. Maybe, the supe wasn't murdered, he just died of natural causes.

She almost snorted when she realized that was about as likely as her seeing the Jingle Bell Forest up at the North Pole.

"Here it is." Sienna pulled out a piece of paper from her back pocket, then paused. Her brows furrowed and her lips parted. "But, this isn't my paper."

The blue paper in Sienna's hand was folded in quarters, like a note.

"Is there something written on it?" Maxim leaned in close to Sienna and noted some writing inside the folded paper.

With a shrug, Sienna unfolded the paper. As she read it, her eyes widened. "This wasn't in my pocket before." She handed it to Sofka.

Maxim must have read it and not liked what it said as his fangs descended, not for the first time that day, and his eyes flashed red.

Sofka took the paper and began reading it out loud. "Tell Sofka Federov that unless she and her two friends leave the island, there will be more dead bodies." Her nostrils flared and her vision blurred. Sofka held her wolf at bay, but she knew her wolf was madder than a hornet's nest.

This was supposed to be their safe place, not the place where their lives were threatened, and bullies attacked them on a regular basis. It took every bit of willpower to keep from shifting and destroying the note. Sofka closed her eyes and took in several deep breaths reminding herself that just about everyone else on the island was on her side. They all wanted to rid themselves of the Bully Boys. It was those no-good, rotten excuses for supes that needed to watch themselves, not Sofka and her friends.

"Alright, I think we need to find KeeKee and the sheriff. I doubt the criminals are still here." Sofka stood and refolded the paper before putting it in her coat pocket.

"What makes you say that?" Sienna asked.

"Because, if they were still around, they wouldn't have used you the way they did to deliver their message. They would have told me directly, or tried to kill me." Sofka shrugged and decided that the boys were cowards, they weren't going to actually go after her.

"So, then who is the dead body?" Maxim stood up and dusted the dirty snow from his pants.

Sienna stood as well. Then she followed Sofka when she headed in the direction of KeeKee.

Sofka put a hand around her mouth creating a makeshift bullhorn. "KeeKee? Sheriff?" She called out loudly. Without worrying if anyone else was around, she gave the body a wide berth, but continued to search for her friends.

"Over here!" KeeKee yelled.

Once the Sheriff and KeeKee were brought up to speed regarding Sienna and the unidentified body, the Sheriff headed toward the male supe in question.

"I'm going to get a look and see if I recognize him, but we need a stretcher so we can bring him back to town and investigate properly." The sheriff's grim face stopped on Sienna. "You're sure you don't know who he is? You've never seen him before?"

With a hard shake, Sienna said no. "I would have remembered him if I had. What do you think happened to him?"

"I won't know until we do a proper investigation and autopsy. You stay here, I'll be right back." The sheriff left them all standing where they were and headed to the pile of debris where Sienna had been discovered.

Chapter 23

No one had seen the male before. At least, no one Sofka and the Sheriff had spoken to so far. They'd worked late into the night going around the island asking everyone they could find about the guy. Even after two days of canvassing, they couldn't find any information about the dead supe.

"I really wish electronics worked here. Then I could have taken a picture of the male and shared it with a select group of supes here on the island and we'd know within an hour if anyone here had seen him." Sofka was sitting in her chair back at the sheriff's station.

She'd not gotten to sleep until close to one in the morning. She didn't sleep much so she got up early and headed into the station. Sofka hoped the Sheriff would know more by now.

"If I had a nickel every time someone wished for electronics..." The sheriff chuckled. "I doubt anyone here knows him. Horatio said he'd never seen the fellow, and I haven't either. So that means this supe never arrived with permission."

Sofka tapped her pen against her chin as she thought about all they'd learned over the past week. "Okay, so if this guy didn't come by Bart's boat, then he had to have come by another means via the water, right?"

The sheriff nodded.

"Have any of the merfolk looked at the dead guy? If he'd not come by boat, then he would have had to swim in. And that means he had to be a merman, or something along those lines, right?" Sofka still didn't know about all of the forms of merfolk, so it was just easier for her to reference them as mermen and mermaids.

Roscoe was leaning back in his chair with his boots up on his desk, as usual. "I suppose so, but he may not be a merman. He could just be a great swimmer, or possibly a selkie."

"Either way, we need to check with Luana, or someone else." Sofka stood and began to put on her outside gear.

"Where are you going? You just arrived." The sheriff's feet thudded against the ground, and he put his coffee mug back on his desk.

She stopped wrapping the scarf around her neck and glared at her boss. "Someone has to check with the merfolk, it might as well be me." Ignoring him, Sofka finished wrapping her scarf around her neck. She enjoyed the softness of the pink cashmere scarf KeeKee had bought her just the other day. It had become her new favorite accessory.

"Hold up now, you know better than to go off by yourself." The sheriff started grumbling to himself as he dressed for the cold weather outside.

Ever since the note, she and her two friends were not allowed to even step outside alone. Ree would have her new mate, Marcus, as her shadow. But KeeKee and Sofka had to rely on a short list of escorts should they want to go anywhere. Today, it was the sheriff who had to stick with Sofka. Horatio was guarding KeeKee.

It was Sofka's turn to grumble under her breath. She hated that she couldn't even go get a coffee without someone tailing her. Some sheriff's deputy she was. The fact that she needed a babysitter really grated on her nerves. "If I find Tony, or any of his little minions, I swear, I'll..." She didn't finish the sentence out loud, but she knew exactly what she would do. And it wouldn't be pretty when she was done with them.

"Now, now, Sofka. You know as well as I do that you can't hurt them, unless you are defending yourself, or others." The sheriff admonished.

This was exactly why she needed to be able to roam the island alone. Should she come upon them, she would first teach them a lesson, then she'd find that supernatural cryo-jail and put all four of them on ice for a very long time. It would be at least two centuries before they even had a chance at seeing the defrost cycle.

Okay, okay, so maybe she wouldn't hurt them. But she sure wouldn't be bothered if they came after her and she just defended herself. No one could get upset with self-defense, right?

Guilt crept in and Sofka knew that even though she'd never intentionally harm another, she shouldn't even daydream about it. Somewhere she'd heard that what you put into your mind will eventually make its way to your heart, and then through your actions it will be out in the world, never to be taken back again. She kicked at a small mound of snow on the ground.

Roscoe grumbled, "I know how you feel. I don't like this either."

A chuckle escaped Sofka. She knew her boss wasn't thinking about the same thing she was. He was probably wishing he was back in the warm office with his feet up on the desk snoring away, as he did most days. "Okay, so we need to find Luana. Is there a place on the island that is best to reach her?"

He nodded and directed them both to the harbor where Bart kept his boat. "So, you think this is all about your old alpha wanting you back?"

She shrugged. "I can't think of anyone else who would want to hurt us, or get us off this island."

"Can't you?" Roscoe stopped at the little wharf and looked inside the tiny shack of an office that Bart used when not on the water.

The only other thing that might be possible was a female who wanted Maxim for herself. But that would be pretty farfetched. Wouldn't it? She gnawed on the idea that a female was behind all of this just so she could get her claws, or fangs, on Maxim. "Would a female supe go to all this trouble to keep me from Maxim? Or Maxim away from me?"

Roscoe held up his large, thick hands. "Hey now, I'm not saying it's a chick fight thing. Although..." He grinned.

"Pft." Sofka rolled her eyes heavenward. "Males. They're all the same, no matter their race."

"Hey now, I resemble that remark," Bart said when he walked out of his little shack. Then he spit on the ground next to the Sheriff's boots.

"Bart, how many times do I have to tell you to change your aim? No one wants your gross spit on their shoes." A small growl emanated from the bear shifter's throat.

"Well, then stay away from me and you won't have to worry about polishing your boots." Bart's laugh was more of a guffaw than a chuckle.

Sofka knew that he could aim better than he usually did. She suspected he intentionally got as close to everyone's feet as he possibly could just for kicks and giggles.

"What can I do for you today? Need a ride to the mainland?" Bart turned his gaze to Sofka and waited for her response.

"Well, I think we need to speak with Luana and see if the merfolk have seen anything recently that might point us toward an intruder." Sofka reasoned with herself that the dead guy had to be an intruder since no one knew who he was. But, if he was there on the island before her, then why was she the target? None of this made any sense.

"We've already spoken with the merfolk, and they said they didn't see anyone lately." Bart's mouth formed as though he was about to spit right on Sofka's feet, but his head moved at the last moment when he noticed her arched brow. He spit his water directly between her and the sheriff.

Roscoe grumbled, but Sofka laughed.

"Good choice. Now, can you help us find Luana? I know the merfolk were already questioned about someone recently showing up, but what about a few weeks back? Maybe even before I arrived?" It was possible her alpha sent someone to Misfit Island to keep an eye out for the three of them. And if that supe had arrived before her, it's also possible he had outlived his usefulness to Kirill and was killed.

The one thing Sofka knew for sure was that she couldn't underestimate her alpha. He was ruthless and cunning. The fact that their pack hadn't caught Santa's attention yet was testimony to Kirill's shrewdness.

Anyone who defied Santa and sold his own pack members to the supernatural traffickers, and did not get caught, had to have a few tricks up his sleeve. She needed to keep that thought in mind. And always look over her shoulder. Would she have to do that for the rest of her long life? Or could they catch him and get him on ice? Or jail? She wasn't really sure who would take control of punishing Kirill for his crimes.

Santa generally policed the Arctic wolf shifters. But the island also stepped in from time to time, especially when the criminals went after the island residents.

"Hmm, you think someone came here before you?" Bart asked.

"Yes." Sofka's eyes widened as she noticed the concern on Bart's face. "Do you remember someone coming here before us? Maybe someone you haven't seen for a while?"

Bart stomped a concrete foot on the ground. "Yes. And I'm sorry I didn't think of him sooner. About a month before you arrived, a wolf shifter came to the island all by himself."

The Sheriff and Sofka both looked at each other before they both bombarded Bart with questions.

"Hey now, one at a time. I only got one mouth." Bart chuckled. "Could you imagine if I was one of those scary gargoyles who had two mouths? That would be fun."

Sofka shivered at the idea that Bart could have been created with two mouths. One was more than enough. All that spit? "Ah, no. Sorry, do you have the name of the supe who came before us?"

"Hmm, let me think. If I'm not mistaken, he gave me a fake name."

"How do you know it was fake?" Sofka's head tilted to the right and her eyes furrowed.

"Gargoyles can always tell when someone is lying. And besides, the name he gave me was John Smithington." Bart spit to the side, not even getting close to either of his guests.

Sofka's brows rose past her hairline and her mouth formed an "O". "Smithington? Are you sure?" She stepped back a few paces until her backside touched the railing. Then she grabbed on and held tight as her head swam.

"Sofka, what's going on? You said you'd never seen the dead supe before. But you know his name?" Roscoe stepped close to her and held her arm.

Words wouldn't form, so she only nodded as tears ran down her cheeks.

"Well, concrete whiskey! What's going on? You know this dead supe after all?" Even though Bart had seen the dead body, it had been dead for quite a while. It probably didn't look much like he had when he first came to the island. And if it was about a month before Sofka arrived, then that was about three months ago. The gargoyle had already forgotten about the man who arrived all alone on the island, so it made sense he wouldn't have recognized him now that he was dead.

Both Roscoe and Bart looked to Sofka for an explanation.

"Sofka, what's going on?" Roscoe's voice was soft, as though he understood what Sofka was going through and didn't want to push.

She really didn't want to talk about it. Shoot, she didn't even want to think about it. Up until that moment, she was pretty sure that Kirill was behind all of this, but not convinced yet. However, with the fake name the male used when getting on the island, Sofka knew without a shadow of a doubt it was Kirill, and his cronies.

The Bully Boys were nothing compared to Kirill. She'd never seen her alpha use the sort of magic that was used on the jail to break out the tundra wolves, but with his connections, it was very possible he had arranged it. With that one name, everything became real for Sofka. It was no longer a possibility, but the truth.

Kirill had been looking for them this whole time. And now he'd found them. Found her. A part of Sofka always hoped that after a few weeks, her alpha would have forgotten about them. Now, she knew he would go to the ends of the Earth looking for them, literally. There was nowhere safe on Earth to hide.

"Are aliens real?" Sofka chuckled. Her mind must have started to crack.

"What? What do aliens have to do with a dead supe using a fake name?" Bart asked.

When Bart first said that name, Sofka's eyes glazed over, and everything blurred. Now, her eyesight began to clear and she could make out the worried faces looking at her. "Sorry, there's nowhere safe on Earth for us to hide. I was kinda hoping we could call some aliens to take KeeKee, Ree, and me away somewhere far, far, far away. A place that Kirill couldn't reach."

Roscoe rubbed the stubble on his chin. "Get your head out of the sky, girl. That dead body wasn't your alpha, so who was he, really?"

"I don't know. But Kirill uses the surname of Smithington when trying to hide his movements from Santa. And so do his henchmen. It's a joke to them all. And John Smithington is one of his favorite names. I'd bet Kirill's henchman used it to send a message to me."

"Is that why he's dead? He didn't find you sooner, so Kirill had to kill him in order to send his message?" Roscoe asked.

Sofka shook her head. "I don't really know why he killed the guy. Or if it was even an order from Kirill. John could have crossed paths with one of the dark supes and lost." She shrugged.

"Or, he was supposed to have done something by now and Kirill did away with him since he hadn't done his job yet," Bart added.

Sofka's nostrils flared. "Could be. Could be so many other reasons, too. But I think we can safely say that Kirill is pulling the strings here."

"I have to concur. The question now is, how do we take care of this?" Roscoe scratched at his chin. He looked out across the water at the far edges of the magical dome that kept them protected from the human realm. "You know, we have all this magic to keep the humans away from us, and yet it does no good when a dangerous supe can get behind the magical walls and hurt us. All without being detected."

Sofka's head fell forward and she let loose a long breath. "I know. Kirill won't give up until he has all three of us."

Roscoe pursed his lips as though he'd just tasted something sour. "I doubt he'd insist on taking the new bride of the Unseelie Prince away from him. Marcus is too powerful to mess with."

"Right, and if anyone did, his family would be here in a heartbeat killing anyone and everyone in their path until they found the killer. Then, they'd probably kill Marcus themselves. But hey no one messes with a prince of Fairie, except for the queen herself." Bart looked toward his booth. "I'm going to go and double check my passenger manifest for the last few months and see if I can find anything else out about this John fellow."

“Good idea.” Sofka worried at her bottom lip. “Should we still reach out to Luana? You know, just to be safe?”

Roscoe shook his head. “No, I don’t think we need to. We know who that supe was now.”

“Right. So now what?” Sofka asked.

“Now, we follow the clues and find out where they lead us.” Roscoe turned and headed back toward the other edge of town where his best thinking spot resided.

"Best thinking spot?" Sofka chided when she found Roscoe in his desk chair with his feet on top of the desk and his eyes closed.

The sheriff grumbled.

"Whatcha thinking about?" She took her seat at her desk and waited for the big lug to wake up. She had just spent the past hour getting Horatio up to speed on what they discovered. And she found both of her besties. They had to know that Kirill was after them all.

Marcus swore he'd destroy anyone who got close to his mate. Not surprising, but sweet nonetheless. He also promised to protect KeeKee and Sofka. They were all family now, after all.

On her way back to the Sheriff's office, she was going to head over to Maxim's place, but he needed his sleep. She knew he hadn't been sleeping lately since he was up all day helping her when he normally slept. At night, he was up doing rounds. She wasn't really sure what that meant, but she did know that he was charged with watching the docks. And with everything going on lately, Sofka knew that was a very important job.

No, today she'd leave him be.

Only, he must not have gotten the memo. Before Sofka had even had time to drink half of her coffee, in walked tall, dark, and handsome. No, wait. She changed her mind. It was tall, dark, and dangerous. Not handsome. She had to stop thinking of him that way. It didn't matter what her heart wanted, she wasn't good for him. Plus, she was most likely going to have to leave the island soon in order to keep everyone there safe.

Kirill wouldn't stop until he had what he wanted. And he'd hurt, or kill, anyone who got in his way.

Over the past couple of weeks she'd come to think of Maxim as more than a vampire. He wasn't the dangerous bloodsucker she originally thought him to be. Now that she'd seen him in action and spent so much time with him, she was coming to like him. And trust him.

Last night she'd even dreamt about them mating. But that couldn't happen. It would gut her if anything happened to him just because she ran from her alpha.

She wasn't blind, she knew he was into her, but anyone around her was in danger. She couldn't act on her new feelings. It was up to her to protect those around her. And she would do just that, even if it meant she would have to leave the island.

Maxim smiled a slow, sexy smile when his eyes fell upon hers. "Hey, gorgeous. How are you today?"

A giggle escaped and she tilted her head down when she stood up and glanced up at him through her eyelashes.

Sofka was such a girl sometimes.

A loud thud sounded on the other side of the room before Sofka could say anything. She turned and noticed the Sheriff's feet had hit the ground and he was sticking his tongue out like he had tasted something bad.

"I don't need to hear this lovey-dovey stuff. If you can't keep it to yourselves, then take a hike." Roscoe continued to grumble to himself as he went to the coffee maker and poured himself a new cup of java.

"Right." Maxim cleared his throat, but he continued to smile at Sofka. "Last night was interesting out on the docks. I thought I should come in and tell you both all about it."

All thoughts of romance and dating fled from Sofka's mind. She straightened up and motioned for Maxim to take a seat. "Can I get you a cup of coffee?"

"No, thanks. I'm fine." Maxim took a seat near Sofka.

"Alright, tell us what's going on." Roscoe turned around from the coffee desk and took a long sip of his hot coffee.

"Something's going on. I saw the magical field around the island flickering out on the water last night. It's almost as if someone is trying to lower the barrier." Maxim ran a hand through his hair and sighed.

Sofka looked closely at his face and noticed that Maxim looked very tired. All energy fled her body and she plunked down on her chair. When the air in her lungs expelled itself, she felt as though she had already lost.

Maxim took her hand in his. "Sofka, you're safe. I won't let anything happen to you or your pack. You know Marcus will give his life for Ree. And Horatio might be a fun-loving polar bear, but he's also very ferocious. KeeKee is safe with him."

"Can any of you defend yourselves against the type of magic that could take the barrier down?" The look in Sofka's eyes hit Maxim hard.

"Sweetheart, please. Don't let this get you down. Now that we know what's going on we can defend against it. The island is going to fight anyone who attacks it directly like this. The barrier held overnight, it didn't come down. And it's still up now." Maxim lifted her hand to his lips and kissed the back of it, not caring that the Sheriff was watching them. Sofka needed his comfort and he was going to give it to her.

She sighed and leaned closer to him. "How do we fight this? None of us have magic in this way. We all are magical beings, but we aren't witches or warlocks. How do we fight them?" Sofka was glad that none of her inner circle were witches. Those creatures usually were so dark, they no longer even had a conscience. Or a sense of right and wrong.

Although, she shouldn't judge a whole species of supernatural creatures by the evil acts of a few. Although, as a species the witches were different. There weren't any covens that helped those less fortunate than others. Usually, it was the witches that caused others to be less fortunate. If they wanted something, they generally just took it. Sonya and the other witches who ended up accidentally bringing gargoyles to life were perfect examples of why witches were all considered evil. Not that what they did was normal.

But then Sofka remembered the dark creatures she'd met recently. Walter, a centaur, was a nice male. Even Sigurd had proved to turn his back on his evil nature. He'd come to the island to escape the need to kill innocent women and children. If Sigurd could change, then maybe there was hope for the darker supes.

While vampires did tend to be on the bad side, a lot of them turned things around once they got past their thirst for blood. Sofka knew there was a thriving market for volunteers to willingly give their blood to vamps. The key word in that market was "willingly". There was a whole system in place to make sure the humans who donated their blood were taken care of and not injured, or worse when donating.

And the opposite was true, too. Arctic wolves could be very good, like Santa and his pack. But they could also be the total opposite of Santa, like Kirill and most of his pack. However, not all of Sofka's former pack mates were evil.

But even knowing that the various races operated in a gray area, she still couldn't bring herself to find a way to use magic to defend themselves. Everything she'd ever heard was that once a supe started to delve into the magical arts, they tended to let more and more evil seep into their souls – their very essence. Using spells tended to turn people and supernatural creatures from light to dark. They'd have to find some way other than magic to defend against Kirill and his attacks.

"I think we should leave the island." Sofka blurted out, not realizing that she'd interrupted plans that Roscoe and Maxim were working on at that very moment.

Two sets of wide eyes quickly turned her way.

"What?" Maxim practically growled his displeasure at her announcement.

"No, I don't think that's a good idea." Roscoe shook his head.

"Wait, just think about it. Kirill is after the three of us. He's already proven he has a way to kill here on the island." As Sofka stopped to take a breath, Maxim interrupted.

"I don't think the Bully Boys killed that supe, John. Or whatever his name was."

"Why do you think that?" Sofka realized she had left her hand in his, but she didn't want to let go. His hand was warm and comforting. Strange considering Maxim's a vampire, but she realized it didn't bother her anymore. Now, she wasn't about to offer up her neck to him, or even watch him feed on anything. But, her only reason to keep him at arm's length was the danger she brought to him and the island as a whole.

"They have only been a real danger in the last couple of weeks. That body is older. My guess is that Kirill contacted them after he killed, or had someone else kill, John." While she wasn't sure who killed John, she did know it was ordered by Kirill, it had to be.

"But, what if he saw something in the Dark Hills he shouldn't have? And that's what got him killed?" Roscoe just had to throw a wrench at her ideas.

"Who says he was in the Dark Hills?" Maxim asked.

That stopped Sofka. She had just assumed since no one knew the dead guy, that he had to have been staying in the Dark Hills. But did he? Could he have been elsewhere? "How do we find out where he was staying?"

"We'd have to have a great sketch artist draw his face, or ask some of the residents from the Dark Hills to come here. I doubt either will happen." Roscoe took a long drink of his coffee. "But, since no one in town has reported anyone missing, we can assume he wasn't staying here, or even close by."

Sofka looked to the back wall, where the Island usually communicated with them. "Island, why aren't you saying anything about this guy? Do you know who he is? Where he was staying? Who killed him?"

Nothing came down from the ceiling. There was no indication whatsoever that the wall was going to communicate with her.

"Ugh! Why do I even try." Sofka shook her head and looked back at Roscoe. "Seriously, why won't the island tell us what's going on here?"

Roscoe being the laid-back bear shifter he was, only shrugged. "The island will communicate when it wants to."

"So frustrating." With a sigh, Sofka gave up trying to get anything from the island. "Alright, we can assume he wasn't staying in town. Which means he was most likely in the Dark Hills. But why? Did he have a contact there? Or was it just the best place for him to hide out until he needed to come after us?"

Maxim shook his head. "I think we first need to discover when he died. Was it before you arrived? Or after?"

"That's going to be tough to determine, isn't it? I mean, the body was found in a dump. It's not like we have a CSI team here who can check the stages of bug larva on this guy. Or his body temperature. Or decomp, never mind. I don't even want to think about that one." Sofka shivered at that thought.

Maxim chuckled and scooted his chair closer to hers. "I think the more important thing here is to find the Bully Boys and see what they know. Someone, most likely your old Alpha, is after you. He must have a plan that involved Tony and his little gang. First thing is to stop them and see what they know. Then, we can find a way to stop Kirill."

"Right, but where do we start?" This was all so new to Sofka. She'd never had any real responsibility when she was back home in the Russian Arctic Circle. She was the leader of her little pack of three, but that really didn't give her much experience with anything other than looking out for Ree and KeeKee.

When she arrived on the island and was given the job of deputy sheriff, she thought it would be fun. Never did she imagine that she'd have a murder to solve, or jailbreakers to search for. Nothing like a trial by fire, she thought.

"I'll head over to the Dark Hills and ask around. They might be willing to talk to me since I've been here so long." Roscoe put his outerwear on and headed out.

"Okay, what about us? What should we do?" Sofka wanted so badly to know what exactly needed to be done, and how to do it. But she'd only been on the job a few weeks. She didn't even have any training. At least humans got a couple of months of training before they were put into the field.

"There is one supernatural we haven't spoken with yet." Maxim arched a brow and waited for Sofka.

It took her a moment, but when she realized who he was talking about, she shook her head. "No, please tell me you aren't thinking that we should seek out the witch."

"Her name is Sherrie. She's not so bad."

Sofka shook her head again. "You know that witches and shifters don't mix. At all. And one who was a part of the coven that tried to steal magic from gargoyles, can't be safe to talk to."

"But, the island will protect us." Maxim had lived on the island long enough to believe in the island's protection.

"No, it won't. There's already one dead shifter. Maybe she killed him for his innate magic. Vampires might not have the same type of magic that shifters do, but I'd say there's enough in you to attract a witch who's out for stolen magic." Visiting a witch was the worst thing Sofka could imagine them doing. "And who's to say she'd even tell us what we want to know? Even if she has nothing to do with this, why would she help?"

"First off, the dead shifter probably deserved what he got. Second, the island has protected you so far, I think it will continue to do so. I..." Maxim sighed. He knew something he'd kept to himself since they arrived. He wasn't supposed to share this information, but maybe it was time Sofka knew. He'd have to discuss it with Horatio first.

"What?" Sofka asked. She could sense he was holding back something and wanted to know why he was holding back.

"Let's head over to see Horatio and see what he has to say. I haven't told him about last night yet anyway, and I really need to." Maxim let go of Sofka's hand to put his coat back on.

When Maxim let her hand go, Sofka felt the warmth and protection she'd enjoyed for the past thirty minutes flee. All she felt now was cold and uncertain. It was silly, really. She knew that Maxim needed his hand back if he was going to prepare to go outside. Shoot, she did too. But that didn't mean she wanted him to let go.

She put her jacket on and turned around and Maxim was right there, in her personal space. He looked directly into her eyes and she felt her stomach somersault all over the place. One second, she was cold and uncertain, and the next she felt a warmth from him that sent her pulse into overdrive. He had to hear her heartbeat picking up. For a vampire it must have sounded like drums at a rock concert.

"Hi." Her words were barely a whisper, but it was all she could get out.

When she licked her dry lips, she noticed his gaze dart down. She saw the look of desire that filled his eyes the instant he looked at her mouth. His pupils dilated and he gulped.

His whispered greeting wasn't any louder than hers.

Slowly, ever so slowly it almost ached, his head began to move closer to hers. Her breathing picked up and she felt her chest heaving with the effort to get enough air. She was no longer cold. In fact, it was just the opposite. Sofka wished she hadn't put her parka on yet. While she wasn't sweating, she knew if this went any further, she would be.

Maxim moved his hand up her arm and cupped her cheek. He rubbed her cheekbone with his thumb.

It felt so good. Sofka licked her lips again. Her mouth was so dry, she couldn't believe it. Her eyes fluttered closed without her permission. Her body was beginning to take over and instincts kicked in. Even though she hadn't kissed anyone since she was a teenager, her body knew exactly what to do. She tilted her head to the side to make it easier for his lips to take hers.

For just a fleeting moment, she felt the softest touch on her lips. But when she moved to get closer to him, he was no longer there. Sofka's eyes opened and she noticed he was across the room from her. "What?"

"I'm sorry, Sofka. I shouldn't have done that." Maxim put a hand over his mouth.

"You're sorry?" Ice shot through her veins. He didn't want her after all? It didn't make any sense. The vampire had been practically throwing himself at her since he arrived. When she was finally ready to give in and kiss him, he didn't want it?

"We should wait until this is all sorted. You can't..." He turned and rubbed his face. "Oh, what am I doing?" Again, he turned around and looked directly at Sofka. One second, he was across the room, the next he was holding her in his arms.

"Tell me this is what you want. If you don't, let me know now." Maxim's whispered words went straight to Sofka's heart.

"Yes." She nodded when no other words formed on her tongue.

Then his lips were on hers and her entire world came crashing down around her. One moment she was uncertain about her future, the next all she could think about was the vampire holding her tightly against him.

His lips were warm and demanding. When she allowed him to deepen the kiss, her world began to reform, and she felt a warmth envelop them both.

"Whoa, what are you doing?" A deep voice yelled into her ear and yanked her away from the only thing she wanted – Maxim.

"What?" Sofka shook her head to clear the haze that had overtaken her.

"Marcus, if you know what's good for you, you'll leave. Now." Maxim growled and fisted his hands at his side once he got between the fae prince and his new mate. For that was exactly what Sofka was, his. And only his. They were destined to be together forever. He knew that the moment they met.

Marcus didn't back down. "Sofka, did you want him pawing you like that?" He snarled his disgust when he looked at Maxim.

"Marcus, um. I don't know what you think you saw, but we were only kissing. And yes, I did agree." Sofka's face instantly heated. It wasn't as though Marcus was her real brother, but since he'd mated with her packmate, and best friend, he was sort of family. She didn't exactly owe him an explanation, but a part of her didn't want him upset. She also didn't want Maxim upset.

"What did you need?" Maxim cleared his throat before he grinned at Sofka's declaration.

Sofka moved out from behind Maxim and stood next to the vampire she had just been kissing, an activity she thoroughly enjoyed. While it had been a long time since she kissed anyone, she remembered enough to know that was no ordinary kiss. Never had anyone kissed her like Maxim just did. Marcus interrupted way too soon.

"I came to see what was happening with the case. I heard from Horatio that the dead guy was most likely hiding out in the Dark Hills. How can I help?" Marcus crossed his arms over his chest and seemed to ignore the kissing scene he had interrupted.

"Where's Ree?" Sofka didn't think that Marcus would leave her alone, but she also didn't think he'd leave Ree's side until this was all sorted and they were no longer in danger.

The Unseelie Prince sighed. "She's at the information center with KeeKee and Horatio. I figured you needed my help. We have to find who's behind this and stop them. And, get rid of those Bully Boys once and for all. I'm tired of them and their antics."

"They have gotten out of control, but until we find them I don't know if we'll know exactly what's going on." Sofka pointed her finger at Marcus. "That means no killing those cretans. We have to interrogate them."

Marcus raised his hands as if in surrender. "I know, I know. Horatio and Ree already read me the riot act. I won't do anything to permanently harm them until they are no longer of any use to us."

The smirk on the prince's face really got to Sofka. She knew that he would stick by his word, but the second they no longer needed Tony and those guys, they'd be toast. The one thing Sofka knew for sure about the fae was that they were not to be crossed. The fae were ruthless creatures, all of them. And fae royalty would smile and tell you they were your friend all the while shoving a dagger in your heart. She still couldn't believe her best friend had mated with one.

"I think you'll have to get in line once that happens." Maxim's eyes were red when he glanced at Sofka.

She wondered if the vampire was thinking he'd be the first in line to harm those tundra wolf shifters. Sofka also wondered if she would be the first to try and deal with them. They had done nothing but bully and harass her and her two best friends since they arrived. And now, they'd upped their game. "Were they responsible for killing that supe in the dump? Or do you think they just found him and used the body to send their message? They didn't kill Sienna, or really hurt her. Not much at least."

"They did kidnap her and tie her up to a dead body after drugging her. It's deplorable and disgusting. A sign of a true psycho, but you might be on to something here. If they'd gone totally off the rails and become murderers, why not kill Sienna and just post their message on her jacket, or something like that?" Maxim's posture relaxed and he rubbed his chin. It was obvious he was thinking about the setting and the message.

"You two can sit around discussing did they or didn't they all you want, but I have to get out there and do something. My mate's life is on the line here." Marcus turned to look at Sofka. "And so is yours. I would think you'd be more interested in finding the culprits than making out with a vampire."

Heat surged up Sofka's neck and into her face. She knew she was blushing, hardcore. Marcus was right, she shouldn't be kissing anyone at this point in time. There was too much to do and not nearly enough time to find Kirill and stop him.

Instead of letting him get to her, Sofka shook off the embarrassment and stared at Marcus. "What do you suggest we do? We've been all over this island looking for the boys, and their puppet master. We've not found anything, but Sienna and the dead guy."

"Who's actually searched the Dark Hills? I know you and vampire-boy here," Marcus nodded in Maxim's direction, "went there, but did you actually search the caves?"

Sofka bit her lip. They hadn't. But, they were only looking for Tony and his gang at that time. "The Sheriff just went out there to search the caves. I offered to join him, but he said he should do it alone."

Marcus mumbled something incoherent under his breath. "That bear shifter can be so stupid sometimes. I know he can take care of himself, but sometimes it's best to head out there with backup."

"Fine, I'll go now, then." Sofka zipped her parka all the way up and put her hat on, ready to head into the cold weather.

"No, don't." Marcus put up a hand to stop her. "I'll go. Most of those residents know me. It would be better for me to go, not you. Besides," he sighed, "I think it might be too dangerous for you at this point in time."

Sofka put her hands on her hips and leaned forward and glared at Marcus. "What does that mean? You don't think I can handle myself?"

"No, not at all." Marcus chuckled and shook his head. "I know you can handle yourself quite well. I just mean that if anyone on the island is helping Kirill, they would be out there at the caves. And that's the last place you want to be. No one there will help you. In fact, most would either help Kirill for the bounty, whatever it might be, or walk away."

"Sofka, he's right. I hate to admit it, but it really isn't safe for you there." Maxim put a hand on Sofka's shoulder. He didn't want to lose her, not now that she was beginning to warm up to him. He wanted to see where this led, but he also knew that they had to solve the case first. Blast that Marcus and his interruption!

"Fine, but I'm not going to sit around here." Sofka continued to dress for the cold weather. "I'm heading over to the coffee shop. I could really use a PSL."

Maxim agreed and they left together as Marcus headed out to join the Sheriff.

As the two walked toward the center of the village, an idea struck Sofka. "Hey, if it was a killmoulis who sprung the boys from jail, whatever happened to it? Can they be tracked?"

"We did sort of forget about that little creature, didn't we? He isn't really dangerous, he could have easily killed us but he didn't. All he did was use his magic to release Tony and the gang. Then of course, he locked us up good and tight. But he didn't harm anyone, not really." Maxim pondered the question. He wasn't too familiar with those creatures, but Marcus probably was. "We'll have to ask Marcus about it. He's probably the only one on this island who knows much, and will share with us, about the killmoulis creatures."

"But, if it's a Seelie court creature, why would it be helping Kirill?" That was the one thing that kept bugging Sofka. "A fae creature that was loyal to a court, wouldn't serve a wolf shifter, would it?"

"That's a good question. I wouldn't have thought so, but it's possible Kirill bought him on the supernatural black market." Maxim looked out of the corner of his eye when he said the next thing, "he was planning on selling you to that sort of trader, wasn't he?"

Sofka sighed, knowing that Maxim was right. "Yeah, but it's still so wrong. I feel for the little creature if he was forced to bond with Kirill. That's just not right. I can't stand the thought of any type of slavery."

"Agreed. Which is why we are going to stop Kirill." Maxim took Sofka's gloved hand in his.

Once they were inside the coffee shop, Sofka began to relax just a bit. The place was hopping. "It sure is nice to see a lot of supes out right now. Even with all the danger, they are still living their lives."

"Hey, Maxim and Sofka. Nice to see you again. Take a seat and I'll be by to get your order." Micky nodded and carried a tray full of various hot drinks to a table in the corner. It was full of supes that Sofka didn't recognize.

"Maxim, do you think that group are the newbs? I've met Aelita, but I don't recognize the rest at the table." Sofka nodded to the rowdy table of five supes.

Maxim looked to where Sofka indicated. "Some are newbs, some aren't. Interesting. It seems they are starting to integrate with the residents."

"Guess that means they plan to stay a while." Sofka nodded and thought it was a good thing. "Let's go sit by them and see if we can get to know them."

Micky stopped at their table once they were seated. "What can I get for ya?"

"I'll take the largest PSL you have. And a coffee cake, warm. Please." Sofka smiled her thanks.

"You know what I like." Maxim had ordered the same exact thing every time she'd seen him at the coffee shop. So, it didn't surprise Sofka that he wanted his regular coffee.

Most people would ask for a coffee with cream or just plain black. But a vampire ordered a black coffee with blood. No sugar needed. Last week, just the thought of a bloody coffee, or bloody Marie as the locals called it, made Sofka gag. Today, though, it didn't seem to bother her. Did that mean she was beginning to accept who he truly was?

While she wanted to take the time to ponder her feelings for Maxim, she knew Marcus had a point earlier, now wasn't the time to think about starting something with Maxim. She needed her total focus to be on the case. Which meant that she should try to meet the supes sitting next to her in order to determine if they may have seen anything before she arrived on the island, or even since her move to Misfit Island.

"Well, no time like the present." Sofka stood up and walked the two paces to the next table. "Hi, I don't think I've met most of you yet. I'm Sofka." She waved and smiled as she waited for them to speak.

Aelita crossed her arms over her chest and glared at Sofka. "What's the fuzz want with us?"

"Aelita, chill. She just wants to be neighborly." The male with light brown hair and a sweet smile looked at Sofka. "Pay her no mind. I'm Chodrak. Nice to meet you."

Not sure how to take Aelita's coldness, Sofka decided that Chodrak would be a good person to speak to. The rest of the supes at the table glared at her just as Aelita did. "Nice to meet you, too. I'm new to the island so thought I should introduce myself." Sofka waited for the other three to say their names.

The rest only grumbled, not bothering to introduce themselves.

Maxim walked up and glared at the three rude supernaturals. "We don't care what you're up to, as long as you aren't helping Tony and his crew. But it would be very much in your favor if you were to share any information you had about the whereabouts of Tony or anyone he's working with."

Chodrak smiled but stayed silent.

Aelita was the first to speak. "I'm not in the habit of helping those who hurt my friends." She didn't say anything else.

Maxim spoke to the largest supe at the table. "Sanford, for someone who prefers the Dark Hills, I must say I'm surprised to see you here. And with new arrivals, too. How'd you all meet?" He tilted his head and waited for the supe who must have been over seven feet tall to speak.

Even sitting, Sanford was head and shoulders above his companions. He also had the steely ice-blue eyes that were prevalent amongst the polar shifters. He was a handsome male, but not like Horatio. This shifter gave off an air of superiority and danger.

"I came in to check on my sister." Sanford nodded toward Micky who was coming towards them with two hot drinks and a slice of coffee cake.

"Sanford, play nice." Micky handed Maxim his bloody coffee. "Sofka, did you want your coffee cake left on your table?"

"Yes, please. And thank you, Micky." Sofka took her drink. "I didn't know you had a brother who lived here."

"Yes, well." Micky shrugged. "He doesn't come into town very often. I'm really not sure what he's doing here now."

"You know why I'm here. I'll not stand by and let some two-bit slugs get away with hurting my little sister," Sanford declared.

For a moment, Sofka thought Sanford might have been someone to question more about Tony. But if he was here, and not back in the Black Hills, then he was either not involved, or he wanted to be close to his sister when the stink hit the fan.

"You know, we're working hard to find Tony and his friends. We know they are up to no good, but someone must be helping them hide." Sofka took a sip of her Pumpkin Spice Latte and almost sighed, it was so good. "This hits the spot."

A tiny smile inched up the side of Aelita's mouth. "That's one of my favorites, too."

"How is Sienna doing?" Sofka knew that Sienna and Aelita were roommates. And she hadn't seen the poor supe since they rescued her from the dump. While physically she wasn't injured, it had to be tough dealing with waking up tied to a dead body.

Aelita's budding smile disappeared, and a look of sheer disgust replaced it. "She's okay. Not ready to go out and about yet. But I'm trying to find out the same thing you are. I want those boys punished for what they did."

"I can understand. I really can." Sofka realized that Aelita must have been cold to her because she didn't think Sofka was looking into the Bully Boys. She decided it was time to start questioning more supes and looked to Sanford. "Do you know anything about the dead guy? He most likely was holed up in the Dark Hills somewhere before he died."

Sanford squirmed in his seat. "Aelita was just asking me the same thing. And I'll tell you what I told her, I don't go over to the Black Hill. My guess is if this guy was in the Dark Hills, he had to have been hanging out in Black Hill. Only the worst of the worst stay there."

Sofka deflated with another dead end. It wasn't like there were a lot of places to hide out on this island. "Could they be moving daily? Or even more often?"

Aelita sat back in her seat. “Hmm, that’s very possible. I know we’ve searched several places and not found anything. I’m guessing you have as well?”

“Yes. They could be staying ahead of us if they are constantly on the move.” Another thought hit Sofka. “I don’t know magic very well, but could they be using a sort of cloaking spell?”

“That would mean they were working with a witch,” Maxim growled. “We only have one on the island.”

“Has anyone bothered to ask Sherrie if she knows anything?” Not that Sofka was volunteering to meet a witch, but it was something that needed to be done. Maybe they could send Marcus over to her when he got back.

“Not possible.” Micky had joined them again. “I went to see her this morning before my shift. She’s not the least bit interested in helping anyone. She wants to stay as far away from all shifters as possible.”

“Well, that’s not a surprise.” While Sofka hadn’t met Sherrie, she had heard enough about the witch to know that she was trying to do better. Which would mean staying clear of any supes that she might be tempted to steal magic from. “But, do you believe her? Is it possible that she attacked Tony and his friends? Stole their magic?” That was something that this witch’s old coven used to do, steal magic from shifters.

Maxim shook his head. “No, the island wouldn’t allow her to do that.”

Sofka laughed. “Really? You still have faith in the island to do its job? Even after it let you and the Sheriff get put in that weird jail?”

"Sofka, we've discussed this before. The island has its limits. Sherrie breaking the rules would be past its limits." Irritation laced Maxim's words.

"He's right," Micky added. "I've been here a long time. I've seen a lot of crap go down here, and there is a line. Death is way over the line."

"Well, we've got one dead body already." The idea that the island allowed that supe to be murdered wasn't sitting well with Sofka.

"What if he was murdered off island and then brought here?" Sanford finally joined the conversation. "It's possible he was killed elsewhere and transported here to be used as part of a larger message."

Sofka wasn't sure if the general population knew that she and her two best friends were the reason for the current issues, but she wasn't about to tell strangers that she was the target. They might decide to throw her into the freezing cold ocean.

It was a good thing she'd ordered the largest PSL they made. Sofka's latte was almost gone, and she wanted more. This conversation was opening up ideas that she wasn't ready for. "If that's true, then there must be a lot more going on than we realize."

Everyone sat there quietly sipping their drinks.

"Um, how about I get everyone refills?" Micky's eyes were wide, and her fingers were gripping her apron, tightly. Talk about the Bully Boys was making her agitated.

"Sure, that'd be great. Thank you, Micky." Sofka could tell the barista was getting close to breaking. She'd been one of the early victims of the Bully Boys' latest round of destruction. Thankfully, she healed quickly. But still, the polar bear shifter could be thinking about the accident that injured her and was the beginning of their increased level of evil.

When Micky had gone back to the coffee machines, Sofka asked in a quiet voice, “is she alright? Is this talk about the boys and their destruction causing her distress?”

Sanford sighed and for the first time since Sofka met him, she saw raw emotion on his face. “She’s stronger than anyone else I know. The fact that she went out to see Sherrie all by herself, says a lot. But, I do think that she’ll feel much better when this is all over with.”

“That’s exactly what I’m going to do. End this before anyone else is hurt, or worse.” Sofka slammed her empty cup on the table.

Chapter 26

Sofka and Maxim left the coffee shop after discussing all of the sites everyone had searched. Between everyone, there wasn't anywhere they hadn't searched. So either the Bully Boys were using magic, or they were on the move.

"I tend to think that the boys are moving around. Maybe even two or three times a day," Maxim stated.

Sofka nodded. "I think I agree with you. But, I don't want to write off the idea that they are getting magical help." She held her hands up before he could say anything. "I know, I know, it's not Sherrie. I've thought about it, and it's possible another witch has given them some powers. Or maybe they found a talisman that granted them invisibility?" she shrugged.

"Grasping at straws now?" Maxim arched a brow.

Looking around to ensure they weren't being watched, Sofka slapped her gloved palm against the side of the building. "Yes, for Frosty's sake! I don't know what else to do. We should have found them by now. The island is small. There aren't very many places to hide out here."

Maxim nodded and then put his arms around her. "Sofka, this isn't your fault, and it's not your responsibility..."

She interrupted him. "Yes, it is my responsibility. This is all my fault. And I'm the sheriff's deputy. I should be able to find them."

After taking a deep breath, Maxim released Sofka. "Actually, the fault lies with the Bully Boys and whoever is helping them. If it's Kirill, then so be it. But that doesn't mean it's your fault. None of this is your fault. And before you start to argue, I know you're the deputy. You and the Sheriff will solve this case. These things take time, we aren't on a TV show. It's not like you can solve it in a day or two. It takes time."

"I know." Sofka sighed and looked up at Maxim. "I just don't want anyone else to get hurt. There have already been so many hurt over this."

"I know. I feel the same way. Take a few deep breaths and let's move on to the next place. I think we should head over to the Island Burger Shack and see if we can find anyone else who might know something. The fact that someone from the Dark Hills is in town, could point to more being in town." Maxim wasn't sure, but he'd never seen Sanford coming to town just to check on his sister. They weren't close. "You could be on to something. It's highly likely something is going on over at the Dark Hills and the so-called innocent supes have left looking for shelter, or safety."

Sofka narrowed her eyes in thought. "You know, I hadn't thought about that possibility. It could also be the presence of the Unseelie Prince that has them jittery."

Maxim chuckled. "Very possible. I used to leave a room whenever he entered."

"Used to?" Sofka arched a brow. Only two days earlier she had noticed Maxim left the room when Marcus showed up. Old habits die hard and all that. So maybe, the supes leaving the Dark Hills was just a coincidence, but maybe not.

An hour later, after a plate of fries for Sofka, and a bloody double-double for Maxim, they had no more information than when they entered the restaurant.

"You know, I'm starting to wonder if the Bully Boys have left the island now." With a long look toward the dock, Sofka put her cold-weather gear back on. "I think we should speak with the merfolk."

"Agreed." Maxim didn't really need to put on cold-weather gear, but he liked to fit in and not call attention to the fact that he was different. So he always wore a black leather jacket with gloves and a scarf. He did tend to leave off the hat whenever possible so as not to mess up his perfect hairstyle.

When they arrived on the dock, Luana was already there, waiting for them. "Good, you're here."

Maxim and Sofka exchanged worried glances.

"How'd you know we were heading this way?" Maxim asked.

Luana pointed to the dome. "Didn't you notice?"

"For all that is cold and frosty." Sofka breathed out and her mouth hung open.

Up in the sky, over the broiling sea, the barrier kept flashing lights as though fireworks were hitting it. Or possibly magical torpedoes.

"Is it holding?" Maxim asked.

"For now. I don't know how much longer the island can keep the shield up. It must be going through a lot of energy right now." Luana bit her nails on one hand.

"Has this ever happened before?" Sofka knew that no magic was endless, but until the Bully Boys had broken out of jail, she'd not seen the island in any trouble, or short on magic at all.

Both Maxim and Luana shook their heads.

Sofka rubbed a hand over her face. "Well, there's nothing we can do to help, unless merfolk possess magic they can lend to the barrier?"

Luana slowly looked from the barrier to Sofka. "No, we don't."

"Okay, then we have to find Tony and his gang. Have you seen any sign of them? Or have any ideas where we can search for them?"

Luana's lips curled in disgust. "If any of us had seen them, they'd be in shreds by now."

"I take it that's a no. What about any ideas? Are there any places where the boys might be able to hide out?" An idea started to form in Sofka's brain, but she wasn't sure if it was even possible. "Could they be in the water? Or maybe..." She held up a hand to keep them from interrupting her. "Just bear with me on this. Are there any small islands inside the barrier where the boys could have swam to without being noticed?"

To call what Luana did "fish lips" would have been too on the nose. But she did open her mouth, move her lips, then close her mouth. Almost like a fish out of water gasping for air. "There is nothing inside the barrier that we haven't checked yet, but there is a tiny island just outside the barrier, but barely. I wouldn't even call it an island. It's more like a rock with a tiny cave on it."

Sofka's eyes bulged. "That would be the perfect hideout."

"It would." Maxim nodded his agreement. "Can you go check? Or send someone else to do it?"

"I'll go." A male voice called out before water splashed right under the dock.

Maxim chuckled. "I should have known Haf would have been close by."

A mermaid's eyes in human form were just like any other woman's eyes, but Luana's had a glow about them that would tell anyone she wasn't truly human. And at that moment, her emerald eyes began to increase in size and luminescence, almost like she was on the verge of shifting back to her mermaid form. A bright green reflected from her eyes and was so bright, it almost blinded Sofka.

Sofka had to put her hands up in front of her face. "Ouch. Care to turn your torch down a bit?"

"Sorry, sometimes Haf can be so overprotective." Luana got her anger under control and shook her head. Her long red hair billowed around her and formed to cover her back like a shield.

"I take it you have the same issue with males that every other female on the planet has." Sofka chuckled and looked out of the corner of her eyes as Maxim bristled.

"Yes." Luana's anger was gone and in its place was her normal emerald green eyes and beautiful smile. Although, if anyone looked closely enough, they'd see her sharp teeth and most likely back up a few paces. "Haf will go and check out the cave. It won't take much time, maybe thirty minutes for him to get there, look around, and be back."

"Would they be able to come and go through the shield at will?" Sofka wasn't sure, but she thought that only Bart's boat could do that.

No other vessel could get through the magical barrier that protected the island from the outside world.

Looking at the barrier, Maxim rubbed his chin and thought about it. "I don't think they could get a boat in and out, but they could swim. The barrier won't hold a supe back. Fish flow in and out of the barrier without any issues, as do the merfolk."

"Correct," Luana nodded. "But, as I said before, there are other ways in and out. They could have a boat sitting just outside the barrier, waiting for them whenever they come and go. And if they have help here, a boat could come for them when they swim through the barrier."

"Could they just swim from the island to the barrier? It's not that far. Any supe would have the stamina, as long as they were good swimmers." Swimming in the freezing cold Arctic waters wasn't fun, but Sofka and her pack used to do it. It was more about training, than fun, but they could all easily swim for a solid hour in the cold waters of her Arctic Circle region. Tundra Wolf Shifters, like Tony, would be just as good if they practiced.

"I suppose, anything is possible. But most likely they have help." Luana looked from the barrier, then off toward her right, where she pointed. "Right about there is where the island is."

Sofka looked where she pointed and noticed that the barrier wasn't being bombarded in that spot. The attack on the barrier was coming from her left. It had to be at least three miles between the spots. As she waited for Haf to return, Sofka wondered if that meant anything, or if the location of the attack on the barrier was randomly chosen. "Are there spots along the barrier that would naturally be weaker than any other?"

"No," Maxim and Luana answered in unison.

They stayed quiet for a bit longer. Then Luana began to pace the length of the dock. Sofka noticed her agitation and looked to Maxim.

"It's been over thirty minutes. If there was nothing to see, Haf should have been back already." Maxim ran a hand through his hair and looked out toward the horizon, where the island should be.

When she heard a splash, Sofka looked at the water, and then back to the dock. "Where's Luana going?"

"Merfolk can communicate underwater over long distances, like whales. My guess is she's going to see if she can locate Haf." Maxim kneeled down on the dock and looked into the clear water. "I can't see her, she must have swum toward him."

They waited for what felt like an eternity, and then an angry face broke through the water. "He's injured. But alive."

Sofka inhaled and put a hand over her mouth. "What happened?"

Luana shook her head. "He's out cold. We won't know anything until he comes to. It's a good thing I jumped in when I did. He lost a lot of blood. Firth is taking care of him now."

"Luana, I'm so sorry. I hope he heals quickly. Is there anything we can do to help?" Maxim took one step closer to the water, as though he might dive in any second.

Luana shook her head. "No, I'll come find you when we know anything at all."

"Do you think it was the Bully Boys? Or could it have been an animal who attacked Haf?" Sofka doubted any animal could hurt a merman like that, especially one as fierce as Haf, but she still had so much to learn about the supernatural community.

"No, it wasn't an animal attack. Someone did this to him. Probably multiple someones from the looks of it." Luana didn't wait around for more questions; she dove back under and the last thing anyone saw was her iridescent tail flapping underwater as she hightailed it away.

Sofka's eyes practically bulged as she took in all of the information. "Do you think Haf will make it?"

"Yes, he's tougher than most. We need to head back to the Information Center and update Horatio. This changes things. We don't need to be searching anymore here, what we need now is a large party to head out to the tiny island and get those boys." Maxim took Sofka's hand and led her away once he took one more look in the direction of the rock cave island.

Later that day, once Marcus was back and everyone who needed to be there, was at the Information Center, Maxim and Sofka explained what they knew so far.

"What are we waiting for? Let's get a posse together and go get them." The Sheriff stood up and headed toward the exit.

"Hold up," Maxim called out. "We don't know exactly what we are in for. Until Haf wakes up, we could be walking into a trap."

"Then we take everyone we can get on Bart's boat." Marcus growled and looked like he was about to shift. Even though fae didn't shift. His aura was murky, and darkness surrounded him.

"Whoa, whoa. Marcus, just relax. We'll get them, we will. But not with you going all Unseelie Prince on us." Ree took his hand and held it between hers, but she stood as far back as she could without dropping his hand.

The Unseelie Prince, in all his royal glory, looked at her and began to calm down. Above his head stood a two-foot crown made out of black ink. But as he calmed down, it turned to a gray mist before evaporating.

"Is that normal?" Sofka wasn't sure if she could ask that part of him to return or be glad the deathly glare Marcus had been sporting had disappeared with his crown.

"Uhhhh, no." Maxim shook his head and with wide eyes, took in Marcus. He noted the prince seemed to stand taller than before. He always had an angular jaw, but now it was as sharp as a sword. It was entirely possible that a hand could be cut if it tried touching his face right then. "I've never seen this side of him before."

"I see. Is Ree in danger?" The last thing Sofka wanted was for her best friend to get hurt by her mate. But, if Marcus' anger could be harnessed as a weapon, that didn't hurt Ree, then Sofka might want to see that side of him again. Even if it was scary.

Maxim looked between the couple and shook his head. "I don't think Marcus would ever hurt Ree. Their bond would keep him from doing so. Even if he lost control of his inner fae prince, I think she would be the one being that would be safe."

"Interesting." Sofka wasn't about to voice her thoughts, but that was one weapon she would keep in her back pocket. Only to be used as a last resort.

"I see what you're thinking. That is very dangerous." Maxim's eyes narrowed on Sofka and he pursed his lips. "Ree might be safe, but I doubt the rest of us would be."

The thought of everyone else's safety, or rather lack thereof, hadn't crossed her mind until just that moment. "I wouldn't want that side of him to come out unless it was a last-case scenario. You know, like a Doomsday option."

"Doomsday is about right." Maxim sighed. "Look, I know you haven't had much interaction with other supes before you arrived here, but the fae aren't to be messed with. There's a reason his family has never been removed from the throne. They have some sort of genetic power that makes it almost impossible to defeat them. But it comes at a cost. One I doubt Marcus wants to pay."

"You're right." Marcus stopped next to Sofka, with Ree's hand still in his. "That demonstration was nothing compared to what I can do if provoked the wrong way."

Another thought entered Sofka's head, and she wondered if someone wasn't trying to provoke the Unseelie Prince. But surely they knew he'd never hurt his mate, right? He might hurt Sofka or KeeKee by accident, but if his mate bond with Ree kept her safe, then using Marcus wouldn't work too well. It would most definitely end badly for whoever instigated his Unseelie Prince side. And then another thought entered, and she really wished her mind would stop coming up with all of these horrible ideas.

"What would happen if someone hurt, or killed Ree?" While Sofka never wanted to contemplate that scenario, she needed to know.

Marcus's nostrils flared and smoke began to surround him. His breathing began to be labored and he growled. "I would destroy anyone who dared to touch my mate."

"Marcus, remember, breathe. I'm right here." This time, Ree got up close and wrapped her arms around him. "I'm fine. It's alright."

"What are you thinking?" KeeKee practically yelled. "Never say those things around Marcus."

Sofka put her hands in the air in surrender. "Fine, fine. I'm sorry. I just had some crazy ideas going through my head, that's all."

Maxim waited for Marcus to calm down. Then he took his own life into his hands. “But she has a point. What if someone is trying to provoke you, Marcus?”

“They might be on to something.” Horatio had joined their little group. “Getting you to destroy the girls might be a smart way to get around the island’s defenses. They’ve tried so many things already. Why not this?”

Marcus shook his head. “If someone did this, they’d have the entire Unseelie Royal Court after them. My family may not like me. Some might even want to kill me themselves, but Ree, Sofka, and KeeKee are now part of my family. And therefore, part of the Unseelie Royal family. They would have the same protections as I would.”

“Meaning?” Sofka asked.

Horatio jumped in with a smile. “If anyone harms, or kills, a member of the family, the entire court would be after them. And no one goes up against Queen Mab and wins. In fact, Mab would probably destroy this island and everyone who has anything to do with it, just to show the world they can’t get away with messing with her family.”

Sofka couldn’t believe Queen Mab would destroy an entire island over this. But when she looked at Marcus, and noticed him nodding his head, she decided she didn’t want to know the truth. “Okay, so we have to make sure that nothing happens to us.” Under her breath, she said, “Easier said than done.”

“Talk about an understatement,” Maxim added.

Everyone began talking at the same time and Sofka’s head pounded. “Okay, enough!” She chopped her hands through the air to get their attention. “There are too many possibilities floating around here. Let’s simplify it a bit, alright? We know that Kirill is somehow involved in this, let's not bring the Unseelie Queen into it as well." The thought of Kirill and Queen Mab in the same room, let alone, the same universe, sent a chill down Sofka's spine.

"We can't just sit here arguing over this. Something has to be done." Horatio took control of the meeting and had everyone quiet again. "It's better if we take the fight to them, they won't be expecting it. We might get lucky and catch them off guard."

"I disagree." A loud, booming, male voice ricocheted around the room and had everyone turning toward the front door. The male who stood just inside the door had to have bent over to enter. Even his shoulders were taller than the door frame.

"Firth, welcome." Horatio moved to greet the leader of the merfolk. "Does this mean you have some news for us?"

Firth stood almost nine feet tall in his human form and even if he wasn't so tall, he still would have silenced the entire village with just one look from his steely aquamarine eyes.

Sofka thought that the leader of the merfolk would carry a trident, like in the movies. But Firth stood there like a sentry with a curved sword on a pole. Its tip was higher than the top of Firth's head. That thing would most likely gut anyone with just one good thrust.

"I do. Haf woke up and he told me what happened. This has moved past the Bully Boys and is so much larger than anyone can fathom." The merfolk leader looked around the room and made eye contact with each and every supe who dared to look at him. Half of those in there looked at the floor, while the other half seemed to quake in their boots when Firth glared at them.

When his eyes met hers, Sofka could have sworn he saw all the way to her very soul. She gulped, then cleared her throat. "Can you tell us what happened?"

"Someone turned the tiny rock cave into an island large enough to hold an army. It seems someone is bent on invading Misfit Island. They are not only building a large army of supernatural soldiers, but they are also amassing an impressive array of weapons." Firth's nostrils flared and he looked back at Horatio.

"I see." The breath left Horatio and he visibly deflated. "I take it they are magical weapons?"

Firth nodded.

"Horatio, a moment?" Maxim nodded toward the far corner of the room.

Both males walked over there and began whispering with their backs to the room. Sofka wasn't sure why they thought they could keep their conversation a secret. The room was full of supernatural creatures who could hear what they were saying. Until they couldn't.

"Great, now the island decides to intervene." Sofka threw her hands in the air and rolled her eyes.

Firth's eyes narrowed and he moved toward the pair that was separated by the island's sound-dividing wall as though a wave was moving him instead of his feet. The sound barrier enveloped him and no one was able to hear him when he spoke. They could see him gesturing to the room, but no sound came from the three.

For just a moment, Sofka considered joining them. Then an arm landed on her shoulder holding her back. She turned her head and pursed her lips. "Marcus, I need to know what they are discussing."

The Unseelie Prince shook his head. "Not now. Let them have their confab and when they are ready, they'll tell us what we need to know."

Since the island had finally done something, Sofka knew she should listen to Marcus. But it did grate on her nerves that Maxim left her out. "I guess, the island can do some things when it wants."

"I think it's been doing a lot more than we can realize. When this is all over, I'm sure we will look back and see the island's hand in everything." Marcus' wise words hit Sofka's heart.

She hadn't been trusting in the island. Not since those Tundra Wolves broke out of jail and caused so much havoc. But maybe Marcus had a point, the island was still in control, even with all of the magical bombardment to the barrier.

Maxim felt Firth's presence inside the sound bubble before he saw the large merman.

"What is so important that you would leave the group? And why did the island shield your conversation from everyone?" Firth leveled his gaze at Maxim, who didn't flinch.

With a quick glance at Horatio, Maxim decided to let Firth into their little secret. It wouldn't be a secret much longer anyway. The vampire realized they could use Firth's help, especially since it would bring the entire local merfolk into their circle. "What I'm about to tell you needs to stay a secret for as long as possible."

Firth nodded.

It felt odd to be saying this out loud, and to someone Maxim didn't know all that well. "When Sofka and her friends arrived here a few months ago, the island let Horatio know something that no one else did." He looked to the Polar Bear shifter, who looked anything but ready to talk about it.

"Right after meeting the girls," Horatio motioned to Sofka, KeeKee, and Ree. "The island told me that those girls would be important to the future of the island. It didn't tell me specifically what was going on, but that they needed to mate with three very different creatures here. And that eventually, someone was going to come and try to stop them."

Firth arched a brow. "The island knew their old alpha would come looking for them?"

Horatio shook his head. "No. I don't know. I think this is much bigger than Kirill, but all the signs are pointing to him. There is something special about those three little Arctic Wolf Shifters. But I don't know what it is. All I know is that they are supposed to mate with males that fate has chosen for them."

"Really? Fate chose Marcus for Ree?" Maxim gestured with his hand toward the couple in question and shook his head. "Poor Ree."

Horatio grinned. "Poor Sofka."

It only took about three seconds for Maxim to get the jab. "Hey, I think Sofka is getting a much better mate than Ree did."

Firth looked between the two males. "Can we get back to this problem? What do three Arctic Wolf shifters and their mates have to do with anything? Why are they important?"

"That's all I know." Horatio shrugged. "The island didn't tell me the details. So, I don't know if we're under attack to stop their mating.

Or if we're under attack for some other reason, and fate has chosen those three, and their mates, to be our defenders."

"There is some correlation between those young pups and what is happening now. I can see that." Firth turned his head and looked at the three females. "The exact reason may not be important, but we do need to do something now before the army gets any larger, or stronger."

"I agree. But the question is, do we bring the fight inside the barrier? Or keep it outside where the humans could see it all?" Maxim had plenty of run-ins with human cops during his time, but even when he was at his worst, he hated when the humans were involved. The less they knew, the better off all of the supernatural community was. The last thing this planet needed was an all-out war between humans and supes.

"Yes, that is the question." Firth agreed.

"I think we should bring it inside the barrier. We don't need the humans getting wind of anything. Especially the fact that the island is here," Horatio added.

"Marcus isn't going to like taking Ree with us into battle." Just the thought of what Marcus might do if Ree was injured, sent a chill down Maxim's spine.

"How do you feel about taking Sofka into battle?" Firth asked.

"I don't like it, but I know her well enough to know that if I try to leave her behind, she'll only follow by herself. Which will be much worse. Besides, I think we are meant to fight side by side with our mates." Maxim looked at Horatio and wondered if he was KeeKee's intended mate. They two spent a lot of time together, and they got along very well, but Maxim hadn't noticed either of them acting like they were potential mates. Which made him wonder who her mate would be.

Horatio, who hadn't picked up on Maxim's thoughts, agreed. "I think you and Sofka, and Marcus and Ree must be together."

"And will you fight with KeeKee?" Firth asked, showing he understood more about the goings on with the land dwellers than he had let on.

Horatio's eyes widened. "Who? Me?' He put his hand over his chest.

Firth only nodded.

"I...um..." He cleared his throat. "I don't have a mate. At least, not yet."

Firth raised his head and looked down his nose at Horatio. "We shall see. In the meantime, who will fight with KeeKee?"

"Man, I think you should. The two of you are close. And I don't think she'd trust anyone else to have her back like you do." Maxim looked to Horatio.

After a moment's hesitation, Horatio nodded. "Yeah, I think you might be right. Besides, I don't think I would trust anyone to have her back like I could. He eyed Firth before adding, "I don't think I can trust anyone outside of our small group." In his heart, he only meant the six of them, not Firth. Or anyone else on the island. Not even the Sheriff was one Horatio felt he could trust with KeeKee's safety. Did that mean that he was her mate?

Chapter 28

Once the decision was made, it didn't take long to get everyone on board. Most of the residents were already in the center of town, just waiting to see what was going to happen. When Horatio stepped up to try and lead them to Bart's boat, Maxim disagreed with who would go in the boat.

Then when Firth got into the argument, Sofka jumped in. "Gentlemen, please. We need one leader, not three." She looked at Horatio, and even though he was the unofficial mayor, she didn't think he should lead the battle. She also didn't think the Sheriff was the best one to do so.

"I think I should be the leader here. I have the most experience." Maxim was of course speaking of his days as a soldier in the Tzar's military.

"I already lead the merfolk. I'm accustomed to giving orders and my supes follow without complaint." First tapped the butt of his long spear on the ground by his feet.

"Yes, but I'm the leader of all those on land," Horatio added.

All Sofka could think of was too many cooks in the kitchen.

"But have either of you practiced any battle drills in the past one hundred years?" Firth arched a brow and looked as though he won the argument.

"That's all fine and dandy for those who swim and don't need to breathe air, but what about the landlubbers?" Sofka returned his arched brow and added a jutted hip with her hand on it.

Maxim chuckled. Most supes wouldn't dream of going up against Firth. Especially once he displayed his sharpened teeth for all to see. Even in human form, he was very formidable. "Okay, how about Firth leading his mer-soldiers. I think we can all agree that would be best."

Everyone around nodded their agreement.

Sofka looked between Horatio and Maxim. "And which one of you will lead those on land?"

Both men stared back at her and smiled.

She held her hands up in front of her. "Oh, no. I'm not a military strategist." Her head began to shake back and forth. As the two strong males continued to stare at her, her head moved even faster until eventually she couldn't see anything past her platinum blond hair that swished back and forth across her face.

"You might want to put your hair up for the battle." The sheriff chuckled and pointed to the mess of tangles forming around her shoulders.

"Roscoe, tell them it has to be one of them," Sofka turned pleading eyes to her boss.

"Enough. If you can't decide, then I'll lead them all." Firth slammed his spear on the ground so hard, it caught everyone's attention.

All of the supes that had been chatting while they had their little pre-war confab, turned their heads and looked at the angry face of the merman in charge.

Sofka smiled. "I think we have our leader." She pointed to Firth.

"Yes, I'm the General, but you are my second in command, little wolf." The edges of Firth's mouth tilted up, almost like he was trying to smile. Instead, it showed off his canine teeth and he appeared more intimidating than he intended.

"Ah, I haven't had much experience with this sort of thing." Sofka took two steps back. Not so much to get away from the scary merman, but more to put Maxim and Horatio closer to Firth.

Just then, Marcus walked forward and grinned at the small group. "Sofka, I think you are the best one to coordinate with Firth. Horatio and Maxim will be your right and left hands. All you have to do is make sure you do what Firth tells you to do. And you let him know what's happening with your troops."

Even though it was completely out of her wheelhouse, Sofka knew that if Firth wanted her to work with him, she'd have to do it. As she agreed, she also realized that by doing this, she wouldn't see much of the battle herself. Which was why both Marcus and Maxim were so happy with the choice.

Sofka narrowed her eyes and pointed at the four alpha males. "I see what you've done here. Don't think I don't realize what you did." She'd get her share of battle, but she also knew that leadership was one of her gifts. And if their fight had any chance of succeeding, she would have to focus on leading the troops, not trying to show she could fight just as well as they could.

As she and Firth discussed who they wanted and how they were going to get everyone ferried over to the small island, she realized that they also needed to leave some back on Misfit Island to help defend those who couldn't fight. Their children and elderly needed to be protected.

"Firth, we must leave some back to defend the island." Sofka bit her lower lip and looked back at a group of young moms holding their babies in their hands. One woman in particular stood out and her heart ached for Melanie and her four pups. Elias was saying goodbye to his little family.

The leader of the merfolk looked to where Sofka was watching. "Yes, there are those who won't be able to defend themselves should the battle move here." He nodded. "I have learned that it's more dangerous to leave fathers behind to defend their brood. They tend to ignore others and focus solely on their family. Elias is needed with us."

"Of course." While Sofka understood, she also hated to take Elias from his family. Then she looked around and found a few strong supes who didn't have a local family. She pointed out twenty different supes from various supernatural races. While all of them would have been very helpful on the battlefield, they would also be the perfect defenders.

Firth looked over Sofka's choices. With the exception of Sanford, he agreed that all should stay behind. "Sanford will be very helpful to us. If the battle moves back here, then he can quickly get back to help. All of us will."

Sofka looked up at the shield protecting Misfit Island from the outside world. The bombardment had stopped earlier, but she knew that the enemy was just regrouping and would come up with something else to use. "Island, I hope you can keep protecting everyone here. I'd hate to go out there and fight for this place, only to see it fall in the end." This was her home now, and she was going to do everything she could to ensure that it stayed that way. Not only for her but for everyone else who called Misfit Island home.

It wasn't even an hour later and she was heading across the water in Bart's boat. There were two smaller boats with oars that held a dozen soldiers between them that weren't too far behind her.

"Don't look so worried. You hear Firth, with everyone we have, we'll beat them just with our sheer numbers." Maxim stood close to Sofka in the bow of the little ship.

"I know, but I don't want to assume that we'll last long enough for Bart to go back and get the last load of soldiers and join us." After a few discussions with Bart, it was decided that he would ferry over the strongest fighters first. His boat barely held one hundred supes. Then behind them would be the dozen who paddled in the two small boats. And Bart would head back to the main island for the other one hundred troops and return as quickly as possible.

"It shouldn't take more than forty-five minutes for Bart to load up and get back here. There is a difference between being confident and cocky. Confidence is what your troops need from you now." Maxim put a hand over Sofka's and squeezed.

While she still didn't understand how she came to be the leader of the ground forces, she made the decision to do everything she could to keep Misfit Island safe.

Before they had even pulled up to the edge of the dome, Sofka noticed a large wave coming toward them. Riding it was a merman holding a large spear. His face looked as turbulent as the waves beneath him. But what caught her attention was his tail. It was larger than she expected. He towered over the other merfolk behind him.

The shimmering aquamarine scales glittered when the sunlight shone on him. "Is that? Does he have a crown on his head?" A golden glow with sharp points all around Firth's head outshone his tail, which was hard to do since as he moved, the aquamarine scales shimmered all of the colors of the rainbow. It was quite spectacular, something she didn't even think was possible, even though this was a supernatural creature.

Maxim's mouth hung open and he gaped. "I've never seen him in a crown. I thought only the king wore a crown. It's rather intimidating to see him like that."

"It is. Maybe that's why he did it? To intimidate the enemy?" Before Sofka could say anything else, she noticed Firth circling his spear over his head and his mouth moved.

"Turn around, we were tricked." Firth pointed his spear back at the island.

Sofka turned to see smoke coming from the spot where the boat would have docked. "Oh no! Look!" She pointed to the black smoke. Behind it, she noted sparks from what appeared to be fireworks. But she knew that was evidence of magic.

"Magical torpedoes. They must have expected us to launch a full-scale attack on their location and waited for us to take our strongest away. What have we done?" Fear etched on Maxim's face, and he hung his head.

"Bart, turn us around, quickly! We have to get back to the island." Sofka yelled as she ran toward the gargoyle.

It still freaked Sofka out whenever Bart rotated his head, without turning his body. It was something only a stone statue could do. The boatman swiveled his head back to look at Sofka and his face mirrored Maxim's. "What happened?" Without waiting for a response, he maneuvered his boat around as quickly as he could. Sadly, it took longer than usual since the boat was so overloaded with heavy supes.

As they turned the boat, Firth and his army of seafaring soldiers overtook them and continued toward their island.

"He'll get there before us," Sofka announced to no one in particular. Once the boat was heading back to Misfit Island, she made her way back to Maxim.

"I can't believe we didn't consider this possibility." The fear Maxim had felt before had morphed into anger when his eyes turned red and his fangs descended.

Sofka watched in fascination as Maxim fully vamped out right in front of her. What would have once scared the bejeebus out of her, now had her marveling at what a fierce warrior Maxim was. For just a second, she wondered if he would feed on the blood of his enemy. Then she realized she didn't care just as long as Maxim stopped the bad guys from hurting anyone who called Misfit Island home.

A flash of red darted over Sofka's head and caught her attention. She wondered if it was a rocket, or maybe another magical torpedo. It was heading toward the island and for just a moment, Sofka feared that somehow the shield fell, and her enemy had set up rocket launchers on that small island, directed toward her home. But when nothing else flew over her head, she realized it was a one-off. Maybe, it was even one of Firth's soldiers. Although, she had never heard of a merfolk who could fly. But, then again, she was still so new to all of the supernatural community. Nothing from her upbringing could have prepared her for all that she had discovered on Misfit Island.

Well, nothing except for the combat training she had received. While she had never had to fight for her life, or for those of her packmates, all of her pack trained in various martial arts and different fighting styles. Sofka prayed that her training, such as it was, would be of benefit once they landed. She also prayed that she wouldn't come upon an island full of dead residents.

"Do you think those from the dark hills who opted to stay behind will help?" At first, Sofka was so angry at the supes who didn't want to get involved she could have spit on them. Now, she prayed they weren't the ones her team was going to battle against.

Maxim shook his head. "At this point, I'd say they will either put their head in the snow or possibly help the invaders. That could have been their plan all along."

"I just hope that Horatio and KeeKee are safe." Sofka had originally thought that putting KeeKee on the second boat would be safest for her, but now she was regretting not keeping her best friend at her side.

"Sofka, you can't beat yourself up over this. None of us could have known this would happen." Ree, who had just walked up to her and Maxim put her arms around her best friend. "You know Horatio will keep her safe. So will the others who were waiting for the second boat. Don't forget, there are one hundred fighters who are on that front line." She pointed to the island.

By now, they could see the smoke where the dock used to be. "They must have blown up the dock, trying to slow us down." Sofka winced.

It was a very smart plan. It wouldn't stop them, since some of those on the boat could fly, and the rest would be able to swim to shore.

"Look!" Ree pointed to a spot through the smoke where something gold caught their eyes. "Is that Firth already fighting?"

As the dark smoke began to dissipate, Sofka could see more of what awaited them on the shore. "It is! Oh!" She winced and turned her head when she saw the damage that just one slice from Firth's sword could do.

"Okay, I don't want to fight anywhere near him." Ree stuck her tongue out and almost gagged. "That is one vicious fish-man."

While Sofka agreed, she also appreciated his efforts to save their home. "Thankfully, he's on our side."

Before Sofka could order anyone off the boat, she noticed the supes who could fly had shifted and began taking off toward the shore. Some of them had family and loved ones who couldn't fight. Hopefully, those were far from the docks.

"Alright, everyone make your way to the mainland. If you can't swim, let me know now." When no one said anything, Sofka smiled. They all jumped in. Most didn't even bother to shift, they jumped in with their clothes on and in their human form.

"See you there," Sofka said to her friends before she did a perfect swan dive into the water. Her wolf scratched and clawed her way out. Before the splash sounded, Sofka was gone, and her wolf was swimming as fast as she could to the shore.

Since the fighting was still centered next to the dock, everyone had to climb up the walls that formed the side of the harbor. Sofka watched as many supes used the dock fenders to help them get up. If she could use the dock fender in her wolf form, then she'd be mostly dry when she shifted back to her human form, only her hair would be wet.

One of the unexplainable parts of being a shifter is where their clothes went when they shifted. Contrary to popular belief, a shifter's clothes didn't tear when they shifted. Instead, the clothes and anything on their body went to a magical holding area while they were in their shifted form. When they returned to their human form, the same exact items returned to where they were before the shift, almost as though they had never even shifted.

She swam to an open dock fender and tried to climb up, but since she didn't have fingers to grab hold of anything, she fell back into the water. Her head went under, and then she bobbed up and shook her furry head to get the water out of her eyes and mouth.

"Here, let me help." A pair of hands she recognized reached down and grabbed under her front legs. Maxim pulled her up as though she weighed nothing.

Once Sofka's feet were safely under her, she quickly shifted back to her human form. "Thanks." Even though a wet vampire was still sexy, she didn't have time to take in his form-fitting clothes. A tiny voice called out to her, *wet t-shirt contest*, but she ignored it and scanned everyone near her.

"Firth is over there." Maxim pointed to the thickest part of the battle.

If Sofka wasn't mistaken, the scary merman was smiling and plowing through the enemy like a hot knife slicing through butter. "Let's get over there and help."

"Wait, your soldiers are waiting for you to lead them." The wet vampire nodded toward most of the soldiers who had waited for her. There was a group who had just jumped right into the battle.

"Right, let's go and help our neighbors save our families and homes." Sofka waved at them to follow her. She figured since Firth was in the thick of it, she could join in as well.

With Maxim at her side, she was confident in their chances.

Chapter 29

Not even twenty minutes into the battle and Sofka was starting to think she had been wrong. Her confidence began to fail her and even though she was better at one-on-one fighting in her human form, she had to switch over to her wolf form. Three wolf shifters came at her in what appeared to her to be a coordinated move. A move she had recognized as one her alpha had taught them all.

While she didn't recognize any of the wolves there, she knew they had trained with her alpha. Too many of them fought just like she did. But, unlike them, she had the past ten years to practice. Time to hone her skills was the only thing keeping her in the fight – cuts, pain, and all.

Sofka expertly maneuvered to her right, then feinted to her left, only to turn right again and jump out of the triangle they had tried to box her into. As she jumped over one of the wolves, she shifted and landed on all fours facing them.

No more Miss Nice Lady. A deep, guttural growl emanated from her bowels, and she chomped her teeth down, hard, when she was close enough to grab ahold of one neck. Like a dog with a bone, she held on tight and shook her head. The wolf in her grasp whined and went limp. She released him, fearing she had killed him. But when he moved his front paws, she knew he was only injured.

It took a lot to kill a wolf. It wasn't something she ever wanted to do, but if it came down to her or him, she'd rather she lived.

In the split second she focused her attention on the downed wolf at her feet, one of the other wolves she had been fighting clamped onto her back leg. She let loose a howl of pain and tried to kick it off her. Sofka knew that going down would mean the end of her, so she did all she could to get her leg loose.

The thought of shifting back to her human form, in order to use her hands and one good foot, crossed her mind, but then before she could act, her leg was free.

She swiveled her head around and saw that a vampire had sunk his teeth into the neck of the wolf that had been using her leg as a chew toy. Thankfully, he had barely broken the skin on her hind leg. While it hurt to put any weight on it, she could use it if needed. And she needed to when she caught sight of the third wolf prowling toward her.

He must have smelled blood for his mouth was watering and he eyed her hind leg. Using that as a distraction, she pretended to be more injured than she really was and limped, then whined in pain.

The act worked.

Wolf number three growled and chomped his mouth before he launched himself toward her injured leg. Letting him think he was going to get her, she waited a few seconds before quickly moving around and grabbed his neck with her mouth. The wolf deserved to die for going after her weakest point, but she still wasn't ready to kill.

Instead, she let him loose only to chomp down on his front leg as hard as she could. When she felt the bone give, and the wolf yell out in pain, she knew she had done her job. She dropped him on the ground to lick his wounds, literally.

An injury like a broken bone would force the wolf to shift back to his human form. He'd be weak and in too much pain to fight any more. It made him a huge target for any fighters who only went after the injured, like Tundra Wolf shifters tended to do, but that was his problem, not hers.

She doubted anyone from Misfit Island would go after an easy kill. There were still too many invaders to fight. Sofka looked around and caught sight of Marcus fighting off an Ice Troll. She prayed it wasn't one who lived in the Dark Hills. Her biggest fear was that those supes would fight for the invaders, instead of helping to defend their home against the evil who sought to destroy the peaceful life they were all working so hard to build.

When she didn't quickly see KeeKee or Ree, she worried about them. But then she caught sight of an Arctic Wolf Shifter next to Horatio's Polar Bear. They were fighting a pair of red hats. "Since when did Kirill work with the dark fae?" Sofka put that thought out of her mind as she scanned the area looking for Ree. Off to the far left of Marcus, she found Ree in her wolf form fighting against a lion. Talk about an unfair advantage. Thankfully, Ree had the same training as Sofka.

But still, she wasn't about to let Ree battle the lion on her own. Sofka took off running as quickly as her wolf legs would allow in the middle of a battle. She had to dodge some fighters and she jumped over a few bodies. She didn't take the time to see who they were, or if they were even still alive. Her main concern was getting to Ree before the lion pounced.

The two were circling each other, moving in time to one another. Every few seconds one would jump closer, but the other would jump back out of reach. It almost looked choreographed it was all so in step.

Before Sofka could get to Ree, a large multi-colored bird jumped in her path and squawked at her. The yellow beak of the beast bolted out and hit her side. Sofka stumbled and rolled over a few times, but she got right back up on her feet ignoring the pain in her hind leg as well as the spot where the sharp beak poked her ribs.

She growled and barked out her anger at being distracted from her friend. The bird, which looked like a giant dodo bird she'd once seen in a kid's book, squawked again and flapped its wings. When the beak tried to stab her again, she quickly moved out of the way.

This time, Sofka was on the defense and ready to study her prey. As a wolf, she chased and attacked many birds in her days. But she'd never fought a bird shifter this large. The bird must have stood close to six feet tall with a wingspan of over six feet wide. To say the shifter was massive would be an understatement. This was the sort of animal that should be fighting a troll, or one of the merfolk. If only they had a dragon on their side. This fight would have been over before it even started.

But Sofka knew that the dragons never left their perches to travel to the bottom of the world. They preferred their mountain top caves, mostly in the northern Arctic regions. Or the largest mountain peaks of the world.

When a swarm of pixies came to her defense, the wolf shifter did its best to laugh. But what came out was a garbled howl that sounded more like an injured wolf, than a laughing one. There had to be at least twenty-five pixies flying around the bird. What most didn't realize was that pixies had super sharp teeth. They were small fae creatures, but their bite hurt. And they were more bite than bark.

The bird quickly lost track of Sofka and began fluttering its wings, trying to get the pixies to leave it alone. While its beak was large, it couldn't move as quickly as a pixie could fly away. Wishing she could stay and help the swarm defeat the strange bird, she knew she had to get to Ree's side. One quick search and she saw that Marcus was still fighting the ice troll, and he looked to be winning. Sofka doubted anyone could beat a Fae Prince. Especially one who had survived as long as he had with Queen Mab, and his brother constantly trying to find ways to kill him.

She caught sight of Maxim, he had another neck in his mouth, but this time, he let it go and spit the blood out. Either the vampire was full, or faun blood didn't taste good to a vampire.

It seemed the enemy had called in many different supes to fight for him. With all of the other signs pointing to Kirill, she wondered if he didn't have a partner. From what she remembered, Kirill didn't care to work with other supes very often. He was a supernatural racist, preferring wolf shifters over anyone else. Arctic wolf shifters were of course on top, in his eyes. But he did work with the variety of wolves who called the Arctic Circle home. Which was why all of the wolf shifters her team were fighting wasn't a surprise.

When she noticed a creature from the dark hills she recognized, she wanted to call out. But in her wolf form it would only be a howl, or a bark. Sigurd was fighting a black bear shifter. One she recognized as living in town. At least, she thought it was Elias. Her fears haunted her as she began searching for Ree again.

Out past Sigurd and Elias, she caught sight of an Arctic Wolf shifter with blond patches that looked just like Ree. Ree was still keeping up with the lion. In fact, Ree looked like she had the upper hand in that battle. So when Sofka heard a bellow coming from Elias, she turned her attention to the pappa bear.

"Sigurd, let Elias go. He's on our side." Sofka shifted back to her human form so she could communicate with the Nixie who seemed to not know who was enemy and who was friend.

The crazed black eyes of the Nixie noticed her. His gaze lingered on her and Sofka wondered if he even knew who he was in that moment. Did he go all crazy in battle like a berserker did? She knew there were ways to defeat a Nixie, but for the life of her she couldn't think of one.

Out of the corner of her eyes, she saw a vampire, not Maxim, sink its teeth into a wolf's neck. Then it hit her, three drops of blood could be used as a way to stop a Nixie from killing. But did it work when the Nixie was using his hands, instead of his voice, to kill?

It was worth a try. Sofka could feel the open wound on her side from when the bird pecked her ribs. She unzipped her jacket and threw it to the side. Then she lifted the side of her sweater and rubbed the wound with her thumb. A hiss escaped her as she felt the pain move down her body and into her toes.

Ignoring the shooting pains, she flicked several drops of blood toward the Nixie and they landed on the snow right next to him. When Sigurd dropped the giant bear to the ground, she noticed his fingers had shifted to long talons. Which must have been what caused the bear to howl so loudly in pain. Elias slowly moved away as Sigurd dropped to his knees and licked up the red snow.

"What has gotten into you? I thought you wanted to live a peaceful life here on this island? Why were you fighting with Elias?" Not wanting to get too close to the crazed Nixie, Sofka stayed where she was.

Only one word escaped the Nixie before he laid down. "Can't."

With Sigurd down for the moment, and Elias wobbling away from the fighting, Sofka turned her attention back to finding Ree. When she located the lion, she smiled. It was down, not dead, but certainly out of the fight for now.

Then she began to scan the remaining supes fighting. The thick of it had definitely passed. Only small groups of battles remained. She noticed Maxim had found her and was heading her way. She looked around and saw that Firth and his army had been particularly destructive in their battle. The leader of the merfolk was surrounded by bodies. It was too soon to take stock of what happened.

Instead, she scanned the rest of the fighters, looking for her family. She noticed Marcus was doing the same, he didn't have Ree next to him. He was frantically running around calling out her name. Which only frightened Sofka.

"Ree!" She began calling out her best friends' names. "KeeKee!" When KeeKee responded, part of her relaxed. Then she intensified her search for Ree. Before she could get very far, Maxim was at her side.

"I don't see her. Do you?" Sofka asked, hearing the desperation in her voice.

The vampire turned in circles looking everywhere. "I don't see her." Then he yelled out louder than Sofka had ever heard, "Ree!"

Marcus came running toward them looking more like the legends of Fae warriors than the prince she knew him to be. His hair was matted on one side with blood. The other side was sticking out in all directions. Blood was covering his chest, but his shirt looked to be in one piece.

Sofka quickly inhaled and covered her mouth. "Marcus? Are you alright?" She put a hand out to his chest but pulled it back when he batted it away.

"I'm fine. Where's Ree? Last I saw her she was fighting a Lion, and winning." With nothing more than a quick glance toward Sofka, Marcus continued to search. "I know she's still alive, I feel her. But I can't see her."

Ignoring the last vestiges of a dying battle around her, Sofka scanned the area she had last seen Ree. "That way." She pointed toward the lion who was still down on the ground.

All three ran toward it. Since the lion was still in its animal form, Sofka knew it was alive, if unconscious. The eyes were closed, so they couldn't demand it turn back into a human.

Marcus kicked the beast. "Get up. Where is my mate?" The growl and force of Marcus' words caused Sofka to jump.

"Geesh. It's unconscious, leave it alone." Sofka looked once more at the lion and noticed the eyelids fluttering. "Wait, it's waking up." She tried to kneel down, but strong arms pulled her back.

"Don't. It might lash out at you. You are his enemy." Maxim's red eyes reappeared and she watched as his fangs descended. They weren't as long as she'd seen them go before, but he was ready for a fight.

The two of them stood there, watching as the lion began to shimmer. It's human form taking shape slowly. One thing Sofka knew for sure, was this animal was injured, badly. A lion should have been able to shift as easily as she could, even with some injuries. Lions were tough. They were some of the strongest shifters she knew of.

"Ahhh," The man lying in place of the lion said before closing his eyes.

Sofka did a double take. She'd seen this male before. Not on the island, but on her journey here. "Adam? No, Adinos?"

"You know this shifter?" Maxim asked.

"Yes, no. We met him on our journey here. He's the one who told us all about Misfit Island." Sofka blew out a breath and took a step back, right into Maxim's firm chest. "We would never have come here if we hadn't have met him."

"It was all planned." a hoarse voice said from the frozen ground. "I'm sorry." The male closed his eyes and didn't wake up again, even when Marcus shoved him around.

"Stop. Leave him be. When he finishes his healing cycle, we can interrogate him then." Maxim ordered. "Now, we need to search for Ree. She's probably somewhere else fighting."

"Or, maybe she ran back to the center of town looking to make sure the kids were safe?" Knowing Ree as Sofka did, the soft-hearted wolf shifter would have run to save the kids without saying anything to any of them, if she thought they needed her.

"Of course! Why didn't I think of that?" Marcus began heading back to town, until Maxim put a hand on his shoulder.

"Hold up. We need to split up. You head into town and we'll stay here and search the area." Maxim's jaw clenched and Sofka noticed the way his cheeks moved with the effort to not say more.

The idea that entered her mind was not one she wanted. Her eyes pricked and her nose itched. She knew that tears weren't far off. Maxim must have been thinking what she was, that Ree's body might be found in the many that were strewn around. Hopefully, Ree was just passed out from the battle with the lion.

While Sofka didn't want to be the one to find her best friend's body, she also feared what Marcus might do if he were to discover her limp body. Ree wouldn't want him going all psycho, even if she died in battle. But Ree wasn't dead. Marcus even said he felt her. If the fates had intended for them to mate, then she wouldn't have died in battle. No, she'd survive this. Surely the fates wouldn't want an Unseelie Prince to lose it on this island.

It may be a group of misfits, but they had become family. The supes living here had made it a home, a safe haven for those who didn't fit in anywhere else. The fates wouldn't want to destroy this place.

No, it only meant that Ree was somewhere else. They just had to find her before Marcus went off the rails. She turned to Maxim when Marcus was out of earshot. "Do you think we should let him go off on his own?"

"I do. Now, where exactly did you see Ree last?" Maxim watched Marcus run toward town.

"The lion was facing that way." She pointed to a shack in the distance. "Maybe she went in there to lick her wounds?" Sofka knew Ree wasn't a quitter, but she was also smart. As a supe who healed quickly, she knew that if she could get to safety, she'd heal up faster.

While the shack looked rickety, everyone on this island knew that looks could be deceiving when it came to buildings. For all Ree knew, there was a massive first aid supply inside. Or maybe even a hospital.

Chapter 30

Sofka's eyes widened when she walked inside the shack. It wasn't a hospital, instead, it was a large hangar. The inside was large enough to fit three private jets, and three limos. But Sofka didn't see any planes, what she did see shocked her to her core. In the middle of the hanger floor was a larger-than-life red sleigh. Then she noticed four giant reindeer. "No, that can't be." She shook her head.

"What in the world?" Maxim exclaimed as he stalked toward the sleigh and reindeer.

"I wouldn't get any closer if I were you." A strong, male voice called out from a darkened corner of the hanger.

Sofka couldn't see who the voice came from, but she felt the presence of at least one person. "Who's there?"

When Sofka took a step toward the darkened corner, Maxim held her back. "Wait, we don't know what side he's fighting on."

"I'm not fighting on any side. I just showed up to find I'd landed next to a battle zone. What side are you fighting on?" The voice was strong, and sounded like it belonged to a confident, if not young, male. His voice was deep, so he was most likely an adult.

"I'm one of the good guys," Sofka called out, hoping he was too.

The disembodied voice chuckled. "I think all sides of a battle believe they are on the side of good. Not too many people would say they were the bad guys."

"Well, we live here on this island and were fighting an invading force." There, she thought, that should tell him who she was.

"And why did they invade?" The voice asked.

"Why don't you come out from the shadows and show yourself?" Maxim demanded.

"I would, but I'm not exactly alone."

Maxim's arms shot out and pushed Sofka behind him. Before his face was out of her line of sight, she noticed he'd gone all protective vamp again. "I'm warning you, if you're part of the invaders, we will defend our island."

"Whoa, I'm not going to hurt anyone. I came to find refuge. Instead, I found a fight. And a woman in distress."

Immediately, the thought of Ree came to Sofka. "Did you find an Arctic Wolf Shifter?"

"Why do you ask?" Now, the voice sounded unsure and tentative.

"Because my best friend is missing. We're searching for her." Sofka sighed and sent a quick prayer that the man had Ree, and she was safe.

"We don't want any trouble, we are just looking for our friend. If you have her, let us take her home and we won't stop you from leaving." Maxim looked back at the sleigh and figured that was how he got on the island.

Sofka noticed where Maxim had glanced, and she took another look. Sure enough, it was the sleigh she thought it was. Even though she'd never met anyone from that pack, she'd recognize the sleigh that had kids all over the world screaming with excitement when they saw it coming. "Santa? Is that you?"

The voice cleared his throat. "No, but close." A man carrying an injured woman walked out from the shadows. His pure white hair and dimpled chin was something any Arctic Wolf would know on sight.

"Chris?" The words escaped Sofka's lips without her even realizing it.

"Ah, guilty as charged." The tall man with broad shoulders shrugged. Then he knelt down and softly lowered the body he was carrying to the ground.

"Ree!" Without any thought for her own safety, Sofka ran out from behind Maxim before he could even touch her. She dropped down to her knees and softly touched Ree's face. "Are you alright?"

When Ree didn't answer, Sofka looked at Chris. "What's wrong with her?"

Chris winced. "She was pretty badly injured when I rescued her from that lion. She had already shifted back into her human form by the time I got to them. I stopped the lion from finishing the job, and then took her here for safety."

Maxim dropped to his knees next to Sofka. "Who is this?" He motioned to Chris.

Without taking her eyes off of her best friend, Sofka introduced them. "Maxim, this is Chris Claus. Chris, this is Maxim Volkov."

"Claus? As in Santa Claus?" Incredulity laced Maxim's question.

Chris put his hand out, and Maxim automatically shook it.

"Yes, but I'm not the big guy. Not yet, at least." Pain crossed Chris' face before he forced a smile.

"Can you help her heal?" Tears streamed down Sofka's face when she finally looked at Chris.

He shook his head. "I'm sorry, but I don't have the gift of healing, like my mother."

Sofka nodded. "I know, only the women have that gift. But surely, there's something you can do."

A long sigh escaped Chris. "She's an Arctic Wolf shifter. The best thing to do is wait for her body to heal itself. We can clean her wounds, which is what I was doing when you entered the hangar. After that..." He shrugged. "Do you have a first aid kit?"

Maxim's head popped up and looked around. "I'll check and see. You never know what the island might put in here."

"Thanks." Sofka looked at Maxim but she couldn't muster a smile.

Before he stood up, Maxim rubbed his thumb across her cheek and cleared away a few tears. Then he stood and began searching the cabinets.

"Vampire? Really?" Chris arched a brow.

"What?"

"You and a vampire? That's kinda odd for an Arctic Wolf shifter, isn't it?" Chris asked.

Sofka chuckled. "This is Misfit Island. And you're one to talk. Didn't two of your aunts mate with dragons?"

"Touché." Chris grinned.

"Ree, if you can hear me, I need you to get better, fast. Marcus is going crazy with fear for you. If you don't wake up soon, I think he might tear this island apart all by himself." Sofka couldn't help but smile just a little bit at her dramatics. Although, she probably wasn't too far off the mark.

"Who is Marcus?" Chris asked.

Sofka looked at Santa's son and a slow smile spread across her face. "If you think a wolf and vampire are strange, just wait until you meet her mate."

After Maxim and Chris finished cleaning Ree's wounds, Sofka took her place next to her unconscious friend again. "Ree, I really need you to wake up. Please." She put her hand on Ree's forehead and tried hard to keep her tears at bay. "She's so cold. That's not good for a shifter."

Normally, a shifter ran hot. Except for when their body was working overtime to heal itself, then it was cold to the touch.

Maxim watched as a tear slowly made its way down Sofka's cheek and splashed onto Ree's cheek. "Sofka, love, come here." He put his arms out and she easily fit into them.

While it was their first hug, it felt right. *She* felt right in his arms. Maxim held her tightly for a few moments before pulling back. One of his fingers ran down her cheek collecting the errant tears. "Don't cry. She'll be alright."

Sofka nodded and leaned into his warmth once more. "I know she will." Then she pulled back and a look of horror crossed her face. "Marcus. We have to find him and tell him where she is."

Maxim sighed and kissed the top of Sofka's head. "I'll go and get him. I'm sure he's going crazy looking for her. You stay and take care of her."

"Thank you." Sofka reached her hand up to cup his cheek. "You really are a great man."

Chris cleared his throat. "I'll...Um, I need to check on my reindeer." He stood up and gave them some time alone.

With a light chuckle, Maxim watched as Chris walked away. "Hey, are you going to be alright here with him?" He nodded in the direction of the young Claus.

"I think so. The Claus family might not care for my kind as much, but they have always been fair to the strays." Not wanting to miss any of this time with Maxim, Sofka leaned in closer and hugged him fiercely.

"Mmm, how I love this. When all of this is over, you and I need some time alone." Again, Maxim kissed the top of her head, wishing he could take her lips in his.

Sofka turned her face up to look him in the eyes. "Yes, yes we do."

When her lips crashed against his, his heart almost beat again. The electricity between them was so strong, and oh so wonderful. He loved a take charge female. Then all thought left him as he took charge and kissed her until a noise broke through their haze.

"Ah, sorry to interrupt, but I think you might want to go and find your friend sooner, rather than later." Chris bounced up and down on the tips of his toes.

Sofka smiled for Maxim and winked. "To be continued later."

"Oh, most definitely." Maxim quickly kissed the tip of her nose and jumped up. Before he left, he looked directly into Chris' eyes. "I expect you'll take great care of my girl."

With a cocky grin, Chris tilted his head. "Oh, most definitely, I will."

Maxim could feel the fangs descend and the red haze in front of his eyes should be enough to convey his message. But, just to be sure, he added a low growl.

Sofka giggled. "Maxim, the sooner you leave, the sooner you'll be back."

Which was very true. He barely gave any notice to the carnage outside as he raced to find Marcus before the Fae Prince could do anything he'd regret.

When he made it to the center of town, Maxim slowed down and looked around. "I sure hope this wasn't done by Marcus." All around him were the bodies of what Maxim assumed were the invading army. He also hoped that none of them were Misfit Island residents.

"Maxim, so good of you to join us." Micky smiled and waved him over to the coffee shop, which had miraculously survived with only a few scorch marks. Of course, all of the windows had been blown out, but that could be easily fixed.

"Micky, thank the island you're safe. Have you seen Marcus?" Maxim walked with purpose over to the coffee shop.

"Oh, yes. And he's inside. None too happy, but he's sitting there drinking his woes away." The polar bear shifter with purple hair pointed to a booth that had seen better days. In it, was a tied-up Marcus.

Maxim arched a brow and looked between Micky and Marcus. "Ah, what happened here?"

"Did you see the windows?" Micky shook her head. "That big blowhard was throwing a temper tantrum."

"And you were able to subdue him?" There was no way Maxim was going to believe that one polar bear shifter, no matter how powerful she was, could have done that.

"Oh no, not I." Micky chuckled, then she pointed to another booth across the room where ten male supes sat drinking coffee and tending to their wounds.

"Ah, I see. Thank you. I found his mate, so he should be doing better." Maxim walked over to Marcus' booth and before sitting down asked, "Is it safe to sit here?"

Marcus snarled at his friend. "Only if you have good news."

With a smirk and a wink, Maxim slid into the booth opposite the surly Fae Prince. "Yes, we found her."

Before Maxim could tell him anything else, Marcus attempted to stand up, and fell back in his seat. "Get me out of this, now! I have to find my mate."

"I will, but I first need to tell you that she's going to be fine. She was injured, but a friend pulled her to safety." Maxim heard the snarl before he saw Marcus move.

The Fae Prince was out of his restraints and jumped over the table and grabbed Maxim by the shirt front. "Is she alright? And where is my mate?"

Maxim pulled Marcus' hands away from him and shoved him back across the table. The booth rocked with the effort and force of Marcus' body being thrown against it. "You need to relax. Ree is going to be fine. She's healing up nicely in a safe place." He looked back over his shoulder and noticed the entire room was watching. "Come with me."

"Where is she!" Marcus bellowed his demand.

"Not here. Let's go before we attract any more attention, alright?" Maxim led him outside and when he was sure it was safe, he told him everything that had happened.

"A Claus? Really? Huh? Why is he here?" Marcus couldn't believe the story and had even stopped walking to scratch his head.

"Let's keep this between us, for now. And get going. I would like you to be there before Ree comes to." Maxim winced when he realized what he had said. He never planned to let Marcus know how badly she was injured before he could see her with his own two eyes.

The anger returned and Marcus had him by the collar once again. His growl told Maxim everything he needed to know.

"Alright, no more talking. Let's get going." Without waiting to see if Marcus would follow, Maxim ran back to the hangar. He could hear the Fae Prince running directly on his heels. When Maxim stopped at the door, he had to physically restrain Marcus. "Dude, you have to calm down. If you run in there like this..." he pointed to the crazed male, "you could scare her."

"You said she was out of it." Marcus tried to reach for the door, but Maxim pulled his hand back.

"She could be awake already for all we know. Take a moment and pull yourself together, man. You don't look good." Maxim looked Marcus up and down and shook his head.

The Fae Prince's hair was even more disheveled than when he found him all tied up in the coffee shop. And now, he had crazy psycho written all over him. What with his clothes all rumpled and the blood on him, it wasn't a good look for the male who usually resembled a human cover model.

"Right." Marcus nodded once, then began trying to comb his hair down with his fingers. Then he moved to straighten his clothes and tucked his shirt in while ensuring his sweater hit his hips just right. Then he leaned down and picked up a handful of snow and rubbed it all over his face in an effort to clean it up just a bit. "There's nothing I can do about the blood on my sweater." He smirked. "Unless you care to lick it off."

"Grow up." Maxim scoffed. "Besides, I don't think I could eat another bite. I probably won't even want anything else for at least a month." Not that he would tell anyone, but he had more than his fair share of enemy blood on the battlefield. If a vampire could gain weight, he'd probably put on ten pounds just from eating his fill.

"Gross. I don't know how you do it." Marcus's lips curled up in disgust before he reached once again for the door. When he opened it, it slammed against the wall and almost came back to hit him. Thankfully, his reflexes were in tip-top shape, and he put a hand up to stop the door from hitting him.

"Nicely done." Maxim chuckled and followed Marcus inside.

"Over here." Sofka called out.

Marcus raced to her side and fell to the ground. "Ree? Honey, I'm here."

"She's going to be just fine. I think now that you're here she'll wake up any minute. She had been stirring before you arrived." Sofka moved to Ree's other side to give Marcus more room. She put her hand on the unconscious shifter's head and smiled. "Her temperature is rising; she should be opening her eyes any minute now."

"Ree, honey. We won. We successfully defended the island, thanks to you. Oh, baby, please open your eyes. I need to see your baby blues." Marcus dropped a quick kiss on Ree's forehead and pulled back when he felt her breathing change.

Before Ree opened her eyes, she called out to him, "Marcus?"

"I'm here. I'm right here." Marcus' voice wobbled as though he was fighting back his own tears. "Baby, I'm here for you." He leaned over and held her close to him.

Sofka stopped trying to be strong and broke out in tears of joy.

Maxim was right there next to her holding her in his arms. "Shh, she's gonna be alright."

Not able to speak due to the crying, Sofka nodded into his chest. Maxim continued to hold her and she knew he was the one for her. He hadn't hardly left her side since everything started. He rescued her when she needed it, and let her do her own thing, too. Sofka never knew that the perfect partner would be everything she needed, not like this.

Since her parents died, she hadn't really seen a good relationship. So many of the couples in her old pack were dysfunctional, which really didn't surprise her. The idea of being with a male whose main source of sustenance was blood still wasn't a turn on, but she could deal with that. It wasn't like she was much better. Shoot, she'd eat raw meat when in her wolf form. And she enjoyed it.

Once Sofka got her crying under control, she realized that she needed to leave Marcus and Ree alone. Well, she didn't realize it as much as they told her to leave them alone.

"Sofka, thank you. But I need to be with my mate right now." Ree smiled and squeezed her best friend's hand. "I need rest, but you need to get back out there and discover what's going on. You're still Firth's second in command, aren't you?"

Sofka sighed. "Yes. You're right. I'll go, but if you need anything, send someone to find me. Alright?"

Ree nodded.

Marcus stood and walked Sofka and Maxim to the door. "Thank you both for finding her and caring for her." He ran a hand down his face. "But, what do we do about this Chris character?"

Sofka had given it some thought. "I think that we keep his being here quiet. I doubt he's gonna want to stay after everything he saw today. So no use in getting anyone excited, or upset." She still wasn't sure how she felt about a Claus being there, but since she doubted he would stay, she decided it really didn't matter.

"Alright. Once Ree is feeling better, I'm going to take her home. If you need us, you know where to find us." Marcus waved as they left the little shack.

Sofka looked back over her shoulder then shook her head. "I still can't believe how the island can pull off that sort of magic. Especially after a day like today."

"Yea, that is strange. I would have thought the island would have exhausted itself fighting off the invaders and their weird magic." Maxim rubbed a hand down his face. "I think we need to find out exactly who was behind this, and if they will try again."

Sofka's face hardened as she thought about all of the destruction the invaders caused. She didn't want to think about the possibility of death. However, with battle came death. It was an inevitable part of war.

As they walked back toward town, she looked around and realized that there were four faces she hadn't seen that day. Faces she expected to see. "Did you ever see the Bully Boys?"

Maxim blinked a few times then turned his head to look around at everyone. "Actually, I haven't seen them since the jail break. Do you think they left the island that day and never looked back?"

It took a moment for the thought to hit her, and then she slowly shook her head. "I don't see how. So much happened after they broke out, it had to be them. Right?"

Maxim rubbed the rough stubble on his chin. "You know, I thought it was them, everyone did. But the weird thing is that no one actually saw them doing any of that stuff. Sienna didn't see who attacked her, right?"

"Right, she just assumed it was them. Like we did. But what if they did leave the island? And that John guy was killed by whoever broke the Bully Boys out? I never really believed they could kill someone. Progression from bullying to murder takes a long time. That was too quick." Sofka wondered if they would ever find out what happened.

"Let's find Firth and see what he's discovered." Maxim led them back to the center of town where most of the combatants had gathered.

Sofka looked around at everyone and felt awful for leaving them to their own devices the past few hours. While she did do some fighting, she really hadn't led them in anything. "Firth, good to see you. How is everyone?"

The leader of the merfolk looked her up and down. "I see you're doing just fine. But was that a limp I saw as you walked over?"

She had forgotten about her injury. "It's nothing. I'll be good as new by tomorrow." She rubbed the side of her head. "Sorry for ditching you during the battle. I had to find Ree."

Firth looked around them and when he didn't see the little wolf, he furrowed his brow. "Where is she?"

With a sigh, she told him a modified version, leaving out the part regarding Santa's eldest son.

"I'm glad Ree will be fine. But you should not have left the battlefield without at least telling me." Firth's compassion had only lasted a moment, then he was the firm leader she had seen earlier.

"Right, well, what's done is done. And it seems you didn't need me after all. The fighting ended pretty much as I left. What have you learned?" While she doubted the fierce warrior thought to keep anyone alive, she figured that someone else would have left enemy combatants alive. Not everyone was a blood-thirsty merman.

The fierce look in his eyes changed for a moment. A look crossed his face, but it was so fleeting that she couldn't be sure it was what she thought it was. It couldn't be that the leader of the merfolk regretted something, could it?

"Yes, well. I didn't have anyone to question. Although, it seems your sheriff found a few supes to take in for interrogation. There was a lion shifter he found injured off to the side." Firth pointed to the jailhouse.

Sofka's eyes widened when she thought about the possibility that it was the same lion she had seen. "Really? What did he say?"

"I don't know. When I saw him, I...well. I didn't want to interrogate him, I wanted to slide my blade through his heart." The regret passed, and for a moment Firth had a wistful look on his face, almost like he was dreaming about sliding his blade through the heart of a lion.

"I see. Well, I'm going to check in with the Sheriff and see if he's found out who's behind this entire situation." She started to turn when Firth stopped her.

"Hold up, I think I can answer that one for you." He waited as Sofka turned back around.

She arched a brow as she waited for him to tell her who was responsible for attacking their peaceful island.

"When it was obvious they were losing, a large Arctic Wolf Shifter called for a retreat. When he was far enough away, he turned and yelled out, "Tell Sofka that Kirill sends his regards."

All of the energy Sofka had in reserve fled her body and her limbs went weak. The only reason she wasn't on the ground was that Maxim had wrapped his arms around her and held her tightly to his chest.

"Sofka, this wasn't your fault. It was his. And you know it. One of his own allies led you here on purpose. He wanted you here for some strange reason." Maxim tried to calm her, but she couldn't believe that it wasn't all her fault.

"I should have just been the dutiful little wolf and let him sell us on the supernatural black market. We could have run away after that, then Kirill wouldn't have been looking for us. Once he got his money, he wouldn't have cared what we did." Tears pricked the corners of Sofka's eyes, and it only served to make her angrier. She was tired of crying, tired of always being thought of as a piece of meat. While she wasn't a human, she still had feelings and rights. And as an Arctic Wolf Shifter, no one should have ever tried to sell her to a slave trader.

If Santa had found out, the entire operation would have been wiped out. And it wouldn't be the first time Santa stepped in and destroyed a bad pack.

Sofka decided it was time she took her power back. "That's it. I'm tired of being the reason for anyone to do anything wrong. From now on, this island is going to be prepared to fight off anyone and anything that tries to take our way of life from us. Tomorrow, we train our own army."

"I like your spunk. But what do you say we wait a few days? Give everyone some time to heal up and clean up first?" The fact that Firth was trying to put off training must mean there were a lot of injured supes on the island.

"Oh, yeah. That would probably be best." Sofka looked around at all of the damage to the little town. While most buildings still stood, there were two or three that might need a total rebuild. She doubted the island would be able to do that so quickly. They would probably have to step in and help with clean-up and rebuilding. "How do you think the island is doing?"

Firth smirked. "Don't worry about the island. I think it's going to be even stronger than before."

"How? Wait." Sofka waved her hands in front of her. "I don't think I want to know, do I?"

"Nope. Probably not." Firth smiled so much, his entire mouth full of sharp teeth were on display. If he hadn't been on her side, she would have squirmed, at the very least.

"Okay, I still better check in with the Sheriff." Sofka waved and turned to leave with Maxim right next to her.

"That is one crazy, scary guy. Did his idea of a smile make you squirm?" Sofka asked as she and Maxim headed to the Sheriff's office.

"Do I have to answer that?" Maxim grinned and showed off all of his teeth while opening his eyes as wide as they would go.

A laugh bubbled up from Sofka's gut and she shook her head. "No, stop it." She put a hand up to hide his face. "That's not scary, it's creepy."

They laughed all the way to the jail. Just before they got there, Maxim stopped her. "Sofka, I'm so glad you made it safely through the battle today." He wrapped his arms around her waist and pulled her close to him. With his forehead touching hers, he whispered, "Tell me you feel this as much as I do."

Her breathy reply was all Maxim needed to take her lips and claim them as his own. This time no one came along to stop them. Sofka gave him back as much emotion as she could. But she felt herself tiring out and knew she still had work to do so she slowed the kiss until it was soft and sweet. “Maxim, is this for real?”

He slowly kissed her cheek, then moved to her ear. “Yes, my love, it is. You are my fated mate. I know it doesn’t make sense to you, but it does to me.”

“Okay.” Sofka kissed him one last time and then pulled away. “Let’s get through the next week, and then we can talk about our future.”

He kissed the tip of her nose and smiled. “Whatever you want, my love.”

Sofka was starting to like it when he kissed her nose. It was intimate and sweet. She hoped he never stopped doing it.

Epilogue

The next week went by quickly. Everyone survived and healed except for three supes. Sadly, Sofka had never met them, so she really didn't mourn their loss. Which only made her feel guilty. She should mourn any loss their island suffered.

"Roscoe, even after talking to those you captured, do you think there is more to the attack then just Kirill trying to get us back?" It was something Sofka couldn't stop thinking about. This was a huge effort. One that must have cost a fortune, more than Kirill could have possibly had. It didn't make much sense if it was all about getting the three of them back. They wouldn't have brought Kirill enough money to cover his losses, even if he had won the fight.

"Sigurd made mention of someone else before he died." Sofka didn't count him as one of their losses since he had been fighting for the other side. "Did you ever discover anything about that mysterious person?"

Roscoe shook his head. “No, but you’re right. There was more to it all than one black marketeer trying to get his *goods* back. I think he lured you to the island since he already had something else going on here. Too much happened too quickly. And all that magic? My guess is he was working with a coven of witches who wanted the island and its magic for themselves. Sigurd didn’t say anything specific, but I got the feeling it was a woman he worked for.”

“That would make sense if it was witches. And I can totally see Kirill working with witches on a heist like this. He would see attacking the island and working with the witches to harness the magic as one giant heist. Something he could brag about for the rest of his life. It would set him up forever. Having the three of us here would just have made it that much sweeter for him.” Sofka pursed her lips and prayed that the losses were too large for the witches, or Kirill, to attempt again.

“Still, I would watch your back.” The sheriff looked her straight in the eyes. “And I think your plan to train the residents of the island to defend against any sort of attack is the way to go. We can’t expect the island to fend off everything for us. It will do a lot, but we still have to do our part.” Ever since the battle, the sheriff had been awake and alert. He took his patrols seriously. And not once had Sofka found him sleeping on the job.

“Right.” Sofka nodded. “But what about Tony and his gang? I still can’t find them. And no one has seen them since they broke out of jail.”

Just then, the screen along the back wall lowered itself. The first communication from the island in a week, causing Sofka to release a sigh. “Finally. What’s it saying?”

Tony and his friends were put on ice after the incident with Sienna. One hundred years should be enough to teach them how to play nice. The screen rolled back up.

"Huh, I should have known. The island isn't the best at communicating with us, is it." While Sofka was elated those boys were on ice, she was still upset that the island didn't inform them sooner. A lot of time was wasted looking for them.

The Sheriff shook his head. "It might not always tell us what we want to hear, but it always tells us what we need to know, when we need to know it."

"Pft." She couldn't help it, but Sofka felt as though that statement was something straight out of the island handbook, or a fortune cookie made by the island. "Well, that's one less thing we need to worry about."

Roscoe's only reply was a half-smile. Then he sat down at his desk and lowered his hat over his eyes. For a moment, Sofka thought he was going to revert back to his old ways. Then she realized why he tried to hide.

"Hey there, gorgeous." A sexy male voice called out from the door. "Are you ready for our date?"

"Yes, I am." Sofka and Maxim were going out to dinner where she knew he was planning on asking her to be his mate, officially. She wanted to have a small ceremony before moving in with him. Kind of like what the humans did. Her parents had done that, and she had thought it was the most romantic thing to do.

She walked toward him as he approached her. Maxim stopped when his foot touched the tip of hers. "You are so beautiful." Then he leaned down and kissed the tip of her nose.

Not for the first time, butterflies zipped around her belly and joy seeped into her bones. Even her wolf was content, which was saying a lot. The inner wolf was rarely content, or happy, unless it was out and chasing its prey. Maybe her wolf saw the vampire as her prey? Sofka could totally see that. She smiled and kissed his soft lips, not caring that her boss was right there watching.

As they walked hand in hand down the street to the newest restaurant on the island, The Blackened Grille, Maxim asked, "So, what do you think about Aelita opening a barbeque joint?"

"I love it. Especially since it's more than a barbecue joint. It's a high-end dinner only restaurant that serves meat grilled over an open fire, or roasted all day on a stick." Sofka's first taste of Aelita's food surprised her. Two days before, she opened up and gave away barbecue pulled pork sandwiches to everyone who stopped by.

"I'm still surprised the island created a new building, just for her restaurant." Maxim grinned. "But I'm so happy that they make the best bloody steak I've ever had."

"Speaking about the island." Sofka informed Maxim about Tony and his three cohorts.

"That's great news. Now, tonight is all about us. Let's not talk about those boys, or anyone else tied to the attack." Maxim had had enough battle discussion and talking about everything that had happened. The last thing he needed was to kill the romantic mood he was trying to get going.

Sofka giggled, hoping this was what her life would be like here on this island. Lots of laughter, good food, and love. "Okay, one last bit of business, then it will be all about us and tonight."

Maxim nodded.

"So, I spoke with Marcus earlier today about the killmoulis. Since we never saw him, I wondered if he had helped to get the Bully Boys off the island. But, now that I know about Tony and his gang, it makes more sense."

"What does?" Maxim asked.

"Marcus said that the Killmoulis would have had to have left the island as soon as his job was done. He can't be away from his master for very long. So, he must have gone back to Kirill. And that's why we never saw him." It still bothered Sofka that Kirill was out there, and planning who knew what, but after their battle, she knew that she and all of her new friends would be able to deal with anything else that Kirill threw at them.

"Okay, we're here. No more talk about anything else, unless it has to do with our future. Got it?" Maxim arched a brow, unsure if Sofka could keep her mind on them all night, or not.

"Got it. I think I'm going to enjoy tonight." She lowered her head and looked up at him through her eyelashes and gave Maxim her best coy smile.

He in turn, kissed the tip of her nose.

And when they were finished with dinner, Aelita brought out a giant glass dish with three different kinds of ice cream, topped with whipped cream, cherries, chocolate sauce, and nuts. The sparklers on top of it all was a special treat just for them.

"Oh, this is wonderful!" Sofka clapped her hands together then gasped when Maxim got down next to her on one knee.

The entire dining room quieted and waited with bated breath to see what the vampire would do. And what the little wolf shifter would say.

"Sofka, you know that I've loved you from the very first moment I met you," Maxim started.

"Oh, how sweet." One patron said before putting her hand over her heart.

Without missing a beat, Maxim went on, "We've been through a lot in the past few months. And we've always done it together. I don't want to spend another day without you. Will you be my mate and marry me?"

Tears of joy flowed down Sofka's face. It was the first time she had cried in a week and she wasn't one bit ashamed of her tears. Her head bobbed up and down. "Yes! I love you so much, Maxim. I want to be yours forever."

She hadn't even noticed the box in his hands until he took the ring out and slipped it on her finger. But she didn't care what the ring looked like, she only wanted to kiss her mate. Which she did. Right there in the dining room in front of everyone.

And the entire room stood up and cheered for them. Cheered for their love and cheered for the sweet way Maxim had declared himself to Sofka.

When they finally stopped kissing, the ice cream had melted, but neither cared. Who wanted ice cream when there were more kisses to be had?

Author's Notes

WOW! It's been a while, hasn't it? I have thoroughly enjoyed writing this new series! I can't wait to write the next one. If you join my newsletter, I'll have more details, dates, cover reveals, etc. Or you can follow me on Amazon or BookBub to get notified when I have a new release.

What did you think about my paranormal light story? Was it fun? Want to see more? Let me know what you think!

It took a long time to write this due to various issues throughout the year. The biggest is a family member of mine developing breast cancer. Please, get your checkups, and if the doctor wants to do more than just a regular exam, don't dismiss it. My family member's cancer was preventable if she would have had the tiny in-office procedure they wanted to do. She is going to be fine, but all of the trouble and illnesses of the past year could have been avoided.

As I was finishing this book, a long-time friend and fan of so many authors passed away. A group of us got together and decided to name a character after her. I had a really cool side character, Michaela, and changed her name to Micky. Everything else about the character stayed the same. Micky was a strong person in real life who had many medical issues to deal with. She loved it when her friends would choose bright colors for their hair. So, my Micky is a tall, purple-haired polar bear shifter. I love this character and was planning on having her take a bigger role in future books. Now, she's probably going to get her own book down the road. My next books are already planned out, so maybe the one after that? I'll let you know when it happens.

I hope you enjoyed this book! A great way to let an author know your thoughts is to leave a review. If something about this book upset you, please reach out to me and let me know so I can address it.

If you want more Misfit Island, check out Island of Misfits! It's a prequel story available now. And keep an eye out in fall 2023 for Misfit Island Book 2.

I pray 2023 brings you much happiness and health!

Chapter header Photo by Derek Oyen on Unsplash

Newsletter Sign-up

Do you love Fantasy, Paranormal, and even a bit of sci-fi, otherwise known as speculative fiction? Then sign up for my newsletter and you'll find yourself immersed in several different universes.

By signing up for my newsletter, you'll not only receive this book, but a couple more free stories as well!

If you want to make sure you hear about the latest and greatest, sign up for my newsletter at: Subscribe to J.L. Hendricks newsletter. I will only send out a few e-mails a month. I'll do cover reveals, snippets of new books, and giveaways or promos in the newsletter, some of which will only be available to newsletter subscribers. (https://jlhendricks author.com/newsletter/)

A Christmas Paranormal Romance Story
J.L. Hendricks
Santa Meets
Mrs. Claus

Contact Me

For those of you who love social media, here are the various ways to follow or contact me:

BookBub: https://www.bookbub.com/authors/j.l.-hendricks
TikTok: https://www.tiktok.com/@jennacleanauthor
Instagram: https://www.instagram.com/j.l.hendricks/
Twitter: https://twitter.com/TinkFan25
Facebook: https://www.facebook.com/JLHendricksAuthor
Website: https://jlhendricksauthor.com